THE YEAR OF THE FIRE MONKEY

THE YEAR OF THE FIRE MONKEY

CHRIS MULLIN

Chatto & Windus
LONDON

Published in 1991 by
Chatto & Windus Ltd
20 Vauxhall Bridge Road
London SW1V 2SA

A CIP catalogue record for this book is available from the
British Library

ISBN 0 7011 3693 6

Photoset by Rowland Phototypesetting Ltd
Bury St Edmunds, Suffolk
Printed and bound in Great Britain by
Mackays of Chatham plc,
Chatham, Kent

To the people of Tibet

'The CIA's becoming engaged in planning assassinations was not a momentary aberration on the part of the handful of men who were involved. In January 1961 the Director of Plans (Richard) Bissell ordered William Harvey, a veteran station chief, to set up a stand-by capability for what was called, euphemistically, Executive Action, by which was plainly meant a capability for assassination of foreign leaders . . .'

Ray Cline, former Deputy Director of Intelligence,
The CIA, p. 211

'I told President Truman . . . about the threats to Tibet's independence and explained your urgent need for assistance. I asked him if America could supply your army with modern weapons and sufficient advisers to instruct your soldiers in their proper use. President Truman did not commit himself in the affirmative or negative. He is sympathetic to your country's problems.'

Letter from the American travel writer,
Lowell Thomas, to the Dalai Lama of Tibet,
10 May 1950

PART ONE

====

Washington, July 1971
Tibetan Year of the Iron Boar

1

ON THE DAY that Harvey Crocker retired, the boys in East Asia Division threw a little party. Everyone who had ever been anyone was there.

Cy Corrigan turned up, along with half a dozen other veterans of that disastrous adventure in southern China in the fall of '51. Gerry Bannister rolled in looking fit and sun-tanned after five years growing grapes in California. In the Fifties he and Crocker had been with the Shan in Burma, signing up opium warlords.

Fritz Neumann put in an appearance, bearing a gift in plain brown wrapping-paper and labelled 'Eyes Only'. Crocker opened the package on the spot. It was a framed black-and-white photograph showing himself and Neumann standing either side of a diminutive Oriental in a white suit. Neumann had worn very well, all things considered. He still had that mop of curly dark hair and a waistline kept in check by a daily run along a beach in Florida. Perhaps there was an extra crease or two on his forehead. Maybe the shadow under the eyes was a little heavier. Apart from that, the picture of Neumann could have been taken yesterday.

Crocker, on the other hand, had gone to seed. Nowadays he had a couple of extra chins and a hairline that had receded out of sight. In the picture he looked uncharacteristically smart in a light-weight tropical suit and a shirt with a button-down collar. You could tell it was Crocker, though, by the insolent grin on his face. As though he knew something the diminutive Oriental did not. Which may well have been the case, for the man was Ngo Dinh Diem, President of South Vietnam, and when that picture was taken he had less than twenty-four hours to live.

Across the bottom of the photo Neumann had scrawled in red ballpoint, 'Remember this one?' and then, 'Saigon, October 31, 1963'. Just what Neumann and Crocker had been doing in Saigon on the night before Diem's assassination has never been satisfactorily explained. Not even the Pentagon Papers shed any light on the matter.

It was the biggest retirement party anyone could remember. The Director had given permission for the executive suite on the seventh floor to be used. From the window there was a clear view down to the Potomac. The younger hands stood around the fringes pointing out the legends from the past. People who hadn't been seen at Langley in years had turned up to wish Harvey a happy retirement.

Halfway through the evening the Director himself stopped by. He made a little speech and presented Crocker with the Agency's Career Intelligence Medal. On one side was engraved the legend, 'FOR CAREER ACHIEVEMENT'. On the flip-side was his name, 'HARVEY Z. CROCKER'. The Z stood for Zebedee – his mother's revenge for his unplanned arrival. If asked what the Z stood for, Crocker always claimed it was Zeus. He liked to claim that his father had been a professor of classics at Yale. Actually, his father had been a salesman of agricultural machinery in South Bend, Indiana. The nearest young Harvey had been to Greece was the kebab takeaway on Second Street.

The Director gave a little speech, the sincerity of which was undermined by the fact that he didn't seem to know Crocker's first name. He kept calling him Ed. 'They didn't make 'em like old Ed any more,' the Director was saying. 'Ed here is the last of his kind and he is going to be sorely missed.' No one dared put the Director right.

'Jesus, what a jerk,' Fritz Neumann muttered under his breath. Mostly, people just put their hands in their pockets and looked at the floor. At the end the Director handed Harvey his medal and shook his hand with exaggerated warmth. There was lots of strong eye-contact and some uneasy small-talk about what Crocker, or Ed – as the Director persisted in calling him – was going to do with his retirement. To begin with, said Crocker, he was going to take time off to do a little fishing in Maryland. Then, before settling, he thought he would take a tour of the country to look up a few friends from the old days. Gerry Bannister and his wife had invited him to stay on their grape farm in southern California. He might even take a look at Mexico while he was down that way. Mexico was one place the Company had never sent him.

The Director gave the appearance of listening for a while, and then slapped Crocker on the back and shook his hand again. 'So long, Ed,' he said, adding, as he turned to leave, 'Keep in touch.'

After the Director had departed, it was a while before conversation picked up again. 'You'd think the old man might have bothered to get his name right,' said a woman from Administration. Someone else said that it wasn't like the old days. In Crocker's day the Company had been one big family.

There was another reason, too. Truth to tell, for the last few years Crocker had been on the back-burner. There was not much call for fieldmen these days. At least not for old-style fieldmen like Crocker who were a law unto themselves. The old guard who had cut their teeth in the Office of Strategic Studies were a dying breed. These days the Company was run by sleek young graduates who sat at desks writing reports and analysing data sent in by other sleek young graduates. What fieldmen there were tended to be younger than Crocker by about twenty years.

Crocker's last-known field operation had been Laos in '65, helping to arm the hill tribes. Even there he had been playing second fiddle to a kid nearly half his age. And, in any case, they hadn't had the scope for personal initiative. Not like they used to have. Every last bullet had to be accounted for.

Since Laos, Crocker had been confined to Langley. It was the first time he had been home-based for nine years and times had changed. Most of his old buddies had either retired or were on the point of retirement. For a year or so he sat around in the cafeteria with Bannister and Neumann drinking bad coffee from plastic cups and remembering the good old days. Then Bannister went off to his grape farm and Neumann retired to a condo in Miami left him by a wealthy aunt. After that Crocker went downhill. His scotch intake doubled. He started telling stories everyone had heard ten times before. Each time his voice seemed to grow a little louder. Once a young secretary on the Cambodia desk complained that he had made a grab for her ass in the telex room. Crocker said he hadn't meant any harm and got off with a warning. Director, East Asia, said he wouldn't tolerate such behaviour from a member of his staff and Crocker went off complaining that no one had a sense of humour these days.

As his significance decreased, Harvey Crocker devised ways to keep up appearances. 'Henry's not going to like this,' he would say loudly each time another piece of bad news came in from Saigon or Phnom Penh. 'No sirree, Henry's not going to like this one little bit.' With that he would rip the telex from the machine and dash off down the corridor in the direction of the divisional director's office. Hearing Crocker talk, anyone who didn't know better might have thought he and the National Security Adviser had breakfast each morning. In fact their paths had only crossed once. They had shared an elevator in the State Department where Crocker had been running an errand for the Laos desk. The National Security Adviser's nose had been buried deep in a confidential file and he had not even offered Crocker the time of day. Undaunted, however, Crocker continued to develop his one-way relationship with the National Security Adviser.

As time passed, it became a standing joke among his colleagues. 'Henry will hit the roof when he hears about this,' one of the secretaries would say when the coffee dispenser jammed.

'We'll see what Henry's got to say about that,' Dick Wiseman on the Thai desk would say whenever a decision had to be referred upward.

Despite the jokes, there was no malice towards Crocker. Most people conceded that he had been big in his day. Some even confessed to feeling sorry for him. 'What Harvey needs is a good woman,' said Margaret Kneppler, the divisional director's personal assistant, one morning when Crocker had shown up in a suit that was more than usually crumpled.

'Are you volunteering?' the director had asked. That shut her up.

According to Records, Harvey Crocker had been married twice – once to a woman from Michigan who had been killed in a plane crash. That was way back before anyone could remember and no one had ever heard Crocker refer to her. His second marriage was to a girl half his age. He had met her in a bar in Bangkok and she had stayed with him just long enough to qualify for American citizenship. She left saying she was going to look up a cousin in Los

Angeles. That was the last Crocker had heard of her. He kept her picture on his desk and spoke as though he expected her to show up at any moment. It was after she departed that Crocker's colleagues began to notice his decline.

When the time came for his retirement, everyone was relieved. He couldn't have lasted much longer. His face just didn't fit any more. One of the older hands organised a collection. Everyone in East Asia Division contributed (even the girl who had accused him of groping her). It raised enough to buy him a set of golf clubs. As the party drew to a close someone suggested a chorus of 'For He's a Jolly Good Fellow'. Crocker gave a little speech thanking them all and saying he would never forget them. One or two of the secretaries cried. It was the end of an era.

Crocker's career, however, was not over. Deep in the files in the basement at Langley, Harvey Crocker had left a time-bomb quietly ticking away.

2

F RITZ NEUMANN WAS the first to raise the subject.
After the party, half a dozen of the old hands had piled into
Gerry Bannister's Chevrolet and driven to a pizza parlour down-
town near the B. and O. canal. It was run by a buddy of Neumann's
– a big, hairy guy of Italian extraction who had been with the
marines at Khe Sanh. Cy Corrigan was lamenting that the Agency
seemed to be going downhill since the golden days of the Fifties. 'In
our day,' he was saying between mouthfuls of anchovy pizza, 'the
guys who ran the Agency thought *big*. If something big had to be
done, they didn't piss around getting clearance from the State
Department, the Pentagon, the National Security Council, Uncle
Tom Cobleigh, and everybody else whose signature is required
these days before you can requisition a new ballpoint. They just
got on with the job and, if anything went wrong, they put it down
to experience.'

The hairy Italian appeared with a bottle of Chianti – the fourth
so far. He hovered briefly, hoping they would invite him to join the
conversation, but no one looked up. 'These days,' Fritz Neumann
was saying, 'everyone is concerned with protecting their ass. You
can't fart in East Asia Division these days without having to send
half a dozen duplicates around the building.' Neumann had been
with Colonel Lansdale in Hanoi in '54, helping to kibosh the
Geneva Agreement. Lansdale was his hero. 'These days,' he went
on, 'the Agency would never touch a guy like Ed Lansdale. All they
want now is paper pushers and analysts. College boys . . .' He
shook his head with contempt. No sir, it wasn't like the old days.

Crocker was sitting quietly puffing on a six-inch cigar, a parting
gift from Mrs Kneppler in the divisional director's office. As she
gave it to him she had planted a kiss on his stubbly cheek.

A morose silence descended. After a while Crocker indicated he
was going to speak. He took the cigar from his mouth and flicked

the ash onto the edge of a plate containing a half-eaten anchovy pizza. He looked at each of them in turn. He was going to say something significant. Eventually he said, 'Kennedy. That's who started the rot. All that crap about cleaning up the Agency after the Bay of Pigs. If Kennedy had kept his mouth shut, everything would have been okay. We could have toughed it out. We might even have fixed Castro if Kennedy hadn't gotten cold feet.'

'Yeah,' said Corrigan, 'it was that Kennedy. Pity he lasted as long as he did. If he'd been hit two years earlier, everything might have been different.'

The Italian brought yet another bottle of Chianti and the talk turned to China. Whoever would have guessed, Crocker said, that Nixon would be the one to throw in the towel on China? An old Commie-basher like Nixon. Now he was going to Peking to shake hands with that son of a bitch Chairman Mao. It just proved you couldn't trust anyone any more. At least you couldn't trust politicians.

It was at that point that Fritz Neumann spoke up. His eyes twinkled at a distant memory. Did anyone, he inquired, remember Operation Fire Monkey?

Did anyone remember? How could anyone forget? The Fifties and early Sixties had seen the Agency up to its neck in some crazy schemes. Deals with opium warlords. Mailing poisoned cigars to Castro. But there were few schemes so crazy as the one that Harvey Crocker came up with in the summer of '58.

It should never have come to anything. Most of the crazy schemes that year ended up in the shredder, but this one would not lie down.

Harvey had been in Washington, killing time between assignments in Taipei and Saigon. That was before the Agency moved to Langley. In those days East Asia Division was housed in a temporary building near the Lincoln Memorial. Crocker remembered it like it was yesterday. It had been his finest hour. He had been lounging with his feet up on a desk in the general office, reading that previous day's baseball results when Cy Corrigan waltzed in clutching a cable from Kalimpong. They had a man in Kalimpong, a Baptist missionary, who monitored the comings and goings from

Tibet. Everyone knew the Chicoms were having trouble in Tibet and there was talk of upgrading Kalimpong station.

Corrigan thrust the cable under Crocker's nose. He seemed excited. 'Could be big,' he kept saying.

In those days cables were decoded manually and a typed translation appended. It read: 'IN TOUCH WITH RELATIVES OF HOLY EAGLE —'

'Who's this Holy Eagle when he's at home?'

'Dalai Lama,' said Corrigan. 'Number One Son in Tibet.'

The cable went on: ' — OFFERING TO SUPPLY YOUTHS TO FIGHT CHICOMS IF WE ARRANGE GUNS AND TRAINING STOP RECOMMENDED ACCEPT STOP REPLY SOONEST.'

Crocker at once saw the possibilities. So did Director East Asia. Within six months the first group of bewildered young Tibetans were being trained in paramilitary warfare at Clark Airbase in the Philippines. Before long Tibetans were being trained, in great secrecy, at Camp Hale in Colorado. It was then that Crocker had his brainwave.

He had come in early one winter's morning and typed an 'EYES ONLY' for Director, East Asia. In those days the post was held by Stan Kumiskey. Stan was short for Stanislaw. He was a Pole who had been recruited into the OSS by Wild Bill Donovan. Like Crocker, Kumiskey was a keen fieldman. He had accepted promotion reluctantly (because his wife had put her foot down) and never settled behind a desk. He made no secret that he would far rather be out in the front line than pushing paper in Washington. Kumiskey and Crocker had a lot in common. In particular, they shared a deep loathing for bureaucrats and politicians.

'Harvey,' said Kumiskey, when he had read the memorandum, 'this could change the course of history.' They had spent an hour discussing the details. Crocker would be given an office of his own and a small budget. The funding would be concealed in the general estimates for China ops. That way no one would ask awkward questions. Secrecy must be absolute. If Crocker needed help, he could bring in Fritz Neumann, but that was all.

Whatever happened, said Kumiskey, those faint-hearts in the State Department must not find out.

*

Within two days Crocker and Neumann were operating from a little office down the corridor. At one time it had been the post room. It had no windows and the walls were lime green. Kumiskey had it checked out for bugs. A telephone with a scrambler was fitted. The wooden door was replaced with one made of reinforced steel and a lock with a timing device was added, the code number of which was known only to the two of them.

Crocker and Neumann became very uncommunicative. They no longer appeared at the morning conference in Kumiskey's room. They took their meals together in the cafeteria, usually after most of the others had finished eating. Sometimes they remained closeted together all day, arriving early and leaving after everyone had gone home. Now and then they would send one of the girls down for burgers and fries or a couple of black coffees. When she returned, the coffees or the burgers would be taken through a half-opened door.

Every so often Crocker and Neumann would take a trip down the corridor to consult Kumiskey. On these rare occasions they condescended to exchange the time of day with their old buddies, but that was about all. Cy Corrigan was sore about it. Everyone in their line of business appreciated the need for secrecy, but this was too much. He guessed it had something to do with the Tibetans at Clark Airbase because a young woman in the library told him that Harvey had ordered everything available on Tibet. He had also withdrawn a report by a defector on the structure of the Chinese Communist Party.

Once Crocker and Neumann disappeared for about two weeks. Their office at the end of the corridor remained sealed. Not a soul went in or out. The cleaners had been told it was out of bounds. When Crocker and Neumann reappeared, neither said a word about where they had been – although it must have been somewhere hot since Crocker's normally pallid features had turned cabbage red.

Meanwhile, the operation in Kalimpong had been upgraded. There was now a colony of Baptist ministers keeping an eye on travellers to and from Tibet.

*

At Crocker's suggestion, the project was dubbed 'Operation Fire Monkey' – after the Tibetan year of the same name. How high the clearance went has never been established. Crocker supposed Kumiskey had discussed the operation with someone upstairs, but he had never specified. Crocker didn't worry. Clearance wasn't his department. Kumiskey had promised to take care of everything. He was as enthusiastic as Crocker about Operation Fire Monkey.

From the Tibetans at Clark Airbase, Crocker had selected three young men. They were picked from different teams at different times. They had not met and each was given to believe that he alone had been chosen. Instead of paramilitary warfare, they were trained for a different mission. They would return to Tibet as sleepers, join the Communist Party (which was known to be short of Tibetan recruits) and work their way up. The young men selected were reckoned to be persons of discretion, dedication, and cunning. They were long-term investments. Fire Monkey would take years to bear fruit. The odds against success were high, but the prize was great. It could trigger the disintegration of the Chinese Communist Party and prepare the way for the recapture of mainland China for the Free World. It would also make up ten times over for all the years of failed operations inside China. It could, as Stan Kumiskey never tired of saying, change the course of history.

Back in the pizza parlour by the B. and O. Canal, the hairy Italian was serving coffee. Half a dozen empty Chianti bottles littered the table. Crocker was still puffing at his cigar. Fritz Neumann was still talking about Fire Monkey.

'Harvey sure invented some fancy names for his operations.'

'What happened?'

Crocker exhaled cigar smoke. 'Got junked after Kumiskey's heart attack. He took early retirement and they brought in some smart ass from Western Hemisphere Division. Didn't know where Tibet was and didn't care.'

'And what about the guys you recruited?' It was the first time Cy Corrigan had heard the full story.

'One got the shakes and pulled out. Last I heard he was running a restaurant in Darjeeling. Second one was picked up within a week of getting home and the third one . . .' Crocker's voice faded. The cigar was sharing the plate with the half-eaten pizza. He made no attempt to retrieve it for it was at this moment that an awful thought dawned on him.

Fritz Neumann had taken up the story. 'The third guy was taller than the others. Intelligent, too. Did a lot of reading. We had one of the linguists translate a Mickey Spillane into Tibetan for him. We always reckoned he was the one most likely to see it through. Aristotle, we called him. Gave them all new names. Can't remember his real name.'

'Ari,' said Crocker quietly. 'His name was Ari.'

'Ari, that's it. We were going to call him Harry but in the end we settled for Aristotle. I can see him now. Cheerful little sod. Always laughing. He had a chipped tooth which showed when he smiled. We taught him to play poker. Before long he could beat us. He wanted to take a pack of cards back with him, but they'd have given him away. Otherwise we might have introduced poker to Tibet.'

'Where's this Ari now?'

It was at this moment that the same awful thought occurred to Neumann. Harvey Crocker looked as if he were about to throw up. 'Jesus,' he whispered, 'if Henry hears about this he'll go through the roof.'

PART TWO

═══

Litang, Eastern Tibet, October 1949
Tibetan Year of the Earth Bull

3

NEWS OF THE revolution in China came slowly to Litang. It drifted up through the lonely valleys and across the high passes. It stopped with the winter snow and started again with the spring thaw. It came with the merchant caravans that passed between Kanting and Lhasa. The news came also with the trickle of ragged soldiers heading south from Chinghai – all that remained of the disintegrating army of the warlord, Ma Pu-fang. They were gaunt, broken men, exhausted by months of wandering through a hostile wilderness. Breathless from the high altitude. Some brought women with children in small bundles tied to their backs. Some rode on horses that were no more than skin and bone. Some limped along in boots that hung in tatters from their feet.

The soldiers walked with their heads down. They looked neither to right nor to left, avoiding the icy stares of the nomads camped with their yaks on the green pasture beside the trail. Children, seeing the approach of such a miserable procession, would run to the road and throw stones. A year ago a Tibetan child throwing stones at a Han soldier would have been fortunate to escape with a sound thrashing. Now the soldiers barely looked up as the stones glanced off them.

Some of the fleeing soldiers would linger at an isolated hamlet long enough to barter a rifle or a pouch of tobacco for a few bricks of tea or a sack of barley. A year ago they would simply have taken what they wanted. Now they did not even haggle at the outrageous prices. They simply loaded their purchases onto the backs of their emaciated ponies and limped away in the direction of the passes that led south into Yunnan and Burma.

By the eighth month the snow had sealed the passes. The trickle of fleeing soldiers dried up and the people of Litang knew they were safe for another winter. They also knew, however, that the world beyond the mountains and the deserts that guarded the entrance to Tibet had changed irrevocably. The civil war that had preoccupied the Han for twenty years was over, and China was now ruled by a dynasty stronger than that of any emperor in history. They understood also that this new dynasty, more than any other in history, threatened their way of life.

This was why, as the Year of the Earth Bull turned into the Year of the Iron Tiger, there was more than usual activity in the Litang lamasery. From the surrounding hamlets and valleys pilgrims came with prayer scarves and offerings of butter and barley to place before the images of the Buddha. And in the prayer halls and dark chapels of the lamasery, lamas could be heard chanting with unprecedented vigour for deliverance from the – as yet unspecified – evil, which hung like a dark cloud over Litang.

Some persons, anxious to acquire exceptional merit, undertook pilgrimages to Lhasa – a journey of nearly three months. Others measured their length in prostrations on the holy walk around the outer wall of the lamasery. From dawn to dusk old ladies were to be seen hobbling, prayer wheels twirling and mumbling the sacred formula, '*Om mani padme hum*' ('Hail to the Jewel in the Lotus') which had for centuries protected Litang from the world beyond.

The Abbot took more practical precautions. He summoned a meeting of local traders and ordered them at once to dispatch a caravan to Kalimpong to purchase a consignment of rifles and ammunition large enough to arm every monk in the valley. To fund the transaction, he authorised an increase in the rents to be exacted from the farmers and herdsmen on the estates of the lamasery.

The Abbot of Litang was a holy man, but he was not so naïve as to throw himself entirely upon the mercy of the Lord Buddha.

In spite of the unprecedented quantity of prayers that ascended to heaven from Litang in the spring of 1950, the omens were not good. The rains were late that year and special formalities had to be carried out by lamas experienced in inducing rain. The building of new houses was forbidden until further notice (because persons building houses prayed for dry weather and this cancelled out prayers for rain).

When the rain came, there was also hail. This, too, was a bad omen. The hail was followed by a huge earthquake, which destroyed many homes in the valley and rent from top to bottom the east wall of the prayer hall in the lamasery. From Lhasa came rumours that the statue of the Jowo, the holiest image in Tibet, had shed tears. The Ganden oracle was said to have had a vision in which he foresaw a land where all images of the Buddha had been destroyed and where monks were forced to work in the fields alongside the peasants.

Had the people of Litang had access to a radio they would also have heard Peking Radio's New Year message. It declared: 'The tasks for the People's Liberation Army for 1950 are to liberate Taiwan, Hainan Island and Tibet.' Four months later the Chinese Nationalists, broadcasting from Taiwan, gave news of a huge Nationalist victory in Hainan. From past experience everyone who heard this knew that it meant the Nationalists had suffered a huge defeat. Sure enough, a few days later the Nationalist radio announced that Hainan was being evacuated. That left only Taiwan and Tibet. In its May Day message, Peking Radio announced that Tibet would be liberated next.

Gradually the news grew worse. Traders from the east brought word that Kanze had been occupied. They reported seeing column after column of marching soldiers entering the city. The soldiers were poorly armed but marched in perfect order. They also, the traders alleged, appeared not to live by looting.

Such reports were greeted with scepticism by the citizens of Litang. They were prepared to believe that a huge army was moving into Tibet but unwilling to accept that there was a single Han soldier who did not live by plunder.

For some months there was uncertainty as to whether the Red Army would enter Litang that summer. The road extended only as far as Kanze. Further progress could only be made on foot or on horseback, and the soldiers did not appear to be equipped for spending winter at fourteen thousand feet.

Any doubts as to the intentions of the Red Army were, however, soon resolved. Early one morning the Abbot awoke to the sound of horses' hooves on the flagstones of the courtyard below his apartment. He peered cautiously from the window and in the half light found himself caught in the gaze of a young Han dressed in olive-green battledress. On his head the young Han wore a cap with what appeared to be a red star on the front. He was accompanied by half a dozen other Han in similar uniforms. Each had a rifle slung across his back and each was mounted on a stout Tibetan pony. With them was a young Tibetan whose brown *chuba* was spattered with mud.

The Han spoke. The Tibetan translated. 'Esteemed sir,' he said, 'I have the honour to inform you that Litang has been liberated.'

4

ARI HAD RISEN early on the morning that Litang was liberated. Even before the first red streak of dawn had appeared in the sky to the east, he had prostrated himself three times before the image of Chenrezi on the makeshift altar in the corner of his room. He had topped up the lamp that burned on the altar with a knob of yak butter, which he kept in an earthenware bowl under his bed. It was there that Ari also stored the few treasures he had salvaged from his childhood. The sling with which he once terrorised the sparrows who pillaged the family fields at harvest time. The knife with which his grandfather had reputedly slain two Muslim bandits in single-handed combat on the Chinghai plateau. A handful of coloured stones taken from the bed of the stream that ran through his family's barley field. These were the only souvenirs of a childhood that had been terminated abruptly when the lamas had come to claim him as their own.

Novices were strictly forbidden to use slings within the lamasery. On summer evenings, however, when his tutor was at prayers, Ari would bring his sling out from its hiding place beneath the bed and take pot shots at the crows who came to rest on the roof of the little chapel across the street from his window. He had never been caught, but there had been some narrow escapes. Another evening, in a shot that went badly adrift, he had accidentally decapitated one of the alabaster snow lions that guarded the entrance to the chapel. Inquiries had been made. There was talk of the direst retribution being visited upon the culprit. For a while Ari had contemplated disposing of his sling down one of the lamasery's deep wells. In the end, however, the incident had been attributed to the demons who were said to be unusually active at that time of year. From then on, however, the crows were left in peace.

*

Dawn at the lamasery had its litany. A cock crowing. Dogs barking. Metal pots clanging on cold stone. Throats being cleared in a series of stomach-turning expectorations. A conch horn summoning the monks to prayer.

Ari was about to leave for the prayer hall when Aten, his little servant monk, suddenly appeared. The boy had been running and his breath formed little clouds like rings of tobacco smoke in the cold air. 'Rimpoche, Rimpoche,' he panted, 'the Han. The Han are here.'

Without a word Ari followed the boy out into the maze of cobbled lanes. Everyone in the lamasery was on the move towards the Abbot's courtyard. It was already packed when Ari and Aten arrived. Half of Litang was there. Wild-looking nomads with daggers hanging from their belts. Women who ran the tea shops in the bazaar. Even the beggars who were usually to be found seated in a row at the south gate.

The Han were on horseback in the centre of the throng. The crowd formed a silent, gawping semi-circle around them, not daring to go near, yet gradually closing in as the pressure from people flooding into the courtyard behind them increased. Ari and Aten pressed forward until they reached the *stupa* in the centre of the courtyard. By clambering onto its base they were able to get a clear view. In normal times the climbing of *stupas* was strictly forbidden, but these were not normal times.

The soldiers remained mounted. The Abbot remained at his window perhaps thirty feet above. The young Han who was their leader addressed the Abbot in a manner that was respectful, but not servile. He paused after every two or three sentences to allow the interpreter to translate. Tibetan people, he said, had nothing to fear from the People's Liberation Army. They came to Litang as friends.

The interpreter spoke in the language of Kham. He seemed nervous and mumbled until the young officer spoke sharply to him. Ari noticed that, unlike the others, the young Han who did the talking had a pocket on each breast of his tunic. From one of these a pen protruded. In later years, when he had come to know the ways of the Han, Ari would learn to calculate the rank of an officer by the number of pens he carried.

The Nationalist bandit regime, the young officer was saying, was rotten, parasitical and finished for ever. He was pleased to welcome the people of Litang back into the Great Family of the Motherland.

This little speech was heard in silence. The people of Litang knew from bitter experience that the Nationalist government was rotten and parasitical, but it was news to them that they had ever been part of the Great Family of the Motherland. And if they had been, they had absolutely no desire to return to its bosom.

The Abbot's parched face registered the merest flicker of comprehension. The young Han officer beamed up at him and said that he would shortly return. The Abbot swayed slightly and then disappeared into the gloom.

With that the soldiers wheeled round on their horses and rode out through the main gate. The crowd parted silently to let them pass. The interpreter kept close behind. He knew that teachings of the Lord Buddha on the sanctity of life did not apply to Tibetans who collaborated with the Han.

Until that day Ari had only once before set eyes on a Han soldier – on the eve of his fifth birthday. His mother had sent him into town to purchase a brick of tea. When Ari had reached the market square he found a crowd held back by ragged soldiers who held rifles fixed with bayonets. He could see at once that the soldiers were not Tibetans.

In the centre of the square a large wooden stake had been driven into the ground. Two soldiers were nailing a crossbeam to it. The people gathered round the square were in a state of great agitation. Some were praying frantically – '*Om mani padme hum. Om mani padme hum*' – others were murmuring imprecations against the Han. Being small, Ari had easily pushed his way to the front and what he saw made his blood freeze. Han soldiers were dragging a Tibetan towards the cross. Ari could see the man's face clearly. His lips were swollen and his eyes were closed by huge black bruises. His bare back and arms were a mass of weals caked with dirt and dried blood. One of the man's legs trailed awkwardly as though it were broken.

Later, Ari learnt that the man was a mule driver who had the bad

luck to be driving his mules across the bridge at the entrance to
Litang town at the same time as a young Han army captain was
crossing in the other direction. One of the mules had brushed
against the captain, who responded by emptying his pistol into the
unfortunate animal. Whereupon he had been roundly cursed by
the mule driver. At once the captain had ordered his men to
administer a beating of exceptional severity to the mule driver, but
this had apparently proved insufficient to assuage the officer's
injured pride. He had, therefore, ordered the wretched mule driver
to be taken to the town centre and crucified as a warning to any
other Tibetan who had the temerity to insult an officer of the
Kuomintang.

The cross was higher than a man. To reach the crossbar, the
soldiers had dragged in front of it a trestle table belonging to one of
the market traders. They had then hoisted the mule driver up by his
arms. Ari could hear the crack as the man's shoulders dislocated.
The soldiers bound each arm tightly to the cross with twine made
of yak skin, which they had soaked in water so that it would
tighten further as it dried. They then took turns to insert slivers of
bamboo behind the man's fingernails, pushing hard to make sure
that each one sank deep. At each insertion the mule man howled.
Each howl was taken up by the crowd, many of whom were
sobbing openly. The sound of their prayers had grown almost to a
chant. Blood ran down the mule man's fingers and dripped onto
the flagstones.

The soldiers thought this was hilarious. They slapped the captain on the back and thanked him profusely for the entertainment.
But the captain was not yet finished. From his pocket he took a
bundle of miniature Nationalist flags. He then clambered onto the
table and attached a flag to each of the splints protruding from
under the fingernails of the man on the cross. Stepping down, he
ordered the table to be removed and stood back to admire his
handiwork. A light wind blew and the little red flags fluttered
gaily. By now the captain and his men were helpless with mirth.
They rocked back and forth, slapping their sides. Tears rolled
down their cheeks.

Ari pushed his way out of the crowd and ran home, sobbing
hysterically. On his way he fell and dashed his face against a stone.

It was only later he realised that half his front tooth had gone. That night, Ari prayed that the mule man would be reborn into a better life. He and his mother climbed the dark stairway to the shrine at the top of the house where they lit a butter lamp in the poor man's memory. But prayers did nothing to erase the memory. He had had his first lesson in the cruelty of the Han. There would be others.

5

ARI'S FAMILY LIVED about an hour's walk along the rugged track that led east out of Litang. His father, whom he had never known, had disappeared on the Chang Tang, the great northern wilderness inhabited by evil spirits and demons. Each spring when the snows thawed, Ari's father and a party of friends would set off for the Chang Tang to trade with nomads who dwelt on the high pastures. Sometimes they would be gone for a month, returning laden with the skins of wild beasts, which they would sell to the traders in the market who in turn would take them to Kalimpong and Calcutta to be sold at a great price.

The year after Ari was born, his father had set off as usual for the Chang Tang. He went with five others – good friends who went every year to trade with the nomads. None of them was ever seen again. Nor was any trace found. The months passed. Each evening his mother, Pema, would sit cradling her infant son on the roof of their small house, watching the track that led into the northern mountains. Sometimes when a horseman appeared she would clamber down the ladder to the ground and, still carrying Ari, run along the track until she was close enough to see that it was not her husband. Then she would walk back slowly, head down, cursing the day that she had ever allowed him out of her sight. It was at least two years before Pema Paljor accepted finally that her husband was never coming back. And years later, she could still be seen on summer evenings sitting on the roof of her house, beneath fluttering prayer flags, gazing towards the northern wilderness.

Like most Tibetan women, Pema grew strong in adversity. Left alone with four young children, she ploughed fields, sowed and reaped barley, sheared sheep, and even negotiated with the lamas for a rent reduction. This last was achieved only after a considerable haggle, the wily lamas arguing that since there was no proof of her husband's death she was not entitled to any reduction in the fifty per cent of her crop due to the lamasery. They were only persuaded to concede when Pema threatened to denounce them for their avarice the length and breadth of Litang.

Although a devout woman, Pema had little time for the lamas and did not hesitate to say so. They were, she said to anyone who would listen, parasites living off the backs of the people. The neighbours were scandalised. To say such things, they said, was to invite retribution. The lamas would put a spell on her. But Pema was unmoved. She was sure, she used to say, that the Lord Buddha did not intend the people of Litang to maintain in idleness a thousand good-for-nothing lamas.

It was, therefore, one of life's richest ironies that Pema Paljor should give birth to an incarnate lama.

Shortly before Ari's six birthday, an event occurred that was to change his life. One summer's evening, while Pema and her children were collecting barley sheaves, two men appeared. They were rough and unshaven, and their *chubas* were thick with dust from the dry road. They had come, they said, to buy a mule. They were, they claimed, on a pilgrimage to Lhasa. One of their mules had fallen into a ravine and they needed another before they could proceed.

Despite their rough appearance they spoke with accents that suggested education. Pema eyed them with suspicion. 'Why come to us? We have but one mule and he will be needed for the harvest.'

The taller of the two men did the talking. The nomads, he said, had refused to trade with them. An old woman they met on the road had said that the Paljor household had a mule for sale.

'What old woman?'

'On the road, about half an hour back.' He was vague.

'She was wrong. We have no mule to sell.'

The man made no move to go. 'At least, sister, perhaps you could take pity on us to the extent of a bowl of butter tea. We have been travelling since dawn.'

Pema might have told him that there was an inn, not twenty minutes' walk away. That she, too, had been on the go since dawn. That she had better things to do than entertain strangers on a summer's evening in the middle of the harvest. Instead, with a sigh, she hurled her barley sheaf onto the haystack and went to her kitchen.

When she returned with two bowls of *tsampa* she found the strangers squatting in the evening sunshine talking to Ari. They did not so much as glance at the mule grazing on the barley stubble not fifty yards away. One of the men had both arms stretched out in front of him. A set of prayer beads dangled from each hand. He was urging the boy to choose between them.

When he caught sight of Pema he returned the beads to the pouch in his *chuba*. Pema said nothing. She handed them the tea and went back to her work in the field.

When she returned, they had gone. The two empty bowls rested side by side on a stone by the kitchen door. She questioned Ari closely.

'What were those men saying to you?' she asked Ari.

'They were playing a game.'

'What game?'

'Choosing.'

'Choosing what?'

The boy would not look at her. It was his secret. They had told him not to tell.

'Choosing what?' Pema demanded.

'Beads, a hat . . . They said they had once belonged to a holy lama.'

Later that summer two more men came to the house. They too said they were pilgrims on their way to Lhasa. They claimed to have been robbed by bandits of everything they possessed. They asked for a bowl of *tsampa* and lodging for the night. One of the men claimed to know an uncle of Pema's who was a minor official in Chamdo. When questioned about her uncle he, too, became vague.

That night, when the children were in bed, the men ate with Pema by the stove in the kitchen. They talked of the war in China. About the price of barley. About the wickedness of the bandits. Eventually the talk turned to her children. Ari in particular.

How old was he? When was he born? They were not satisfied with the year. They wanted to know his exact date of birth. One of them claimed to have a boy of the same age. Had the omens at the time of his birth been auspicious? Had she ever thought of sending him to the lamasery?

No, said Pema firmly. She had not. She had borne three sons and only Ari had survived the year of his birth. With her husband gone, he would be the only man in the family. She was counting on him to look after her in her old age. The men did not pursue the subject, except that one said something about the benefits of education in the lamasery. When they departed next morning, Ari followed them as far as the road into town. Pema stood at the window and watched them go. Deep in her heart she knew that the lamas would soon come for her only son.

They came one grey day in the eighth month. They came as the first streaks of powdery snow appeared on the mountains. They came with much clashing of cymbals, beating of drums, and blowing of horns.

The Abbot came in person with a retinue of a hundred monks, a yellow parasol held high over his shaven head. With him came a procession of devout citizens. Neighbours, aroused by the spectacle, peered from windows and rooftops.

Pema heard the horns and cymbals when they were still a long way off and she knew at once that this was the day. When the chaotic procession arrived, she was at her door, ready. She stood with her children gathered about her. Three young girls, their hair in long pigtails, and her son, her only son, his hand clasped tightly in hers. Only Ari appeared not to understand.

When the procession reached the Paljor household, the clamour ceased abruptly. The line of monks parted to reveal the Abbot preceded by a huge, stave-bearing bodyguard.

The guard side-stepped. The Abbot advanced two paces so that he stood alone confronting Pema and her son. At first he afforded them scarcely a glance. Instead he surveyed the outside of the house as though he were a prospective purchaser. He looked at the places where the rain and wind had eroded the white paint from the front wall. He inspected each of the windows, noting with apparent approval the flower pots where, in the summer, Pema grew chrysanthemums. He looked up at the ragged prayer flags fluttering in the autumn wind. Then he looked beyond the house to the meadow where the mule grazed and at the mountain beyond the river, the upper slopes of which were powdered white.

Yes, said the Abbot. This was the house. Exactly as he had seen it in his vision. Accurate even down to the number of flower pots on the window sills. 'And this,' said the Abbot, turning at last to Ari, 'this is the Rimpoche.'

A murmur of approval went up from the crowd. There was a renewed outbreak of cymbal clashing and drum beating. A horn sounded. And then silence again, broken only by the sound of Pema sobbing softly.

Six years ago, the Abbot explained, a holy lama had died. The lama had lived for nearly forty years in a walled-up cave on a hill behind the lamasery where he had given over his life entirely to fasting and contemplation. A search for his reincarnation had begun at once. Deputations of learned monks had combed Litang, but to no avail. In desperation they had even searched the neighbouring valleys. Then, three months ago, the deceased lama had appeared to the Abbot in a dream. He had been reborn, he said, as the only son of a widowed farmer's wife living within sight of the lamasery. The Abbot's dream had included a snapshot of the house. It was to the east of the town, at the end of a small lane, and looked out over a pasture, dissected by a stream. It had three floors and flower pots on every window ledge.

Search parties had been dispatched at once. Monks disguised as pilgrims had visited all the likely houses in the vicinity of the lamasery. They had visited the Paljor household posing as pilgrims who had lost a mule. The Abbot apologised for the deception. It was, he added, occasionally necessary to devise such pretexts in the service of the Lord Buddha.

On the first occasion the monks had brought with them two sets of beads, one of which had belonged to the dead lama. They had offered them to Ari and he had chosen the correct one. They had shown him two hats and he had chosen the one that had belonged to the late lama.

To obtain a second opinion, two more senior monks had visited the house. This time they had posed as travellers who had been robbed. They had stayed the night and taken the opportunity to observe the boy closely and to inquire as to the date and time of his birth. These coincided almost exactly with the moment when the holy lama had evacuated his earthly presence. (It was difficult to be precise as to the moment of his passing since the hermit lama's cave had been visited only once a week.) The investigating monks were therefore satisfied, concluded the Abbot, that they had discovered the reincarnation.

At this the pandemonium resumed. There was more clashing of cymbals and beating of drums. Neighbours pressed in upon Pema to congratulate her on her good fortune. Ari's three sisters fled indoors and shut themselves in an upper room.

The bodyguard, making liberal use of his stave, beat a path to the front door for the Abbot and two other monks, whom Pema recognised as the men who had inquired about the mules. Ari was taken inside and dressed in his best *chuba*. Prayers were said. Water and barley grains were sprinkled in various places about the house. A smell of incense pervaded.

Outside again, the bewildered boy was mounted upon a white horse. A monk bodyguard held the reins. A yellow parasol, similar to that which sheltered the Abbot, was held aloft. Pema stood on the doorstep weeping. Her daughters, their faces stained with tears, clutched tightly at her skirts. At a word from the Abbot, the procession set off in the direction of the lamasery where Ari might have remained for the rest of his life, but for the coming of the Han.

6

IN TIBET THERE are many worse fates than to be born an incarnate lama. As he grew older Ari often reflected that he might have been a mule, an earthworm, or even one of the little servant-monks like Aten, assigned to the lamasery by impoverished parents in lieu of unpaid rent. Every morning, as he watched boys no older than himself weighed down by baskets of nightsoil running between the living quarters and the vegetable gardens, Ari gave thanks to the Buddha for allowing him to be reborn a lama.

He was one of half a dozen young Rimpoches who had been discovered in the villages around Litang. Each was allocated a comfortable room and a servant and placed in the care of a tutor. Ari's tutor was a kindly, wrinkled old monk called Phuntsog who had lived at the lamasery since he was five years old. As a young monk, Phuntsog had been struck down by a palsy and had, as a result, lost the use of his left arm. It hung withered and useless by his side. Phuntsog's job was to teach Ari to read, write, and pray. He could be strict but, unlike some lamas, he was not a bully.

'A Rimpoche is supposed to set an example to others,' he would say when Ari refused to move from his bed before dawn on a cold winter morning.

'If you are not careful, you will be reborn a mule,' Phuntsog would say with a twinkle in his eye when Ari became bored with writing practice.

On winter nights Phuntsog would tell stories about the spirits and demons who inhabited the high plateau. In particular, Ari liked to hear about the exploits of King Gesar and his mythical kingdom of Ling. Gesar was said to have haunted the northern plains for one thousand, three hundred years and, to this day, travellers on the Chang Tang report occasional sightings.

With Phuntsog, Ari had climbed the hill behind the lamasery to inspect the cave where, he was assured, he had lived for nearly forty years in his earlier incarnation. The path up the hill had been worn smooth by generations of pilgrims seeking blessings from the holy hermit. The entrance to the cave was sealed by huge boulders. Devout pilgrims had chiselled prayers into the rock face. About six feet above the ground there was an aperture just big enough for a human body to pass.

'If he was an old man, how did he get out?' asked Ari.

'He didn't.'

'Never?'

'Not for the last five years of his life.'

'Then how did he eat?'

'His food was brought by monks and passed through to him.'

Ari had climbed onto the boulders and was peering through the aperture. The cave was very dark inside. He could see no more than a few feet. The air stank of damp or worse.

'Did the monks talk to him?'

'No. They never saw him.'

'How did they know when he was dead?'

'Because the food remained uneaten.'

All the way down the mountain Ari was silent. That evening when Phuntsog came to bid him goodnight he said: 'When I am old, will I have to live in a cave?'

Phuntsog smiled. 'No,' he said. 'There are many different ways of serving the Buddha. For you he has reserved a special mission.'

From the window of his small room, Ari could see out across the town to the pasture that led down to the river. He could see yaks grazing and, at night, he could hear the tinkling of the bells around their necks.

On summer evenings, if there was no sign of Phuntsog, Ari would sometimes (after murmuring an apology to the Buddha) requisition the makeshift altar and place it by the window. By standing upon it on tiptoe he could see the top of his mother's house. Just before sunset, he could occasionally make out her lonely silhouette looking towards the monastery that had taken away her son.

After the first week, Ari was not troubled by homesickness. He was fortunate that his family lived so close by. His mother and sisters often visited and plied him with sweets and barley cakes. During the spring and summer he went with them on picnics and played hide-and-seek with his sisters among the rocks by the river. Once or twice he even sneaked home and helped with the harvest.

The other young Rimpoches were not so fortunate. Their families lived several days' or even weeks' walk from the lamasery and rarely came to visit. At first some cried out for their parents. One small boy tried to run away home, but was brought back by peasants who found him wandering along the road out of town.

Because they were reincarnations, the young Rimpoches inherited worldly goods from their previous lives. In Ari's case this did not amount to very much since his first incarnation had been as the austere hermit. A walking-stick, a string of prayer beads and an eating bowl made from the cap of a human skull: these were the only souvenirs of his earlier existence. With the bowl came a spoon skilfully fashioned from a piece of rib cage. Ari couldn't bring himself even to touch the bowl and spoon. They lay unused beside the butter lamp on his altar to Chenrezi.

Other Rimpoches had more to show for their earlier existence. Some inherited treasure houses piled high with offerings from generations of devout pilgrims. One small lama owned a Russian cuckoo clock given him in a previous life on a journey to Mongolia in the company of the late thirteenth Dalai Lama. The clock was a source of wonder throughout the lamasery and, each day, a posse of young monks would assemble outside the chamber of its owner to see the clock strike noon.

It worried Ari that he could not recall a single detail of his previous existence. 'If I lived in that cave for forty years,' he said to Phuntsog one day, 'then at least I would remember the smell.'

Phuntsog was ready with an explanation. 'It is not at all surprising. Your first life was spent in deep meditation. All worldly thoughts were banished.'

'Even the smell?'

'Yes, even that.'

'Supposing there has been a mistake?'

'Mistake?'

'Supposing I am not the Rimpoche?'

'Of course you are. The Abbot had a vision. He saw your house. Remember?'

'There are many houses like ours.'

'The Abbot is a very wise man with much experience of finding Rimpoches.'

'But he could still be wrong.'

Phuntsog was unruffled. When the boy was older he would realise that the Abbot was never wrong. The Abbot of Litang was renowned throughout Tibet for the accuracy and significance of his visions. 'In any case,' said Phuntsog, 'there is the rosary and the walking-stick. You recognised those.'

'Yes,' said Ari. He remembered them. Or at least he thought he did.

When Ari was ten years old his eldest sister, Drolkar, married. She married the son of a merchant family who had made a fortune trading between Litang, Lhasa, and Kalimpong. Ari's mother, who had engineered the marriage, regarded it as the greatest triumph of her life. Almost every *sang* of Pema's modest savings was invested in providing Drolkar with a dowry.

Like all girls from the Kham region, Drolkar wore her fortune in her hair, which – according to tradition – was braided into one hundred and eight strands. Silver coins and turquoise brooches were attached to the braids and, when the day of Drolkar's wedding came, the coins hung down her back in three rows as far as her waist.

Sonam, the boy she married, was a member of a minor branch of the Pangda Tsangs, one of the greatest trading families in Tibet. Like most of the young men of Kham, Sonam was tall and proud and walked with a swagger. He wore gold earrings, his hair was in two long plaits, and he excelled in feats of horsemanship. Among the young women of the neighbourhood, his capture was considered a triumph as a result of which the Paljor family gained much face.

But Pema was not concerned with face. Nor was she concerned with Sonam's looks or wealth. She had arranged her daughter's marriage because the Pangda Tsangs, with their warehouses in Kalimpong and Calcutta, had a foothold in the outside world. Like

35

everyone else in Litang she had heard the rumours that the State Oracle in Lhasa had prophesied the imminence of a great misfortune. If and when misfortune struck, Pema was determined that her family should have a foothold in the world beyond the Himalayas.

By his fourteenth birthday Ari had grown into a fine young man. He was tall and strong and his skin was unusually fair. Even with his shaven head and his maroon monks' robe, it was clear that he was uncommonly handsome. His mother told anyone who would listen that it was an awful waste of a young man's life to be cooped up with those avaricious lamas. The neighbours were appalled by such blasphemy. What an ungrateful woman, they said, not to appreciate the rich blessing bestowed upon her in giving birth to an incarnate lama. But Pema would have none of it. She loathed the lamas and she didn't care who knew.

By the time he was fourteen, Ari could recite by heart long passages of the holy texts that formed the basis of his education. He could recount page after page from Sakya Pandita's *Knowing All*, and was well acquainted with the writings of Padmasambhava. But he knew virtually nothing of the world beyond Tibet. Of India he knew only that it was the home of many of the greatest Buddhist teachers. He also knew that it was a place to which traders, such as his brother-in-law, went with salt and yak skins and returned with such wonders as watches and oil lamps.

China he knew because it was the place from which the soldiers came who had crucified the mule driver. Sometimes Han soldiers came to the lamasery, demanding taxes for their government. China was also the source of many of the goods on sale in the market at Litang, including bricks of tea with names like Flaming Jewel and Double Thunderbolt.

Apart from Han soldiers, Ari had only once set eyes upon foreigners. That was when two men with pale skins had passed through Litang on their way to Lhasa. They were said to have come from a far-off country called Yingland. When Ari had asked Phuntsog where Yingland was, the old monk had said vaguely that it was many months' walk to the west of Lhasa. That was all the information he could offer. It was the first time that Ari had seen Phuntsog stumped for an answer.

The two Yingland men visited the lamasery. Ari had seen them one evening near the great prayer hall. With other young monks he had trailed them for hours in and out of the temples. Unlike Tibetans they did not remove their boots before entering the temples and they did not make prostrations before the images of the Buddha. They also had big noses and fair hair – features much remarked upon by the crowd that followed them.

No other foreigners came to Litang, although it was rumoured that at Chamdo, some way to the west, there was a man from Yingland who was employed by the Tibetan government. He was said to have a machine through which it was possible to speak to people in Lhasa and also in India and China. Sonam confirmed that this was so. He had seen the man and his machine. It was a miracle.

Sonam said that the Han also had such machines and this news caused Ari deep gloom. How will we ever defend ourselves, he wondered, from foreigners with talking machines? He put this to Phuntsog one evening. Phuntsog considered the matter gravely and said there was nothing to worry about. 'We have something no other country has. His Holiness the Dalai Lama will watch over and protect us.'

Three days later, the advance units of the Red Army reached Litang.

7

THE RED ARMY did not stop at Litang. Throughout the Year of the Iron Tiger and into the Year of the Iron Hare, long columns of Han soldiers marched through Litang on their way to central Tibet. They had come, they said, to liberate Tibet from foreign imperialists. No one could recall seeing a foreign imperialist unless the Han were referring to the two foreigners who had passed through several summers ago. Evidently they were. There was much discussion in the tea houses of Litang as to exactly what constituted a foreign imperialist.

The Han did not find the going easy. Their soldiers were not equipped to operate at such heights. Many were boys, not much older than Ari, from the teeming coastal provinces of eastern China. Their thin cotton uniforms were inadequate for the cold Tibetan nights and their stomachs, used to a diet of rice and vegetables, did not easily adapt to barley porridge and yak meat. Rumour had it that they were dying like flies. People who lived near the Han encampment claimed that the air was thick with smoke from funeral pyres.

Such rumours gave rise to false optimism. People seeing the pale, sickly Han soldiers loitering in the market-place said that they would soon give up and go home. Traders began taking bets as to how long it would be before they departed. Gradually, however, the Han acclimatised. Supplies of yak and sheep skins were purchased and, before long, Han soldiers were seen in warm boots and jackets. It was whispered that some traders were doing very well out of the Han presence. A damn sight too well, some said.

By the end of the Year of the Iron Hare, it was clear that the Han had come to stay. Batang, Kanze, and Jyekundo had been occupied. The Upper Yangtse had been crossed in at least three places. At Chamdo, the Tibetan army had disintegrated and the governor, Ngapo, had been captured. So, it was said, had the foreigner from Yingland and his talking machine. The Han were apparently making much of this since he was the first foreign imperialist they had captured in Tibet.

From Lhasa came word that the Dalai Lama had fled in the direction of India. This was followed by news that negotiations were underway between the Han and the Tibetan government. The prospect of negotiation with the Han was treated with derision in the tea house of Litang. How typical of those cowardly aristocrats in Lhasa. No self-respecting citizen of Kham would rest until the last Han had been driven from Tibet.

And it wasn't all talk, either. From the north came stories of whole regiments of Han soldiers being cut down by Kham warriors. Young nomads from the Chang Tang appeared at the lamasery seeking blessings that, they hoped, would make them invincible to Han bullets. Caravans of wounded Han soldiers were seen on the trail leading back towards China. Sonam whispered that his uncles were organising the resistance.

A winter passed and then a summer. Snow powdered the mountains and dissolved with the first rays of spring sunlight. Nomads came down with their yaks and sheep from the high pastures and went back again. Fields of barley ripened in the sun and were harvested. Caravans of traders continued to ply back and forth between Litang, Kalimpong, and Lhasa.

Sonam made his first trip to India and returned with tales of iron horses that ran on rails and pulled carriages containing hundreds of people. In due course word came from Lhasa that the Dalai Lama had returned. There was talk of an agreement with the Han, which would enable Tibet to remain free. The prophecies of the oracles became less apocalyptic.

In Litang the Han soldiers kept to themselves. They rarely ventured out of their encampment and when they did so it was only in groups of half a dozen or more. Gradually the Han encampment began to assume an air of permanence. Tents gave way to neat rows of stone barracks. The Han soldiers started cultivating vegetables and keeping chickens. A network of talking machines on wooden poles was set up around the camp. At dawn each morning these machines emitted loud music and barked instructions in the unintelligible Han language. The soldiers would line up outside their barracks bending and stretching in time with the music. This was a source of much hilarity among local farmers, who gathered outside the perimeter to watch. Ragged nomad children whiled away the daylight hours imitating the mysterious ways of the Han. In due course the novelty wore off, but not before some time.

It had to be admitted that the Red Han were quite unlike any other Chinese soldiers seen in Litang. They took nothing without paying for it. In their dealings with local people they were courteous. They respected the lamas and made no attempt to interfere with local customs. When summer came they were even to be seen helping poor farmers gather in their harvests.

When the new year dawned, the Han officer in charge of the camp invited the Abbot and the senior lamas to a banquet. The heads of several leading families were also invited. There was much debate as to whether or not the invitations should be accepted. One school of thought said that it was a fiendish Han trick and that, once inside the encampment, they would not be permitted to leave. Others said it was better to accept the invitations – otherwise the Han would be insulted. In the event the invitations were accepted. The party carried on until nearly dawn and some of the lamas returned a little unsteady on their feet. They came with tales of a banquet the like of which they had never seen. There had been much toasting with rice wine and talk of undying friendship between the Tibetan and Han peoples. There were those among the common people who thought that their leaders were getting on just a little too well with the conquerors.

As to the intentions of the Han, little was said at first. There was talk that the road was to be extended from Kanting. Some said it would eventually go all the way to Lhasa and beyond. This was dismissed as wild talk. Word came that a seventeen-point agreement between the Dalai Lama's government and the Han had been signed in Peking. This occasioned another banquet at the Han military encampment and once again the feasting went on well into the night.

Whatever the terms of the agreement, it did not seem to provide for the departure of the Han. On the contrary, with every day that passed the Han encampment seemed to grow ever more permanent. The commanding officer now had his own residence: a little white-washed stone house built around a tiny courtyard. When that was completed, a concert hall began to rise. With each spring more troops arrived in Litang, resting for a few days before marching on into the interior. It was said that they would be used to build the road, but there were those who voiced doubts.

There was no more talk of saving Tibet from foreign imperialists. Instead, the Han began to speak quietly of liberating Tibet from feudalism. The citizens of Litang were puzzled by this new word. Various wise men were consulted as to its meaning, but no one could shed any light. Not even the Abbot knew. The senior lamas puzzled over it for days until, eventually, the oracle was consulted. The Abbot remained closeted with the oracle for over an hour. There is no record of what was said, but it was soon after that the Abbot sent to Kalimpong for another consignment of .303 rifles.

The Rifles arrived at dead of night. They came in a caravan of mules whose hooves were bound with sacking to muffle the sound on the flagstones of the lamasery courtyard. Ari knew they were coming because Sonam had told him. Sonam had also made him swear to tell no one. 'The Han have many spies,' he said.

The rifles had been purchased in Kalimpong by one of Sonam's uncles. The Han had not yet occupied the high passes leading to India. So it was an easy matter to smuggle the guns into Tibet. For the last three stages of the long journey, the caravan had travelled only at night, avoiding the main trails. It was perfectly safe because the Han never ventured out of their encampments at night.

Ari watched the boxes being unloaded. The Abbot's bodyguard supervised. The Abbot himself watched discreetly from an upper window. Half a dozen of the brawniest servant-monks had been entrusted with the unloading. One of the boxes fell and the contents spilt with a clatter onto the flagstones. The guns were long and sleek – quite unlike the crude muskets that the Khambas used for hunting. They gleamed in the moonlight. There were also

41

boxes said to contain ammunition, so heavy that they took two men to carry. The unloading took the best part of an hour. The Abbot ordered the weapons to be stored in a vault below the great prayer hall. It was a secret place known only to the most trusted lamas.

'Why do we need so many guns?' asked Ari when Sonam came to the monastery next day.

'To kill Han.' Sonam gave a wicked smile and drew a hand across his throat. 'Many Han, many guns,' he added unnecessarily.

'But how can a Buddhist kill?' From an early age Phuntsog had drummed into Ari that he was not to kill even a fly.

Sonam's white teeth flashed another of his wicked smiles. 'The Abbot has talked to the Buddha. Buddha says that in the case of Han he will make an exception.'

8

THE YEAR OF the Iron Hare gave way to that of the Water
Dragon. The Years of the Water Snake and the Wood Horse
followed. The Year of the Wood Sheep loomed. By now the
Han encampment had expanded considerably. Every building
was made of stone. The Han flag flew from a stout wooden
mast in the centre of the parade ground. Timber had to be
imported across great distances, since Litang was above the tree
line.

In spring and summer Han soldiers could be seen at all hours of
the day tending their vegetable gardens, which now extended
down to the river. The Han had also rented pasture land from local
farmers and started to keep sheep and pigs. A number of local
people had been employed as labourers at the Han encampment.
They were paid above the going rate, which caused some grum-
bling from the lamas and the local gentry.

In their dealings with the people, the Han remained as courteous
as ever. Each summer Han troops toured the countryside helping
with the harvest and would not accept so much as a cup of *chang*
without paying for it. Concert parties at the encampment were
now a regular feature of life in Litang. Everyone was invited. Even
– to the disgust of the lamas – beggars, who clogged the south gate
of the lamasery.

Relations between the lamas and the Han remained cordial, if
formal. There was much bowing and scraping on the part of the
Han towards the Abbot and his retinue. There was talk of undying
friendship between the Tibetan and Han peoples. Those who
observed closely, however, claimed to detect a hint of strain in the
fixed smiles of the Han.

For their part, the lamas took turns in giving senior Han officers
conducted tours of the lamasery. In the prayer hall the officers
stood upon the very stone that marked the entrance to the secret

43

vault where the guns were stored. It was not only the Han who could deceive.

As for the Abbot, he remained aloof – venturing out to the Han encampment twice a year to celebrate the Chinese and Tibetan new years. In return the Han commander and his officers were invited to the annual celebrations for the birthday of the Dalai lama.

Meanwhile, consignments of guns continued to arrive at regular intervals. Younger monks began leaving for the Chang Tang where, it was rumoured, the nomads gave training in the use of the weapons.

Work began on the road that, the Han claimed, would bring prosperity to Tibet. There were those who had doubts, but the rates of pay offered to labourers were generous and there was no shortage of recruits. Work continued even in winter. Some of the labourers became ill and died. This caused some resentment, but the work went on.

The presence of so many Han began to distort the small economy of Litang. The prices of grain and meat rose until they were beyond the reach of ordinary citizens. The Han, it seemed, were buying up everything. By the end of the third winter, and for the first time in living memory, there was hunger in Litang. People began to complain. A deputation of citizens went to see the Han commander. He was sympathetic, but unhelpful. Everything would be fine, he said, once the road was complete.

The lamas did their best to discourage the road. Word was spread that all those who worked on it would be cursed. Every possible piece of ill fortune was ascribed to the coming of the road, but it advanced remorselessly. It ascended the high passes that led from Kanze, and ran along the floor of the valley into the town. In places it was no more than a perilous ledge skirting the summit of an impossible mountain. Elsewhere it descended in wide loops into sunless chasms. Those who had been furthest along it reported that the people of other valleys were also engaged in road building. It seemed, in that Year of the Wood Horse, as if every creature in the east of Tibet, man and beast, was employed upon the construction of that accursed road.

*

The day came at last when the road was complete. At the suggestion of the Han commander, the Abbot declared a public holiday. Everyone who had worked on the road received, by way of bonus, a sack of barley. The very barley that had been purchased in the local market and was now beyond the means of ordinary citizens.

The Han erected a makeshift arch across the road near their encampment, which they decked out with flags and flowers. At the top, in the centre, they placed a large portrait of a moon-faced Han. A picture of the young Dalai Lama was placed alongside. It was considerably smaller, a fact that did not go unremarked by the lamas. There was much discussion about the identity of this moon-faced Han. In answer to inquiries, the soldiers would say only that he was the Great Leader and Wise Teacher of all the peoples in the world.

'As great as His Holiness?' ventured one of the traders who had a smattering of the Han language.

To which the only response was a patronising smile.

That was the first the people of Litang had heard of Mao Tse-tung.

The first vehicle to make the journey from Kanze to Litang was a truck containing more Han soldiers. So was the second. And the third. A band played. Soldiers marched, carrying, as they did so, another large portrait of the Great Teacher and Wise Leader. Tibetan spectators were given tiny paper flags to wave. They reminded Ari of the flags he had seen inserted into the fingernails of the crucified mule driver.

There was some excitement since few Tibetans had ever before seen a motor vehicle. They approached the trucks with caution. A youth reached out and touched the bonnet. It was hot and he withdrew his hand swiftly. By and by someone plucked up the courage to stand on the running-board and to peer into the cab. He was invited inside by the Han driver and permitted to sit holding the steering wheel. This drew a great cheer from the crowd. Before long, Tibetans were clambering all over the truck.

A little platform had been erected. There were to be speeches. The drivers of the first vehicles to traverse the road were formally welcomed. The commander made a little speech in which he talked of the road as yet another glorious achievement of the Chinese Communist Party. No one was quite sure to what he was referring. The commander thoughtfully added that the road was also a fine example of co-operation between the Han and Tibetan peoples. This provoked polite applause though Ari noticed that some people conspicuously abstained. When the speeches were over there was much hand-shaking and back-slapping. Everyone seemed happy, but most of all the Han. After all, it was their road.

Ari's guardian, Phuntsog, died soon after the road opened. He had been in decline ever since the first Han had arrived in Litang nearly five years ago, though there was no reason to suppose any connection between the two events.

For the last year of his life Phuntsog had been confined to his bed. Ari visited him every day, sometimes taking medicines recommended by his mother. They made no difference. Phuntsog slowly grew thinner and weaker until his whole body was as decrepit as his withered arm.

Sometimes they talked about the Han. Ari would report on the progress of the road or the latest increase in the price of tea. Phuntsog would shake his old head sadly.

'Our life will never be the same again,' he said.

When Ari asked what he meant, Phuntsog said that these Han were not like those who had come to Tibet in the past. 'These Han are much cleverer. They have iron horses and talking machines. They will never go home.'

'We can fight them.'

'No,' said Phuntsog, 'It is no use to fight. There are too many. They would kill us all. We must find another country to help us. A country with iron horses and talking machines like those of the Han.'

'India?' said Ari. It was the only other country he could think of.

'Maybe. But there are other places, far away, more powerful even than the Han. I have heard it said that they have machines that fly.'

Flying machines. Phuntsog had spoken of these before. Ari had asked Sonam who had confirmed that such things existed, but he offered no details.

46

'Yingland?' Ari remembered the two fair-skinned foreign imperialists who had passed through Litang many years before.

'Perhaps, but there is also another place.' Phuntsog, too, was vague. His memory was failing and he was tired. Ari did not press him further and the subject did not arise again. Within three days Phuntsog was dead. His body was dismembered and fed to the vultures on the funeral rock.

Later, after the remains had been picked clean, Ari went back to the funeral rock and collected the bones to prevent them being ground up for fertiliser. Phuntsog had been a good man and he deserved better than that. Ari put the remains in an earthenware flower pot and buried them in the vegetable garden that he and Phuntsog had tended. Except for one small piece of thigh bone, which he placed by the butter lamp on his altar on Phuntsog's memory. It was Ari's only souvenir of the man he had loved like a father.

By the end of the summer the road reached Chamdo. Before long, said the Han, it would reach Lhasa. The iron horses soon became a familiar sight in Litang. Long convoys rumbled through the valley, clouds of dust rising in their wake. Some went no further than the Han encampment; others rested the night and then moved on.

The opening of the road brought to Litang other Han who were not soldiers. These Han did not wear the olive-green uniform of the Red Army. They were clad in blue or grey cotton tunics and trousers. In winter these were padded against the cold. In fact, the Han seemed to find the weather cold for most of the year and they walked around looking as though they were wearing all the clothes they owned. Some of the more important Han had sheepskin coats, which came down to their ankles, and hats made of yak hide that covered their ears. For the first time Han women appeared, among them the commander's wife. And in due course children.

Except at official functions the Han did not mix with Tibetans. Compounds were built to house the new arrivals. Their houses were not built in the Tibetan style, but were long barrack-like structures with metal roofs. Eventually a small school was opened for the handful of Han children and Han teachers were brought in to teach them. A hospital was built that catered exclusively for Han. The Tibetans became alarmed. 'Soon they will out-number us,' people said. Everyone knew that on the great plains of China there was an inexhaustible supply of Han.

After the opening of the road, Ari thought he detected a change in the attitude of the Han. They no longer appeared so obsequious in their dealings with the lamas. For the first time there were reports of fierce arguments between Han and Tibetans. Usually over prices in the market. Instead of paying whatever was asked, as they had done until now, some Han resorted to abuse. The gist of which usually seemed to be that Tibetans were greedy, dirty, and incompetent. At about this time there was also a reduction in the rates the Han paid to labourers.

Soon there were reports that the Han had imposed a tax on traders returning from India. There was talk also of a land tax. The proceeds, it was said, would go towards making Tibet into a modern country, like China. The ears of the lamas pricked up as soon as they heard of this. The Abbot dispatched his chief steward to the Han encampment to make inquiries. Instead of being received with the usual courtesy, the steward was kept waiting two hours before the commander would deign to see him. And when at last he was received, the steward was treated to a long lecture about the feudal and backward nature of Tibetan society. The time had come, said the commander, for great changes. What changes, he did not specify.

The details were not long in coming. From outlying villages came reports that the Han were telling farmers that they were no longer required to pay so much rent to the lamas. Drastic reductions were proposed. Large farmers were told they should hand over surplus land to the landless. The Abbot immediately dispatched a mission to investigate. They were gone for two weeks and what they reported on their return only confirmed his worst fears. He ordered a new tax to be imposed. Farmers were ordered to contribute an additional five per cent of their annual income. This was to be called a 'Save Tibet' tax. It was to be collected discreetly. The proceeds would be spent on the weapons Sonam's uncles were buying in Kalimpong.

Now it was more difficult to bring guns in from India. The caravans were being searched. There were reports that guns had been found and that the Han were recruiting beggars and vagabonds to act as their spies. They were rumoured even to have spies inside the lamasery.

Although no one in Litang had any love for the Han, there was support for the proposed rent reductions. 'These Han can't be all bad,' said Ari's mother when he told her what was happening.

Ari was shocked. 'How can you say such a thing?'

Pema refused to be drawn. 'You know what I think of the lamas,' she said. 'My opinion has been the same since long before the Han came to Litang.' The years of hard work had told on Pema. She walked bent double from a pain in her back for which there seemed to be no cure. The colour had drained from her face, despite the long hours spent in the open air. She had no husband. The lamas had taken her only son. One of her daughters had already married and moved away. It was only a matter of time before the others went too. Then she would be alone.

One day in the late summer, after the barley had been harvested and spread out along the road for the trucks to pound under their wheels (the Han road had its uses), the steward of the lamasery received a summons to the Han encampment. Here he was handed a letter for the Abbot. It was addressed in perfect Tibetan script, bound with a red ribbon, and sealed with wax. The contents were, however, relayed orally to the steward: a plump man with small pig-like eyes and a tendency to belch involuntarily. He was, said the Han commander, to provide the Han with an inventory of the entire possessions of the Litang lamasery. The extent of its lands and the assets of its satellites. The contents of its treasure houses. Income from rents. Even the offerings of pilgrims were to be accounted. And to ensure that nothing was omitted, said the commander, a team of Han inspectors would in due course be making a tour of the lamasery and its estates.

When the news was conveyed to the Abbot he was said to have flown into a fearsome rage. All manner of curses were invoked upon the loathsome Han. Oracles were consulted. Special prayers were said. A meeting of head men from all the villages in Litang

49

was summoned. There was dark talk of an uprising. The Han made no attempt to interfere, but they were watching. They now had checkposts on all the roads into and out of the valley and on most of the high passes leading to India. Every traveller was asked to state his business and, more often than not, his baggage was searched. It was even said that the Han had spies among the beggars on the south gate of the lamasery, taking note of everyone who entered.

A summer passed. No more was heard of the new taxes. The barley was harvested and the serfs contributed their tithes as usual. It was noted that Han soldiers had abandoned their practice of helping with the harvest, but beyond that nothing much had changed. After the harvest the usual picnics were held on the banks of the river. There was dancing, displays of archery, and horse racing. Han soldiers mingled unarmed with the crowds. One or two even joined in the festivities.

Winter came. The nomads descended as they did each year from the high plateau with their sheep and yaks.

In the last month of the Year of the Wood Sheep a delegation of Han officers appeared at the lamasery. Four officers and a Tibetan interpreter. The same one who had accompanied that first group of Han five years earlier to announce that Litang had been liberated. It was obvious that they were important Han because they wore thick coats and hats of yak fur and they came in two small iron horses covered at the back with a canopy. 'We wish to speak to the Abbot,' they said. They had come unannounced. Usually they were scrupulous about making appointments in advance. Asked to state their business, they were evasive.

After being kept waiting all of an hour, they were shown into the presence not of the Abbot, but of the steward. 'We have come to see the Abbot,' said the leading Han. The interpreter translated.

'He is praying.' The steward's piglet eyes showed fear.

'Then we will wait until he has finished.'

'The Abbot will be a long time praying. Maybe for two days.' The steward belched. His chins quivered. 'He has asked that you state your business to me.'

The Han who was talking stamped his foot impatiently. There

were other lamas in the shadows. One had his hands buried deep inside his robes.

'It is about the inventory. I have been sent to tell the Abbot that it must be produced by the New Year.'

The steward belched again. It was the first he had heard of the inventory for six months. He had rather hoped it had been forgotten. Apparently not. 'You have no right . . .' he said.

The eyes of the Han spokesman flashed anger. Without pausing for his remarks to be translated, he launched into a long diatribe to the effect that, if the inventory were not forthcoming and if it were not accurate to the last grain of barley, there would be unpleasant consequences. Chairman Mao's name was mentioned. Nowadays it was a prominent feature of every conversation with the Han.

The spokesman was still in full flow when there was a sudden movement in the shadows. The lama whose hand had been concealed inside his robe had withdrawn it. He was clutching a pistol. He took a step forward into the light. He was a big man and his face was pock-marked. He held the pistol at arm's length, the barrel pointing directly at the head of Han who was speaking.

The Han stopped in mid-sentence. His face registered more amazement than fear. The interpreter took a step backwards. The lama with the gun remained stock still. The other lamas advanced from the shadows.

A full minute elapsed before the silence was broken. With a flourish of his hand towards the lama with the gun, the Han turned on his heel and stalked out of the room threatening dire retribution. The interpreter and the other Han bustled after him. The lamas stood at the window overlooking the courtyard. They watched the Han climb into their iron horses and depart.

Within days word of the incident had spread throughout Litang. The people waited fearfully for the Han to respond. There were prayers and prostrations. The name of the Buddha was invoked with a fervour exceptional for the time of year.

But nothing happened. The Han could be observed going about their business as usual. When the Han New Year came, there was the customary invitation to the Abbot and his retinue to attend the festivities at the encampment. In the circumstances, however, the Abbot thought it wise to decline. He did so politely.

The Tibetan New Year passed without incident, although for the first time no invitations were issued to the Han commander and his officers. It was not until the early hours of the last day of the first month of the Year of the Fire Monkey – which corresponded in the world outside to 28 February 1956 – that Ari was woken by the sound of gunfire from the direction of the Han encampment. The Litang uprising had begun.

9

THE BATTLE BEGAN gradually. A rapid outburst of firing followed by silence. Then another outburst. And another. At first Ari thought someone was setting off the firecrackers left over from the New Year celebrations. He lay on his bed listening. In the alley-way beneath his window he could hear voices. Someone was banging on the door. It was his servant, Aten. He sounded agitated. 'Rimpoche, you must get up. The Khambas have attacked the Han.'

Ari was wide awake. The crackle of gunfire was now almost continuous. He groped in the darkness for his robe and pulled it over him. There was an explosion. A dull, muffled sound repeated at regular intervals. Aten was outside, waiting. He indicated the ladder leading to the roof. 'From the roof, you can see, Rimpoche.'

The other novices were already on the roof. So were some of the little servant-monks, chattering excitedly. Someone lit a butter lamp; a gruff voice from below told him to put it out. The darkness was total. There was no moon. Ari shivered, as much from excitement as from cold.

And then, in the distance, there was a fire. First a flicker, then a blaze fanned by the icy wind. A series of unrelated explosions followed. 'The Han ammunition store.' Aten seemed surprisingly well informed.

Suddenly the sky was set alight by something fired from within the Han encampment. The angry clouds were tinted red. Ari could make out the silhouettes of men on horseback. A ferocious outbreak of gunfire followed. It seemed to be coming from inside the encampment. The Han were fighting back.

The light faded and darkness was restored but, from then on, at intervals, the sky was set alight in this manner. Each illumination was followed by a tremendous burst of firing from within the Han encampment. There was much talk among the novices as to the cause of this phenomenon. No one could explain it, beyond saying that it must be some new weapon of the Han. The working of miracles, it seemed, was no longer exclusive to the lamas.

By dawn the battle had receded. What firing there was appeared to come from farther away. The fires in the Han encampment seemed to be out. Glumly, Ari and his fellow novices concluded that the rebellion had failed.

Daylight showed the plain in front of the lamasery to be empty. There was no sign of the old women who came each morning to tread the holy walk around the lamasery, twirling their prayer wheels and clutching their beads. No sign either of the little servant-monks commuting back and forth between the lamasery and the river, buckets swinging from their narrow shoulders. Even the beggars had gone from the south gate.

From the Han encampment a plume of black smoke spiralled upward to the sky.

The tolling of the bell in the Abbot's courtyard summoned the senior lamas to the prayer hall. Ari and the other young Rimpoches went too. The excited chatter of a few hours earlier had given way to gloom and fear. They sat cross-legged on their cushions, talking in whispers. There was the sound of bells and drums and the droning of lamas at prayer. The smells were of incense, rancid butter, and unwashed bodies. Two boy servants served butter tea from an enormous urn, which would comfortably have accommodated both of them.

The Abbot was seated on his dais, his parched features more grim than ever. He cleared his throat loudly, as he always did when he had something important to say. There was, he said, no time for formalities. Khamba warriors had attacked the Han encampment. The attack had failed, but there would be others. In the meantime the lamasery must be defended. He had given orders for the gates to be closed and barricaded. No one was to be allowed out or in. Fortunately the Lord Buddha had endowed him with the foresight to lay in a considerable quantity of guns and ammunition. There was also food enough to last for three months. Deep wells had been dug to ensure the water supply. They were being completed even as he spoke. A number of younger monks had recently returned from the Chang Tang where they had received training in the use of firearms. They would teach those who lacked such skills.

This news was greeted with a rumble of discontent. Like everyone else, the senior lamas had heard the rumours, but this was the first they had been officially told. The Abbot again cleared his throat, emitting a gob of spit that landed squarely inside a stone spittoon a good yard from where he was seated. He expressed regret that he had not been able to take all the senior lamas into his confidence, but these were extraordinary times and demanded exceptional measures. He was sure there was no one present who begrudged the few practical steps he had felt it necessary to take to safeguard the heritage of Litang and its people. He paused to run a beady eye over the assembly. No one met his gaze and he continued unchallenged. He had, he said, consulted all the appropriate authorities including the oracle and at least three holy hermits. Many hours had been spent in prayer and contemplation. He spoke vaguely of visions, the contents of which were unspecified. He had, he said, even dispatched messages to the government in Lhasa. (These last, he added acerbically, had produced no response whatever. Not so much as an acknowledgement.) Such advice as he had received was unanimous: buy guns. That he had done. Indeed, a considerable store of rifles and ammunition lay in a vault directly below the very flagstones upon which they were now seated.

The lamas shifted uneasily.

He now proposed to issue the guns to the younger monks. Anyone who could not bring himself to shoot Han would not be obliged to. But he had consulted all the relevant authorities and could assure anyone who had doubts that no penalties would accrue to anyone who killed in defence of the faith. On the contrary, the Buddha would regard such an act as one deserving exceptional merit.

The vault was opened and the weapons brought up, still in their wooden crates. An eager queue of young monks had assembled at the steps of the prayer hall. Each was given a rifle and a hundred rounds. They held out their robes, like housewives' aprons, to receive the ammunition. The rifles were British made .303s, sleek and well-oiled. The sort only the richest families could afford. The boys handled them with the confidence of those who had been reared since birth in the company of guns. There was hardly a family in the whole of Kham that did not own some sort of weapon, if only an ancient flintlock bequeathed by forefathers who had traded in India or China. Indeed, if truth be told, not a few of the lamas had weapons of their own stashed discreetly in their chambers. Officially, they were used for warding off wolves and bandits during spiritual missions to the high plateau. In practice, it was not uncommon on warm summer days to see a party of monks setting off on a hunting expedition to the forests in the lower valleys. Nor was it unknown for the vicious feuding that, on occasion, broke out between one lamasery and another to be resolved by an exchange of gunfire.

Beyond the walls of the lamasery, the silence persisted. The nomads who inhabited the plain during winter had disappeared overnight, taking most of their animals with them. Here and there a yak or a sheep grazed unattended. In the town the streets were empty. The shops remained shuttered. Smoke from kitchen stoves was the only sign of life. Not a dog or a beggar stirred.

Only at the Han camp were there signs of activity. At intervals a siren sounded. Tiny figures scurried hither and thither. The Han talking machine barked instructions. The plumes of smoke gradually dissolved into a clear blue sky.

By and by, half-a-dozen horsemen appeared from the direction of the town. They were wild, ragged men from the high plateau. One of them had what appeared to be a bullet wound in his left shoulder, which was bleeding profusely. The gate was opened just wide enough to admit them. They brought with them a heavy gun and a belt of ammunition that ran through its middle. Captured, they said, from the Han during the previous night's fighting. On the orders of the Abbot it was erected above the main gate from which was to be had a clear view of the road leading from the Han encampment.

The men brought news of the rebellion. Many Han had been killed, they claimed. There had, it was true, been a withdrawal, but this was only temporary. There would be another attack that night.

Nightfall, however, brought no new attack. Only the occasional crackle of gunfire and that from much further away than the encampment. When dawn broke the monks awoke to find the lamasery surrounded by Han.

Ari watched in dismay from the roof of his chamber. The Han were everywhere. Behind rocks and boulders that cast long shadows in the early morning light. In deep trenches that had somehow appeared overnight. They had even, despite the snow, erected a heavy gun halfway up the hill overlooking the lamasery.

'What are we going to do?' Ari asked Lobsang, the elderly monk who had befriended him since the death of Phuntsog.

'Stay calm and await the guidance of the Buddha.' That was Lobsang's answer to everything.

'We are trapped. They will kill us all. Look.' Ari waved his arm towards the huge gun on the hillside behind them. Even as he spoke, two Han were inserting a shell in the breech. The shell was so big that even two men could only carry it with difficulty.

'The Buddha will have a plan.' With that the old man went back to telling his beads. He did not give so much as a glance towards the gun on the hill.

Yesterday it had seemed good news to hear that so many Han had been killed. Today it did not seem so fortunate. The Han were unlikely to be generous in victory.

Ari looked towards his family's house. It was but a short distance from the Han encampment. There was no sign of movement. He wondered if he would ever see his mother and sisters again.

'ESTEEMED ABBOT, RESPECTED LAMAS, PEOPLE OF LI-TANG.' The voice, speaking the language of Kham, boomed across the valley, echoing off the hills. From where was it coming? No one could see. Heads appeared cautiously above parapets. Was this yet another Han trick? 'WE REGRET THAT THERE HAS BEEN AN UNFORTUNATE MISUNDERSTANDING.' At last the source was located. A metal basin propped on its side atop a pile of rocks by one of the Han trenches. Some sort of string led from it and disappeared into the trenches. 'BANDITS AND REACTIONARY ELEMENTS HAVE ATTEMPTED TO DESTROY THE UNDYING BROTHERHOOD BETWEEN THE HAN AND TIBE –' The voice was silenced by a single rifle shot, which toppled the metal basin backwards into the trench. From the lamasery wall there was cheering and laughter.

Within ten minutes the voice had resumed. It began again as though the interruption had not occurred. 'ESTEEMED ABBOT, RESPECTED LAM –' This time the voice was silenced by a fusillade of shots. The metal basin disappeared. Hunched figures could be seen scurrying in and out of the Han trenches.

It was an hour before the voice resumed. Louder, clearer, and altogether more menacing. 'WE ARE VERY PATIENT. WE CAN WAIT. BUT WE WILL NOT WAIT FOR EVER.' There was a further volley of shots, but to no effect. This time the Han were using not one, but many metal basins. The voice paused to allow the firing to cease and then calmly resumed. 'YOU HAVE UNTIL NOON TOMORROW TO COME OUT OF THE LAMASERY AND SURRENDER YOUR GUNS. IF YOU DO SO, YOU WILL BE TREATED LENIENTLY. IF NOT, YOU WILL PAY A HEAVY PRICE.'

Another night passed. By dawn there seemed to be more Han than ever. The trenches had been extended so that they now encircled three sides of the lamasery. The Han talking machine had been rigged up out of rifle range. Patriotic music was playing. Smoke rose from within the trenches where cooking pots boiled over dung fires.

In the lamasery the older lamas busied themselves with rituals imploring deliverance. Hideous devils were carved from blocks of coloured butter and then cast into flames amidst much clashing of cymbals, blowing of horns, and beating of drums. Every chapel hummed to the sound of incessant prayers. A smell of incense pervaded. As the deadline set by the Han approached, the murmuring of prayers assumed unprecedented urgency. But to no avail.

On the dot of noon the Han talking machine sprang to life. The same unseen voice. It began with the usual homily about the undying friendship alleged to exist between the Tibetan and Han peoples and concluded with an assurance that Tibetan religion and customs would be respected by their Han brothers. There was a pause and then the voice said: 'WE WOULD LIKE NOW TO KNOW WHETHER THE MONKS OF LITANG WILL CO-OPERATE WITH US IN BRINGING THIS UNFORTUNATE MISUNDERSTANDING TO A PEACEFUL AND HAPPY CONCLUSION.' The reply was a hail of bullets that clattered uselessly on the stones piled high in front of the Han trenches.

Five minutes later a loud report echoed off the sides of the valley. The earth trembled. A large hole appeared in the roof of the prayer hall. A whiff of smoke drifted from the barrel of the gun on the hillside. The unseen voice was mocking. 'OH, FOOLISH LAMAS, BY YOUR STUBBORN ATTITUDE YOU WILL BRING RUIN UPON LITANG.'

That night a small party of monks, led by one of the nomads who had taken refuge on the first day of the siege, slipped out of the lamasery under cover of darkness. They returned safely after two hours. When dawn broke the Han gun was found to have slipped its moorings and to have plunged onto a rocky outcrop far below, where it lay damaged beyond repair. As for the custodians of the gun, they were discovered lying face down in the snow with their throats cut. When the Han talking machine came on the air next day, the unseen voice spoke no longer of brotherhood but of retribution.

The attack began with a barrage of unexplained explosions. Later, Han soldiers were seen feeding large bullets into a metal tube. In the years ahead Ari and his friends would become familiar with the 55-mm mortar, but now it was yet one more mysterious instrument of Han repression. The explosions ignited a series of small fires, which were easily extinguished. They also caused the first injuries – hideous wounds that no amount of magic from the lama doctors could cure.

The first mortar attack was followed by a full-scale assault. To the amazement of the monks, hundreds of Han soldiers rose from their trenches and charged the walls. Some carried ladders, others hurled small bombs. Most were cut down before they reached the

wall. The machine-gun above the gate was used to terrible effect –
at least until the bullets ran out. The Han retreated in disarray.
They left behind a score of bodies and a fine selection of guns and
throwing bombs. When darkness fell two young servant-monks
were lowered from the wall in a basket to collect the abandoned
weapons.

This first defeat of the Han led to a somewhat premature
outbreak of festivity. The Buddha was thanked profusely. Offerings of butter and barley were laid on all the altars. A great deal of
chang was drunk. Guns were spontaneously discharged into the
night air. It occurred to Ari that, had the Han chosen to return that
night, they might have entered the lamasery unopposed.

Happily, however, the Han remained in their trenches and
contented themselves with loosing off the occasional mortar
round. In order to limit the damage, the Abbot directed that the
treasures be stripped from the chapels and temples and stored
underground.

On the fifth day a message was received. It was brought by a
woman who had worked at the Han encampment. The poor
woman was shaking with fear. The message proposed negotiations. The Han encampment was suggested as the venue. The
Abbot rejected this out of hand. If the Han wished to talk, they
could come to the lamasery. In due course the Han commander
himself appeared at the main gate. He had with him half-a-dozen
officers and an interpreter. The one who had been present when
the previous Han delegation had been unceremoniously evicted.

The commander was as charming as the day he had first set foot
in Litang. He talked only of misunderstanding. Several of his
officers had exceeded their instructions. There had never been any
intention of expropriating the assets of the lamasery. In due course
there would have to be some changes, but these would be gradual.
As a gesture of goodwill he proposed to postpone all talk of reform
for at least three years.

The Abbot listened stony faced. The interpreter looked neither
at the Abbot nor at the Han. He knew that a special place in hell
had been reserved for him. There would be no reforms, said the
Abbot. None at all. Not now. Not ever. The people of Litang had
been entirely content before the coming of the Han and their

accursed road. To restore contentment among the people, it was necessary only to set a date for the departure of the Han. That, he assumed, was what the commander had come to discuss.

The Han commander's smile faded. 'We Han are very patient people,' he said through clenched teeth. 'We can wait for weeks, months if necessary, until you change your tune.'

It was not until the siege of Litang entered its eighth week that despair began to set in.

There had been no more frontal assaults by the Han. A lama from Amdo had busied himself concocting potions that, he claimed, would make the wearer invincible to Han bullets. A renewed intake of mortar fire had swiftly disproved this, since when no more had been heard of the lama and his potions.

Contact with the outside world had been lost since the fourth week when a messenger, sent out through the Han lines to scour the countryside in search of help, succeeded in re-entering the lamasery. He reported that the rebellion appeared to be at an end and that the Han were firmly in control. He also brought word of a vast new construction project in which the Han were engaged at the far end of the valley. Local people had said it was to be a base for the iron birds whose imminent arrival had long been rumoured.

Food was now rationed to one small bowl of barley meal each day. Ari's cheeks were hollow and for the first time he could count the bones of his rib-cage. 'If we don't get help soon, we will all die,' said Aten as they stood one evening on Ari's roof looking towards the trenches where the Han were still dug in.

'What have we to fear from death? It is the Han who have no gods.'

'It is all right for you, Rimpoche. You will be reborn into a good life. As for me, I could be reborn a donkey or even an earthworm.'

They had had this conversation before. Aten was convinced he was destined to be reincarnated into an even lower form of life than the one he at present inhabited. His father, he asserted, had been reborn a dzo on an estate in Ba. How Aten knew this was unclear, but his confidence was absolute.

'Don't worry. I shall speak to the Buddha. He will take good care of my friend Aten. You will see.'

The Han were in no hurry. The days were growing longer. The snow on the passes was melting. Reinforcements and heavy guns could soon be brought in by road. Then they would teach these lamas a lesson they would not forget.

It was on the sixty-fourth day of the siege that morning prayers were disturbed by a low droning sound unlike any that had ever been heard in Litang. It seemed to be coming from the sky. The look-outs on the south wall cupped their hands around their eyes and gazed eastwards.

At first there was nothing. Then a speck against the clear blue. Growing larger as the sound grew louder.

One of the little novices was first to realise what it was. 'An iron bird,' he shouted. 'The Han are bringing their iron birds.' All winter there had been talk of such things. A lama who had lived in China had talked with foreboding about the awesome powers of the iron bird against which all known weapons were useless.

'The iron birds are coming.' As word spread, shaven heads appeared at windows. Young men scrambled onto walls and rooftops. Ancient lamas shuffled out of shadows. Everyone looked upwards and eastwards, towards the speck in the sky.

At first it looked no bigger than a sparrow. Then it was an eagle. Then it was as big as one of the vultures that hovered over the funeral rock. By the time it was overhead the monks could see that it was far bigger than any bird they had ever seen. As it crossed the plain its wings cast a wide shadow. It swept so low that the watching monks scattered in panic. Some hid in doors and alleyways. Some spread themselves flat, as though prostrating. So great was the noise that many held fingers in their ears until the bird had passed.

From beyond the wall there came the sound of cheering. When Ari looked he could see that the Han soldiers had climbed out of their trenches and were waving their hats in the air.

*

No sooner had the monks recovered than the iron bird returned. This time it circled the lamasery but did not descend. On the underside of its wings and on the back of its body Ari could see red markings, like the flag that flew above the Han encampment.

At about this moment the Han talking machine came to life: 'ESTEEMED LAMAS.' The tone was mocking and arrogant. 'ESTEEMED LAMAS, YOU HAVE SEEN OUR IRON BIRD. WE ARE NOW GOING TO GIVE YOU A DEMONSTRATION OF ITS POWERS. WATCH CAREFULLY.'

Without warning the iron bird descended and roared towards the lamasery from the east. The Han had disappeared back into their trenches. Most monks had also scattered again, but a few braver souls stood their ground, pointing their rifles into the sky. As the iron bird approached an unidentified object was seen to fall from its belly. Seconds later there was a huge explosion followed by a murderous rattle of gunfire. The earth moved. A hailstorm of rocks and earth scattered over roofs and courtyards.

Ari and Aten had concealed themselves behind tea urns in the kitchen. There was a clatter of falling cups and bowls on the stone floor. Through the doorway they glimpsed what seemed to be a line of hailstones advancing rapidly in a line across the courtyard, biting into the flagstones. It was only when they went outside that Ari realised that the hailstones had been bullets. Deadlier bullets than any that Ari had ever seen. A row of huge bullets was embedded in a wash-house door, spaced at precisely equal intervals, like stitching in a robe. When Ari turned from the door he came upon a sight that made him retch. One of the young servant-monks had been directly in the line of fire. The boy was on his back. His mouth was open as though caught in a cry of pain. A trickle of blood ran down his chin. His arms and legs were spreadeagled. And his torso was separated from his abdomen by a hand's breadth.

The iron bird did not return. It circled once and then disappeared in the direction from which it had come. Ari stared after it until it was a tiny speck. Several of the younger monks fired uselessly into the sky. The Han speaking machine came back to life. This time there was no talk of compromise. The message was blunt:

'LAMAS. LISTEN CAREFULLY. YOU HAVE BEEN ABANDONED BY YOUR GODS. YOU HAVE NO CHOICE BUT TO THROW YOURSELVES UPON THE MERCY OF CHAIRMAN MAO AND THE PARTY. SURRENDER BY DAWN TOMORROW OR THE IRON BIRD WILL RETURN TO DESTROY YOUR LAMASERY AND KILL YOU ALL.'

10

'WE MUST GO, Rimpoche.' It was Aten. All day the younger lamas had sat in urgent little groups discussing what was to be done. Some were for fighting to the death. Some for surrendering. Some for praying. Only Aten seemed to think there was any other possibility.

'Go where, Aten?'

'I don't know, Rimpoche. Maybe America.'

They had first heard of America on the Han speaking machine. According to the Han, American imperialists were behind the revolt in Litang. Just what constituted an imperialist had never been clearly established, although the word had featured in Han propaganda for some years now. It occurred to Ari that America might be the place Phuntsog had been trying to think of when he was dying. Now every reference to America on the Han speaking machine was eagerly seized upon. Obviously the Han regarded America as an enemy and, since they referred to it so many times, Ari reasoned that it must be a powerful enemy. Any enemy of the Han must be a friend of Tibet. He had explained all this to Aten and Aten had agreed. America had featured for some time in the prayers of Ari and Aten.

'It's no use, Aten, there is no way out.'

'Yes, Rimpoche, tonight when the Han are sleeping. That is our chance.'

They waited until the fires went down in the Han camps. The moon was hidden by cloud. Somewhere on the mountain, a wolf howled.

Aten produced two pistols. 'Good for killing Han at short distance,' he said.

With Aten there were four others. Servant-monks with coarse features. All strong. No longer prepared to entrust their fate to the

Buddha. One, a youth of no more than fourteen, had an ear missing. A fight, he said, grinning through blackened teeth. They were armed with kitchen knives, which they had passed the day sharpening.

'We can go up the hill,' said Aten. He waved towards the place where the Han artillery had been. The dying embers of a fire gave away the position of the soldiers.

Before he left, Ari had taken a last look round his little room. It had been his home for twelve years and he would never return. This was where Phuntsog had taught him to read and write. Where he had learned to pray. Where, in the early days, he had cried for his mother and sisters. Now he was leaving for ever. He took his sling from its hiding place under the bed and tucked it under his tunic, next to the pistol. He refilled the butter in the lamp and left it burning for good luck. He prostrated three times before the altar. Finally, he attached the piece of Phuntsog's thighbone to a piece of yak hair and hung it about his neck. Then he was ready.

They made their way up through the narrow, sloping streets. Past the library and the prayer hall. They could hear the urgent droning of prayers and smell the incense as they passed.

'Too late now for prayers,' whispered Aten.

To avoid attracting attention, they cut across the vegetable garden where Phuntsog's ashes were buried. Past the temple of the oracle. Past the treasury, now empty of its treasures. Past the dormitory of the servant-monks who fetched and carried for the Abbot and his retinue. Ragged prayer flags fluttered.

They came to the high wall. There was a small door, but it was bolted and barricaded. It opened onto the path that led to the sealed cave where Ari was supposed to have lived in an earlier incarnation. He had been this way with Phuntsog.

There were guards on the wall. Bodyguard monks and nomads who had taken refuge at the beginning of the siege. They sat talking in low, urgent tones, rifles leaning against the wall. There was no light. They were just black shapes.

'Here,' Aten indicated a door into one of the outhouses, which abutted the wall. It had been used to store grain, but was empty now. Dark and cool. Two of the young servant-monks had gone ahead. Invisible in the gloom. Ari groped his way along the inside wall.

'Go on,' hissed Aten.

Ahead he heard a grating sound. A stone moved upon a stone. One of the servant-monks was removing stones from the wall. Ari stumbled against a block of granite on the floor. He stopped and ran his hand lightly along the rear wall until he came upon an aperture. One of the servant-monks had already climbed through. The other followed. Then it was Ari's turn.

'Go quickly, Rimpoche.' Aten's hand was in his back. The butt of the pistol tucked beneath his robe was cold against his stomach.

Inside the wall there was a passage, just wide enough for one man. The stone was damp. Water dripped. Cobwebs trailed. Ari could hear the servant-monks ahead of him. Behind he heard Aten scramble through.

They followed the passage for about fifty paces. In places it was so narrow that he had to turn sideways to squeeze through. Once he had to duck down on hands and knees. Then he felt cold air against his cheek. Another aperture. This one smaller than the other. Ari inserted himself head first, pushing with his feet against the inside wall.

Outside the air was cool and clear. There was a drop about the height of two men. Then Ari found himself beside the first two servant-monks, pressed against the wall. Aten followed. Then the other two.

They started up the hill, still in the same order as before. Two servant-monks before and aft, Ari and Aten in between. They moved carefully. Staying clear of pathways. Freezing when one of them dislodged a stone.

Behind, in the lamasery, they could hear the monotonous chant, '*Om mani padme hum. Om mani padme hum. Om mani padme hum.*' A bell tinkling. A gong sounding.

When they were higher they looked back and could see the glow of the butter lamps. On every altar, in every temple. A last, desperate appeal to the Buddha.

Above, embers still glowed, giving away the position of the Han. They steered well away from the fire. One of the servant-monks went ahead, a knife clenched between his teeth. Ari was breathless. His legs ached. It was so long since he had eaten a good meal. Someone tapped his shoulder. He looked round. It was Aten, smiling, 'Okay, Rimpoche?'

Ari was too tired to smile. 'Okay, Aten.'

Twice they had to turn back because the servant-monk who had gone ahead reported that the way was blocked by Han. Once they caught up with the first monk to find him crouched behind a rock, pointing. Ahead, not twenty paces away, there was a lone Han, seated on a rock, smoking. He had his back half turned towards them. His rifle rested across his knees. Ari made to turn back, but Aten stopped him, gesticulating frantically. Ari half withdrew the pistol. Aten shook his head. Then Ari remembered the sling. Aten must have seen him pocket it before they set out.

Ari made as if to hand the sling to Aten, but the young monk again shook his head. Ari was the better shot. When they were young they had competed, aiming at a row of brass butter dishes on the wall behind the refectory.

Ari hesitated. The servant-monk, the one with the missing ear, was fingering the blade of his knife and gazing wistfully in the direction of the Han. Ari glanced at the Han and then at Aten. Then, without another thought, he selected a large round stone. Silently he stood, steadying himself on a rock. He put the stone in the sling, twirled it once, twice, three times about his head, and hurled with all his strength.

The Han must have heard the whistle of the sling. He made as if to stand, bringing his gun round to face them. But too late. The stone caught him square between the eyes. He made no cry. Just toppled backwards, legs still trailing over the stone that had served as his seat. From where Ari, Aten, and the others were crouched only the soles of the Han's feet were visible in silhouette. When they reached him, the cigarette was still alight between his fingers. The rifle rested loosely across his chest. His cap had dislodged and lay on the ground nearby. Red blood was seeping through his thick black hair and dripping onto the stone that had become his pillow. His forehead had split open. The break was clean, from the bridge of his nose to the line of hair. Ari had killed his first Han.

*

He walked past quickly, trying not to look. One of the servant-monks relieved the dead Han of his rifle and ammunition pouch. Another stole his watch. Later, when they were further up the hill, he displayed it proudly. 'The watch belongs to Rimpoche,' said Aten sharply. 'He killed the Han.'

Instantly the watch disappeared.

'Forget it, Aten. I don't want it.'

Already Ari was haunted by the face of the dead Han, his forehead split. He had been no older than Ari. Younger probably. No doubt his parents were farmers too. Perhaps he was also an only son. With a mother waiting for him to come home. It would be a long time before she knew . . .

'What are you thinking, Rimpoche?' It was Aten again.

'I am thinking about that Han.'

'Why should you care about him? He came to Tibet to kill us.'

'Before, I have never killed even an earthworm.'

'A Han is lower than an earthworm.'

'What would Phuntsog say?'

'Phuntsog? He would be proud of you, Rimpoche.'

Once they were clear of the Han lines they turned right along a ridge overlooking the valley. There was no moon, but the sky was clear and the stars were bright. After they had been walking for about an hour they heard the gunfire. Not one shot, but many and coming from several places. Now and then they heard shouts. Sometimes a scream. It was surprising how far sound carried.

'The lamas have attacked,' said Aten. 'The Han cannot use their iron birds at night.'

The shooting went on for the rest of the night. At first it was single shots. Pistols and rifles. Then came the crackle of the Han machine-guns. Then mortars, shaking the sides of the valley. Crump, crump, crump. Several times the Han fired rockets, which set the sky alight. There were brief glimpses of figures, struggling. Then the vision faded, leaving only the sound of battle.

'We must go, Rimpoche,' said Aten. They had been watching for about ten minutes from their vantage point on the ridge. There was no sign of the four servant-monks. They had vanished into the darkness.

They carried on for another hour – sometimes breaking into a trot, pausing occasionally to look back on the battle. The fires were raging out of control. The curved roofs of temples stood out clearly against the flames.

'Which way to America, Aten?'

'I don't know, Rimpoche. South, maybe?'

11

PEMA PALJOR AND her two younger daughters had spent the
night on the roof of their house, huddled against the biting
wind. Earlier that day they had watched the iron bird circling the
lamasery. The explosion that followed had caused the house to
tremble. As darkness fell they heard the rumble of trucks on the
highway. Pema knew that the Han were moving in for the kill.

She was dozing lightly when the first crackle of gunfire echoed
round the valley. Gunfire was now a familiar sound in Litang, but
Pema knew that this was the end. The firing steadily increased. At
first it seemed to be coming from within the lamasery, but soon
they recognised the big guns of the Han – the dull thump of the
mortar, the muzzle flash of the Han cannon. The sky was alight
with red and yellow flares. The hillsides shook. Nearby a dog
howled and before long it had been joined by every dog in the
valley.

It was well over a month since the last news of Ari. A neighbour's son had escaped from the lamasery and brought word that
Ari was alive and well. There was no shortage of food, the
neighbour's son had reported, the lamas had stocks enough to last
at least another month. That much Pema believed. Those lamas
knew how to look after themselves.

As the weeks passed without any sign of relief, Pema found
herself praying again. She had not prayed since her husband had
disappeared on the Chang Tang. It was nothing personal, she
explained to the Buddha. For him she had only respect. It was
those greedy, good-for-nothing lamas she could not stand. It was
they who had brought this disaster on Litang.

As a token of goodwill, Pema had cleaned out the prayer room
near the top of the house. The butter lamps had been lit again.
Prayer scarves draped the image of the Buddha. The altar was piled
with offerings of barley and dried meat. Dechen, Pema's youngest

daughter, had even donated her gold earrings. The Buddha, she said, was welcome to them, if he delivered Ari safely.

Drolkar, the oldest girl, had departed several weeks ago with her husband, Sonam. For India, where Sonam's family had a big house. She had wanted Pema and the girls to come with them, but Pema had refused to leave without Ari.

Every night, for the sixty-four nights of the siege, Pema and her two remaining daughters had sat on the roof looking towards the lamasery, praying. More than once, during the day, Pema had made her way along the road towards the town until turned back by Han soldiers. She could see the Han in their trenches and clustered around fires. They were boys no older than Ari, blue with cold, stamping their feet to keep warm. She might have felt sorry for them had they not been Han.

Once she had come within a hundred paces of the lamasery wall. Faces peered down at her. Boys, monks, wild nomads from the Chang Tang. They did not seem cold and hungry like the Han, but that was in the early days of the siege. Pema anxiously surveyed the faces, but there was no sign of Ari.

'Will the Han kill the lamas when they take the lamasery?' asked her second daughter, Nyima, during one of the small silences that punctuated the gunfire.

'I don't know,' said Pema. These Red Han did not kill and loot like the Han who had come to Litang in the old days. It was well known that, when they first came to Tibet, the Red Han had released all the captured Tibetan soldiers and sent them home with a good meal inside them. In the early days many Tibetans had been impressed by this. Later, it had come to be regarded as yet another trick of the Han to win people to their side. Even so, it was a hopeful omen.

On the other hand, since that road had been completed, the Han had grown steadily more arrogant. And since the early days of the siege they had made no secret that retribution was in store for the obstinate lamas and their running dogs. As yet the retribution was unspecified but with each day that passed, the rhetoric of the Han grew more severe. On balance, Pema thought that she would be lucky ever to see her son again.

*

The thought had not long passed when they were disturbed by a tapping sound. Dechen heard it first. 'Listen, there is someone at the door.'

'At this time? It is the middle of the night.'

'Shh. There it is again.' Almost inaudible above the distant din.

Dechen went to the edge of the roof and peered down into the gloom. There were two men. Shadowy figures. One of them saw her and looked up, gesturing to be let in.

'It's Ari!'

'Don't be silly, girl. And keep your voice down. The neighbours will hear.'

But Dechen had already disappeared down the ladder. Her sister followed.

By the time Pema had climbed down, the two men were inside. The door was closed and Ari's sisters had their arms about his neck, sobbing with joy.

It was like a dream. Ari was home. Transported from the lamasery in the midst of the siege. The Buddha had worked a miracle.

When they had embraced once, twice, three times, Pema stood back to look at him. Even in the light of the butter lamp he looked pale and tired. His jaw was unshaven. She ran a hand lightly across his face. His cheeks were hollow. But it was Ari. Of that there was no doubt.

When the excitement had temporarily subsided, Ari introduced his companion.

'This is my friend, Aten. Without his help I would still be trapped.'

Aten bowed in the direction of Pema and stuck out his tongue. He was a year or two younger than Ari. His cheeks, like Ari's, were hollow, but his eyes sparkled.

The girls were put to work preparing a rich butter tea and a stew of yak meat. Pema unrolled her best rug and spread it on the floor of the big room on the middle floor. They pulled off their boots and left them in the kitchen. In due course the odour of feet was overcome by that of yak stew.

Ari told of their escape. About the hole in the back of the grain store. About the climb up the hill and the long walk along the ridge. Aten interrupted to say that Ari had killed a Han with his sling. Ari paled at the memory. Pema said they should pray to the Buddha so that he would have mercy upon the spirit of that Han. After all, it was not his fault that he had been sent to die in Litang.

Later, after they had eaten, they went up to the roof. The first streaks of dawn were in the sky. The dull crump of the mortars had ceased. The crackle of gunfire was sporadic. A cock crowed. Dogs barked. Trucks rumbled back and forth on the Han road. On nearby roof tops, they could see outlines of people looking towards the lamasery. Low voices carried across the semi-darkness.

'You must go down,' said Pema as daylight broke. 'No one must see you. Maybe the Han will come looking.'

Pema made beds for them in her best room. They should get a good sleep, she said, and while they were sleeping she would try to find out what had happened at the lamasery. The girls were told to stay at home and keep the door barred. They were to let no one inside. Not even their closest friends.

Ari drifted quickly to sleep, the sound of gunfire still ringing in his ears. His last thought as he closed his eyes was for Phuntsog. He touched the piece of Phuntsog still hanging from his neck and thanked the old lama for his safe deliverance.

When he awoke there was no sign of Pema. Daylight streamed in through the cracks in the wooden shutters. Dechen and Nyima fussed in and out with bowls of steaming tea. Not having lived at home for so long, it was the first time Ari could remember seeing them with their long dark hair combed down over their shoulders. He was fortunate to have sisters so beautiful.

He went to open the shutter, but Aten stopped him.

'No, Rimpoche. It is not wise. Someone may see you.'

They strained their ears for the sound of gunfire. There was one short burst, like a fire cracker at New Year festival. It seemed to come from further away than the lamasery.

After a while Pema returned. It took her a moment to catch her breath. How old she looked, thought Ari. There were deep caverns below her eyes and lines on her face that he had not seen before. The siege was over, said Pema. The monks had not waited for the return of the iron bird. Instead they had tried to shoot their way out under cover of darkness. Some had escaped, but many were killed or wounded. Many Han had also been injured. Iron horses with red crosses on each side were running back and forth between the lamasery and the Han encampment.

Hundreds of captured monks were being held in a large pasture by the river. The Han were making a wire fence around it, but it was not yet complete. She had been able to go close enough to talk to some of the monks. Soldiers had tried to shoo her away but she had told them she was looking for her son. The Han were now combing the hills in search of monks who had escaped. One or two were still said to be hiding in the lamasery. The Han were searching. As for the Abbot, he had last been seen being taken under escort to the Han encampment along with several senior lamas.

'You cannot stay here,' said Pema. 'Already there is talk that the Han will search every house in the valley. They may be here within a day or two.'

'Where can we go?' Until now it had not dawned on Ari that he would not be safe in his mother's house.

Pema thought for a moment. Her face was clouded with the thought that she would soon lose her son again. 'To India,' she said. 'To stay with Drolkar and Sonam.'

'India?' Until now it had been just a name to Ari.

'Sonam's family are rich. They have a big house in . . .' She could not remember the name of the place.

'Kalimpong,' said Nyima.

'Yes, that place. You can stay there until it is safe to return.'

Once India had been decided upon, Pema and her daughters set about preparing Ari and Aten for their journey. The problem was that none of them knew exactly where India was or how to get there. Pema made discreet inquiries and returned with the dismaying news that it was a journey of at least three months with horses. Without horses it could take five or six months, maybe longer. Since the Han were patrolling all the main trails out of Litang, they would have to travel at night and to stick to high paths where the Han were unlikely to venture.

Pema dug deeply into her storeroom and provided Ari and Aten each with a satchel of *tsampa*, dried meat, and salt. She boiled a dozen eggs and divided them equally. Pema insisted that they take off their monk's robes and replace them with warm *chubas*. From a large chest in her bedroom she drew out two that had belonged to Ari's father. Ari's fitted perfectly, but Aten's was so long that it came to his ankles. Dechen made him take it off while she raised the hem. Dechen seemed to have taken a shine to Aten. She would not take her eyes off him and giggled helplessly whenever he looked at her. Ari wondered whether it was wrong for a lama to go with a woman. It was well known that they sometimes went with boys.

They stayed a second night. Before deciding that it was safe, Pema went out to see what the Han were up to. She reported that they had not yet started searching the houses. She had also obtained more details of the journey to India. First, she said, they must head west to Lhasa. They would have to pass through Batang and Markham Gartok. They must be careful because there had also been uprisings against the Han in these places. They would have to cross wide rivers, too. At Gartok there was a ferry. They should try to avoid crossing at the main points because the Han would be watching these. Pema said she had heard that there were not so many Han in Lhasa. Maybe it would be safe for them to stay there. If not, they should continue south to Gyantse and from there down to Kalimpong.

'You are blessed,' said Pema, 'you will see Lhasa. It is the dream of my life.'

'Come with us,' said Ari. A moment's thought would have told him it was impossible.

Pema did not hesitate. 'No, it is too late. I am too old. I will delay you. Besides,' she smiled weakly, 'who will look after your sisters and find them good husbands?' Aten winked at Dechen and she dissolved into giggles, hiding her face behind long hair.

'We can go together,' said Ari.

'Yes,' said Aten and Dechen in unison, 'we can all go to India.'

Pema shook her head. Ari did not press the point for, even as the words had left his lips, he knew it was an impossibility.

*

They set off soon after dusk on the second night. There were the beginnings of a moon and the stars were diamond bright. Pema, Dechen, and Nyima walked with them through the bare fields down to the river. In a few weeks they would be ploughing these fields ready for the barley crop. Ari wished he could have stayed to help.

When the snow melted on the high plateau the river would surge through the little gorge it had carved for itself from the hard earth, but now it was a frozen stream meandering between big rocks. Ari remembered how he and his sisters had played hide-and-seek among these rocks. A distant memory from the summer before the lamas had taken him away.

They crossed the river, stepping from one rock to another. A path zig-zagged up the side of a hill. The way was well trodden.

Pema and the girls stayed with them until they were at the top. Several times Ari suggested they go back, but Pema would have none of it.

Before setting out they had burned their monk's robes and transferred the pistols to their *chubas*. Ari suggested they throw them away, but Aten insisted they keep the guns.

'If the Han find us with pistols, they will certainly kill us.'

'They will kill us anyway,' Aten had said. 'This way at least we can take some Han with us. Han have only one life. We will be reborn.' Aten grinned. Even in death there would be victory.

As they were leaving the house, Pema had pressed upon them a silver bracelet and some gold rings. The bracelet had belonged to her mother, she said. When they needed more food they could sell it. Ari had tried to refuse. He knew it was all that remained of his family's meagre inheritance. But Pema had insisted. Dechen removed her earrings from the family altar and pressed them upon Aten. Ari was shocked at the sacrilege, but Dechen was composed. The Buddha would understand, she said firmly. Their need was greater than his.

When they reached the top of the hill they parted. Ari and his mother embraced. She held him tightly, just as she had done all those years ago when the lamas had come to take him away. This time he had been at home for just one day and two nights. Now he must go again. Pema did not know exactly how many years she had seen, but she had calculated it was nearly fifty. That was a good age for a Tibetan. She wondered if she would ever see her son again in this life.

'I will come back.'

'I don't think so.'

'Then you must come to India. When we get there, I will ask Sonam to make arrangements for you and the girls to come out with one of his trading caravans.'

'There will be no more caravans. The Han have forbidden them.'

'We will find a way.' Ari could not see his mother's face in the darkness, but he knew she was crying. He kissed her forehead and released her from his arms. Dechen and Nyima kissed him, too. Once on each cheek. They did the same to Aten. Dechen lingering, or so it seemed to Ari. She was crying, too.

They sat on a rock watching Pema and her daughters make their way back down the hill, Pema holding Dechen's hand. They were soon gone. Black shapes disappearing into the night.

From their vantage point Ari and Aten could see hundreds of small fires burning around the lamasery where the Han soldiers and their prisoners were camped. Now and then the lights of an iron horse moved silently through the darkness, tracing the route of the Han road along the floor of the valley. In the distance they could see the lights of the Han encampment, flickering. Once or twice the sound of voices floated up to them. Whether Han or Tibetan was impossible to tell. It was surprising how far sound carried in the darkness.

Aten stood up, swaying slightly under the weight of the bundle on his back. They had enough *tsampa* for one month.

'Well, Rimpoche,' said Aten, 'we must be going. It is a long walk to America.'

12

KALIMPONG SAT ON a ridge between two mountains. An insignificant sprawl along the face of Kanchenjunga – a mountain more magnificent than any Ari and Aten had seen on their long trek. Wherever they went, Kanchenjunga looked down upon them, immense, brooding. An infinite blend of pastel shades starting with the rhododendron forests on the lower slopes and working upwards through green, brown, yellow, blue, and pink, merging into permanent snow. Sometimes the summit was obscured by cloud or snow storms. Sometimes it stood out stark and jagged against a crystal sky. Even on the darkest nights Kanchenjunga was there, watching over them. A vast black mass blotting out the northern skyline.

The town began with houses of mud and thatch and progressed through wood, plaster, and corrugated iron to the shops of bricks and concrete before petering out again in mud and thatch. It was strung out along a single tarred road.

High on a hill overlooking Kalimpong was a cluster of solid, spacious buildings, the most prominent of which was a tower that tapered sharply to a point. This, according to Sonam, was the foreigners' temple. And, sure enough, foreigners with fair skins and light hair – like those whom Ari had once seen passing through Litang – were to be seen in the market rubbing shoulders with Hindus, Tibetans, Bhutanese, and people of many other races who came to do business in Kalimpong.

Sonam's house was grander than any Ari and Aten had ever seen. True, they had not been to Lhasa where, it had long been rumoured, the aristocrats lived lives of unimaginable luxury, but so, it appeared, did Sonam.

Sonam's house was at a little distance from the town. It stood alone on a small hill surrounded by a high wall, enclosed within which was a garden of bright flowers and fruit trees. Beyond the garden and the wall, Kanchenjunga rose stark and magnificent. From his bedroom window each morning Ari watched the great mountain emerging from the mists and the darkness, the first rays of sunlight reflecting pink in the snows. He had seen such scenes many times in his life, but none to compare with the view from Sonam's residence.

Like most grand Tibetan houses, the outside walls of Sonam's house were painted white, save around the doorways and windows, which were bordered in dark red. Inside, however, instead of bare stone, the walls were plastered smooth.

There were no wells. Water appeared, as if by magic, from metal instruments embedded in the walls and disappeared into subterranean passages. Light came, not from candles or oil lamps, but from the flick of a switch. Electricity, Sonam had said. El-ect-ric-ity. Ari grappled with the word, but eventually gave up. There was so much to learn.

After three weeks at Sonam's house the sores on their feet had healed without trace. A doctor had been summoned to examine them. He had poked and prodded their intestines and departed leaving a bottle of yellow pills with strict instructions as to consumption. Within a week the curse that had haunted their bowels for the last month of the journey had disappeared and Ari and Aten began to gain weight. By the third week, Ari could no longer count his ribs, and colour had returned to his cheeks.

At the end of the first week, Sonam had taken them to a tailor to be measured for new *chubas*. The tailor was a Hindu: an obsequious little man who bowed and scraped as though Sonam were a great lama, but he did make good *chubas*. Sonam ordered two for each of them. And also a pair of yak boots. Before long they were strutting proudly through Kalimpong showing off their new clothes.

Later, Sonam gave them a guided tour of his uncles' warehouse. A dark, cavernous building. Bigger even than the prayer hall in the Litang lamasery. Piled high with bales of wool, tobacco, bricks of tea, and spices. Guarded by snarling mastiffs that threatened to dismember anyone who approached within thirty paces.

As for Drolkar, she was more like a grand lady from Lhasa with her silk dresses and jewellery. She had even begun to take lessons in the Lhasa dialect from a Drepung lama who was visiting India on a pilgrimage. What would their mother have said?

There were meetings. Secret meetings. With men who came to Sonam's house after darkness and who stayed for hours drinking strange liquids and talking in low voices. They came in iron horses smaller and shinier than those of the Han. As they lay in their beds, Ari and Aten could hear engines running, doors slamming. Rinchen, the servant girl, went back and forth with jugs of *chang* and bowls of tea. One afternoon, when Sonam was at his uncles' warehouse, Ari questioned Rinchen about the meetings. Who were these men? What were they discussing? Rinchen, usually a cheerful girl, became agitated. She claimed to know nothing of anyone or anything. Ari probed. She must know something. Most of the men, whispered Rinchen, spoke the Lhasa language. Once or twice there had been foreigners. No, they were not Chinese or Indian. They had yellow hair and white skin. Men like those she sometimes saw in the bazaar. That was all Rinchen knew. Or at least all she would admit to knowing. Ari later recounted this to Aten who was in no doubt as to the strangers' origin. 'America men,' he said solemnly. As far as Aten was concerned all men with fair hair and pale skins were Americans.

One day, without warning, Sonam said to Ari, 'There is a place where one man like you can learn to use machines which can challenge a thousand.'

'America?'

Sonam's face clouded. He liked to bask in secret knowledge. It irritated him to think that Ari already knew. 'Yes,' he said sullenly, 'America.'

'America is a big country?'

'Yes.'

'And rich, too?'

'Yes.'

'Bigger and richer than China?'

'Much.'

'America will help Tibet?'

'America is a friend of all small countries seeking freedom.' Sonam seemed to be repeating something he had learnt by heart. Like a young lama reciting a new prayer.

'What about Aten?'

'He can go too.'

'How many days' walk is this America, from Kalimpong?'

Sonam nearly died laughing. He slapped his knee with the flat of his hand. 'Walk? You cannot walk to America.' He was still laughing. His eyes were wet with mirth. Walk to America. He had never heard anything so funny in his life. Ari sat without expression. He was thinking that six months ago Sonam might have made the same mistake.

'So how do we get there?' he asked when Sonam had recovered his composure.

Sonam was mysterious again. 'It can be arranged.' To that he had nothing more to add and a repetition of the question only led to a repetition of the answer. 'It can be arranged.'

That evening a man came. A Tibetan. Fat with skin almost as fair as a foreigner's. To judge by the fuss that everyone made he was also very important. Drolkar and Rinchen had to be restrained from prostrating.

The fat man and Sonam were closeted for some time in the room where Sonam entertained his guests. It was the best in the house. Light and airy with windows opening onto Kanchenjunga. Rinchen fussed in and out serving tea and sweetmeats.

After a time, not less than one hour, she came to fetch Ari and Aten.

'They want you.' The fat man was seated on a pile of silk cushions. An enormous cigarette was clamped between his teeth. Many of the senior lamas at Litang smoked ragged cigarettes made from various types of weed that inhabited the high valleys. Some even smoked weed that came from India or China and that could be purchased in the Litang market, but Ari had never seen a cigarette so big as that smoked by the fat man. He was also drinking. Not tea or *chang*, but a deep yellow liquid in a clear glass. A half empty bottle of the same liquid stood open on a nearby table. Sonam, too, was drinking the yellow liquid. The tea and the sweetmeats were set to one side, untouched.

Had they been at home in Kham, Ari and Aten would by now have been flat on their faces out of respect for so significant a personage. But here in Sonam's guest-room an air of informality prevailed. The source of the informality was impossible to locate. Perhaps it had to do with the yellow liquid and the huge cigarette. Ari and Aten hovered uncertainly, heads bowed.

Sonam and the fat man were deep in conversation. In due course, but not before a full minute had elapsed, the fat man deigned to notice them. He inspected them carefully, pausing midway to flick the ash from the end of his cigarette. It fell upon the carpet, which was decorated with the image of a snow lion. The fat man said something to Sonam. It was in the unintelligible language of Lhasa. Sonam nodded. The man tossed a few words at Ari who shifted uneasily from one foot to another.

'His Excellency wishes to know if you have experience of fighting Han?' said Sonam.

Ari was dumb, but Aten spoke proudly. 'The Rimpoche,' he indicated Ari, 'killed a Han. With a stone in a sling.' Ari flushed. He wished the earth would open.

The Excellency nodded. He seemed satisfied. He spoke again. 'Excellency wishes to know if you are prepared to go to America to learn how to fight Han?'

Ari and Aten indicated that they were.

'He says,' continued Sonam, 'that the Americans are our good friends. They will help us drive the Han out of Tibet.'

The fat man sipped the yellow liquid and continued to address them. 'Excellency says that you will be the first Tibetans to go to America. Later, there will be others. Many others. You are honoured.'

The Excellency exhaled vigorously. A shroud of thin blue smoke enveloped him. 'He says that he is authorised to bestow upon you the blessing of His Holiness the Dalai Lama.' Ari and Aten bowed low. The Excellency murmured incomprehensibly. Again, Sonam translated: 'He says your mission is a secret. A big secret.'

Two days later a man came to see Sonam. A lean, spare man whom Ari had seen hovering at Sonam's gate during the visit of the Excellency. He came in the early morning, as the first rays of sunlight tinged the snows of Kanchenjunga. He stayed only a matter of minutes and, after he had gone, Sonam came in person to rouse Ari and Aten. 'It has been decided,' he said, 'you go tonight.'

There was very little preparation. Sonam presented each of them with bone-handled knives sheathed in yak leather. They were engraved with an image of the Buddha. 'For good luck,' said Sonam as he handed over the knives. In exchange, however, Sonam confiscated the pistols they had carried with them since Litang. 'You will not need these in America,' was all he said by way of explanation.

Drolkar made a tremendous fuss and ordered Rinchen to provide little bags of *tsampa*. She also presented them each with two mangoes and would have given them half-a-dozen apples apiece had not Sonam put his foot down. 'It is not necessary,' he said, 'American people are very kind. They will have plenty to eat.'

Did American people eat *tsampa* and drink butter tea, Drolkar wanted to know. Sonam said he was sure they did. Everything was available in America. The source of his knowledge was unclear.

For the journey Ari and Aten dressed in their new boots and *chubas*. Sonam said it would not be wise to dress as lamas since they would be unnecessarily conspicuous and this, after all, was a secret mission.

They debated whether Ari should bring his sling. Aten said that in America there would be many modern weapons. They would not need a sling. In the end Ari made a present of it to Sonam's eldest son. The boy was delighted and immediately commenced a reign of terror against the local bird population. Ari felt a pang of regret at being parted from his sling. It had been with him since childhood.

Finally, they went to pay their respects to the Buddha and to ask his blessing for a safe journey. They lit butter lamps, left prayer scarves on the altar, and made many prostrations. Later, Drolkar said she had consulted the spirits and they had assured her that it was an auspicious day for a journey to America. To ensure good fortune she sprinkled them with grains of barley.

When it was time to go Sonam said he would accompany them to the edge of town. When they had passed the last house Sonam announced that he would have to turn back. They should carry on down the road and in due course they would meet a man who would take them to America. As to what that man would look like or where he would meet them, Sonam would not say. Possibly he did not know. He embraced each in turn, first Ari then Aten. They had nothing to fear, he said. The Buddha would protect them and bring them safely home. One day the Tibetan people would look upon them as heroes who had helped to liberate their country from the Han. With that, Sonam turned and disappeared into the gloom. They stood and watched until he became invisible.

They walked for some hours. There was a good moon. Several times they were overtaken by Hindus riding the two-wheeled machine Sonam had called a bicycle. There were many of these in Kalimpong. Sonam had said there were even bicycles in Lhasa nowadays. 'Do Americans have bicycles?' Aten had asked. Sonam had expressed no view.

They passed houses with groups of Hindu men squatting outside, talking in low voices. Oil lamps glowed. A radio played loud music. Since coming to Kalimpong they had become familiar with the talking machines known as radios. Even Sonam had one.

'How far must we walk?' asked Ari.

'Until someone comes to take us to America.' Aten's faith was great.

'Supposing no one comes?'

'Of course they will.'

'But if they don't?'

'Then we will have to walk.'

There were lights in the distance. Small at first but growing bigger. They came from behind. From the direction of the town. Then a sound they recognised. 'An iron horse,' said Aten.

They stood still and watched the lights coming towards them. Bright lights. So strong that it was impossible to see the machine or the men inside. Aten wanted to hide, but Ari insisted they stay on the road.

As it approached, the vehicle slowed. They raised hands to shield their eyes from the light. A hundred paces further on it stopped. The lights went out. There was no movement. Only a black shape in the moonlight.

They approached with caution. There was no sign of life. Drawing near they could make out two men. This iron horse was like that which had brought the fat man to Sonam's house. It was entirely enclosed and had four doors. They had seen several such vehicles in Kalimpong. Sonam called them motorcars and said they belonged to rich merchants and officials of the Hindu government. Soon, Sonam had added, he too would drive one.

As they drew alongside a rear door opened. 'Get in. Get in.' The voice was agitated. Ari peered cautiously inside. There were two men in front and two in the back. The two in the back were youths, also from Kham. Their hair was in long plaits. They had huddled together in a corner to make room for the new arrivals. One indicated the space on the seat. It seemed hardly enough for two people.

They scrambled inside. To make space they put their bags of *tsampa* and the mangoes that Drolkar had given them on a shelf at the back.

'Close the door,' said the agitated voice. Aten made several attempts, but it would not shut. The man in front cursed and climbed out to force the door closed. Ari was seated half on top of Aten. Phuntsog's thighbone pressed hard into his chest.

The car started with a jolt. After they had travelled a short distance the lights came on again, illuminating the road ahead. When his eyes had adjusted, Ari could see that the car was driven by none other personage than the Excellency. He no longer looked particularly exalted, hunched over the steering wheel, a hat pulled down hard over his head. Ari recognised the other man as the lean one who had called that morning at Sonam's house to tell them to prepare for the journey. They drove for hours without stopping. The road was rough and the car bounced, bumped, and weaved. It was not a straight road. There were sharp bends every few paces. Soon they had lost sight of the black mass of Kanchenjunga. The road sloped steeply downwards. On one side there were deep, dark chasms and on the other black hills dotted with little houses visible in the moonlight. At times they drove so close to the chasm that Ari feared they were about to plunge to their deaths. They passed through villages, all in darkness. Once they skirted a large town. Now and then they passed another vehicle. They could see it coming long in advance. Lights weaving back and forth on the road far below. By and large, however, the road was empty. Gradually the hills grew smaller, the valleys less deep, and the air became sticky. They were leaving the mountains.

The two men in the front sometimes talked quietly to each other, but to the four young men in the back they addressed not a single word. At some stage the Excellency produced one of the fat cigarettes Ari had seen him smoking at Sonam's. He proceeded to smoke for the rest of the journey. The smoke drifted back causing Ari's eyes to water. One of the other young Khambas had a fit of coughing. Aten said he felt sick. The Excellency was oblivious.

The other two young Khambas were called Lotse and Muja. They came from Batang. Ari and Aten had passed that way on their journey to Kalimpong. It was a place of golden barley fields. Richer than Litang. Lotse and Muja had come to India as guards with a caravan of wool destined for one of the warehouses operated by Sonam's uncles. 'We did not hear about the uprising until we reached Kalimpong,' said Muja. His shoulder was bare and badly scarred. His white teeth smiled in the gloom. 'We were preparing to return. To fight the Han. Then we are summoned to see a big man.' He indicated the back of the Excellency's head. 'He told us there was a place where we could go for learning how to kill Han.' Just where this place was, he seemed unclear.

'America?' asked Ari. It rang no bells. Muja just smiled and said it was some place where they could learn to kill Han by magic.

They spoke in whispers. The Excellency and his attendant displayed no interest. A window opened. There was a sudden rush of cool air. Aten said he no longer felt sick. The hills were now much smaller. The road was straightening. Lotse and Muja were overwhelmed to discover that Ari was a Rimpoche. They would have prostrated there and then but for the lack of space. Ari told them about the siege at Litang. Lotse expressed surprise that a Rimpoche would take part in fighting. Muja remarked sourly that most of the Rimpoches he knew just prayed and collected taxes.

'This Rimpoche killed a Han,' said Aten proudly. Whereupon Lotse and Muja offered hearty congratulations.

*

Towards dawn they turned off the main road and headed east. They could tell as soon as the first red streaks appeared in the sky. The road was dead straight. The hills were but a distant memory. There were trees on both sides. Trees unlike any that Ari had ever seen. They had tall, bare trunks surmounted by a sudden outcrop of leaves. A cock crowed, a dog barked. The Excellency urged the car on ever faster. He seemed anxious to complete the journey before daylight. The vehicle jolted and swayed. Several times the passengers' heads hit the roof. They clung tightly to each other.

The car stopped. The lean man got out and walked to the side of the road. There was writing on a white board. The characters were obscure. What language was this? The lean man examined the board closely and then returned, shaking his head. There was a muffled conference. A piece of paper was examined.

They drove a short distance and then stopped again. Another board with strange writing. The same procedure: the lean man studying the paper, shaking his head, and returning to the car. The Excellency cursing loudly. They stopped a third time. The Excellency himself got out. Ari could no longer feel his legs. He wished that he could get out, too, but dared not ask. There was a road to the right. No more than a track. The Excellency examined it carefully. He seemed to be looking for a sign. A Hindu appeared. He stared for a long time at the car. Then at the Excellency. Then he relieved himself by a tree. The Excellency spoke sharply to the Hindu and he moved away, pausing every few paces to look back.

Eventually the Excellency was satisfied. This was the place. He looked at his watch and then at the rising sun, huge and blood red. He signalled impatiently.

'Out, out.' The order came from the lean man. Aten struggled with the door, but it would not budge. Eventually it was opened by the thin man. Aten tumbled out. Ari, Lotse, and Muja followed. They were stiff and sore. Ari stamped his feet until sensation returned to them. The Excellency was standing some distance away. He signalled impatiently, glancing anxiously at the rising sun. Why was he afraid of daylight? Perhaps he would melt like ice.

The Excellency was giving orders. Now and then Ari caught a word. 'Over there.' He was pointing down a track that led away from the road. In the distance there was a clump of trees. Tall and bare, crowned with green. 'Over there,' the Excellency was saying, and then another word Ari recognised. 'America.' America, over there. Surely not.

The lean man was talking now: 'Walk down this road,' he indicated the track. 'Over there, beyond the trees, there is another country.' He said the word slowly. 'Pak-ist-an.' Pakistan. What was this place? Sonam had said they were going to America. Ari felt a flash of panic. Had they been tricked?

The lean man was explaining. 'When you get to the border, you will find men waiting. They will take you to America. Now go.' He indicated the track with a flourish. The Excellency had already climbed back into his car. Without even saying goodbye.

13

THEY STARTED WALKING. Behind them, doors slammed.
When they had gone only a few paces, Ari remembered that they had left the *tsampa* and mangoes. He turned to go back, but the car had turned too. Ari glimpsed the Excellency as he sped past, looking neither to right nor to left.

They stood, staring as the vehicle disappeared in the direction from which they had come. Dust rose in a cloud. The sound of the engine faded. There was silence.

'What will we eat?' said Aten.

'Maybe Rimpoche will work a miracle for us,' said Lotse.

They laughed, but their situation was not in the least amusing.

A child appeared – a girl with long hair and dark eyes, clutching a ragged baby. She said nothing. Only stared.

The track led across fields of stubble. The earth was dry and cracked. And very flat. The sun was almost risen now and very hot. Much hotter than Kalimpong. The air was still. A trickle of sweat appeared on Ari's brow. He wished he had not worn his sheepskin *chuba*. The girl with the baby followed at a distance.

They passed a house. A flimsy affair compared with those in Tibet. Made of mud and the leaves from the tall trees that were all about. People emerged, staring. A man stood by a barrel, dousing himself with water. He was wearing a sort of skirt wrapped tight about his waist and reaching to his ankles. His brown chest was bare. As they passed, he called out to them in a language they did not understand. They ignored him. A dog followed, barking hysterically. Muja threw a stone and it ran off, yelping.

The trees were further away than they appeared. By the time they reached them the sun was well clear of the tree tops. The shade was welcome. Ari wiped his brow with the sleeve of his *chuba*. Lotse's forehead was bathed in sweat. Aten said he could do with a cool drink from a mountain stream. But there was no sign of any mountain and the only stream they passed was dry.

The track narrowed to a footpath. It wove from side to side between the trees, well trodden. 'Supposing no one comes to meet us?' said Aten.

'Of course there will be someone,' said Ari uneasily. He had noticed that neither the Excellency or his henchman had felt able to look them in the eye as they parted.

The path through the trees extended only a few hundred paces. It came to an abrupt halt in front of a river bed. The mud was dry and scarred with the footprints of cattle. Beyond the river bed the path resumed across more fields of stubble and cracked earth. There was a clump of trees in the distance and beneath them men, waiting.

They crossed the river bed and moved out of the trees back into the sunlight. The sun was hotter than ever. It was hard to see the men clearly because the sun was so bright. Ari shielded his eyes so that he could see. There were four, maybe five men, he said. Two squatting in the shade. One pacing up and down. One, maybe two lying flat out in the grass.

'Farmers,' said Aten wearily. He, too, had cupped his hand over his eyes. They approached with caution.

In the distance, some way beyond the waiting men, sunlight glinted on hot metal. 'Iron horses,' said Aten.

Ari looked again, eyes straining. Yes, there were at least two motorcars parked discreetly.

'Congratulations, Rimpoche,' said Lotse. 'You have worked your first miracle.'

The men had seen them now. They were on their feet. One, two, three, four, yes, five. One of them was running, well in front of the others. He was the first to arrive, and was wearing a uniform.

'Welcome, brothers.' He was panting. Still out of breath from running. They looked at each other, hardly able to believe their ears. This man, wearing the uniform of a foreign army, was speaking the language of Kham. 'My name is Wangdu,' he said. 'I have been sent to welcome you to the Free World.'

The others had caught up now. Three brown men in light cotton

91

uniforms, like Wangdu's. Two carried rifles. Another had a pistol in a pouch on his waist. The fourth was a foreigner, his eyes shaded by a hat, perspiration trickling down the side of his face. He stood head and shoulders above the others, a short-sleeved white shirt hanging loosely over light trousers. His arms were hairy.

'You are now in eastern Pakistan,' continued Wangdu. 'These gentlemen,' he indicated the tree brown men, 'are soldiers of the Pakistan army. This is Major Satish.' The man with the pistol saluted stiffly. 'And this,' Wangdu indicated the white man, 'is Captain Hank. HAA-NN-K,' he spelled it out. 'Captain Hank has come to take you to America.'

The American walked towards them, hand extended. 'Sweet Jesus, I sure am glad to see you boys.'

Captain Hank was the boss. He barked orders. Major Satish repeated them and the two soldiers went running off across the field. By the time they had reached the road the soldiers were each sitting behind the wheel of a small truck, engines running.

'Made in America,' said Wangdu, patting one of them with his hand as though it were a favourite yak.

They set off down the narrow road. Ari, Lotse, and the American in the first jeep. Aten, Muja, and Wangdu in the other. Captain Hank's armpits were damp.

'Ain't you guys hot in those things?' he said, fingering Lotse's sheepskin *chuba*.

But there was no one to translate so they just stared blankly at him.

They drove only a short distance and then turned off the road into a compound. Where they were going it was not easy to see because the back of the vehicle was covered by a small tent, the rear flaps left open. They passed men on bicycles, a cart drawn by oxen with wheels as high as a man, chickens scratching in the dust. It occurred to Ari that, unlike Tibet, this was a very crowded country.

The compound was full of single-storey white-washed build-ings. There was a flag on a pole, as there had been at the Han encampment. Soldiers lounged in the shade.

They were shown to a room. It had a high window, barred.

Captain Hank did not come with them. A soldier with a rifle stood at the door. 'We are prisoners,' whispered Muja.

A ceiling fan turned lazily, barely disturbing the heavy air. The only furniture was a table with wooden benches along either side. On the table there was a flask and cups.

'Sit, please.'

They sat. A soldier poured tea. It was unlike Tibetan tea, thin and weak, but they sipped it gratefully.

Food came. A steaming white substance in a big bowl. Beef cooked in spices. Green vegetable. Sonam had said that Pakistan people did not eat barley.

'Rice,' said Wangdu. 'Please eat. It is very good.'

Ari knew what it was. The Han ate rice. So, both the Pakistan men and the Han were rice-eaters. He considered the implications silently.

When they had eaten, Captain Hank reappeared. He made a little speech. 'Er, gentlemen.'

'Brothers,' translated Wangdu.

'We are, er, going on a long journey. You will understand that, since our mission has the, er, highest security classification, it will be necessary for you to maintain a low, huh, profile. I, therefore, have to ask . . .' A soldier appeared with a bundle of clothes over his arms. '. . . that you, er, undergo a change of, er, apparel.'

Wangdu struggled with the translation, but no one was listening. They were watching the soldier distribute the clothes in four bundles, one for each of them.

'First, however, you might like to take a shower.' Captain Hank indicated another room. There was a barrel full of water and four ladles. The Captain gave a cheery smile and left them to it. He was, he remarked, proud to be serving alongside four such brave young men.

The new clothes caused much hilarity. The Pakistani soldiers fell about when they emerged. The white trousers were far too large and were held up only by a cord knotted around the waist. The shirts extended almost to their knees.

Aten was angry. 'They make fools of us,' he said, but even he had to laugh.

Wangdu did his best to explain. 'This is what the Sikh people wear. Very light and cool.' That much at least was true. It was a relief to be out of the cumbersome *chubas*. Wangdu was also about to explain that Sikh people also wore something on their heads when Captain Hank reappeared, carrying four long strips of blue cloth. They trailed over his hairy arms.

'These, gentlemen, are turbans.'

'T-U-R-B-A-N-S,' said Wangdu.

Captain Hank offered to demonstrate. 'First, you must tie your hair like so.' He gathered up what hair he had and tried to hold it in a bunch at the top. The demonstration was a failure. Sikhs apparently did not have crew cuts. A genuine Sikh was called for. He wore a thick beard and a soldier's uniform.

The problem was explained to him while he stood rigidly to attention. He saluted and proceeded to unwind his turban, still at attention until Captain Hank told him to relax a little. When the turban was unwound they could see that his hair was gathered in a tight bun secured on the crown of his head by a small net.

The net, it seemed, had not been anticipated. The Sikh, his turban rewound, was dispatched to find four such nets.

He returned with three colleagues. All Sikhs, all marching stiffly. Each was allocated a Tibetan. There was much hilarity, shared by everyone except the Sikhs and Captain Hank, who looked anxiously at his watch. In due course the job was done and the Sikhs departed in perfect formation.

Captain Hank then went into a huddle with Wangdu. 'The Captain says,' said Wangdu nervously, 'that you should place your daggers on the table.'

Nobody moved.

'I have explained to him,' said Wangdu, 'that it is the Khamba tradition always to carry a dagger. The captain insists. He says your daggers will be returned as soon as you reach your destination.'

A silence. Then Ari raised his shirt and untied his dagger. He dropped it heavily onto the table beside his *chuba*. Aten did likewise. Lotse and Muja followed, sullenly. A Pakistani soldier collected up the clothes and the knives.

Wangdu and Captain Hank conferred. There was a disagreement. Wangdu appeared to be angry. Eventually he spoke, choosing his words with care. 'The captain says that because our mission is very secret, he is going to pretend that you are prisoners. It will, therefore, be necessary for you to wear these.'

Captain Hank grinned sheepishly. He was holding up a pair of manacles. A long chain was attached.

Without warning Muja sprang. With a blood-curdling whoop he leapt across the table straight at Captain Hank. The manacles went flying. Muja and Captain Hank collapsed in a bundle on the floors, Muja's hands around the Captain's throat.

Wangdu tried frantically to restrain him. 'You have tricked us,' Muja was screaming. 'You are no different from the Han.'

Soldiers came running, pistols drawn. One was pointed at Lotse who was about to spring to Muja's aid. Muja was prised loose by two of the burly Sikhs who had assisted with the winding of turbans. His hands were manacled behind his back. Captain Hank was helped to his feet. The blood had drained from his face. There was a red mark on his throat where Muja's hands had gripped. His elbow was grazed. 'Gentlemen,' he said, 'there has been an unfortunate misunderstanding.'

14

CALM WAS RESTORED. Muja was unmanacled and returned to his seat. He sat muttering the foulest curses while Captain Hank repeated that there had been an unfortunate misunderstanding. It was, reflected Ari, the very phrase the Han had used after the attack on their encampment.

Regarding the manacles, a compromise was agreed. The first part of their journey would be by truck. Since the back of the truck would be covered it would not be necessary for the Tibetans to be chained. Later, however, they would come to a big river. Here they would take a boat. There would be many people on the boat. It would be necessary to pretend that they were Sikh prisoners. On the boat they would have to be chained. Armed guards would also accompany them. Under no circumstances should anyone know they were Tibetans. They must speak to no one. If they needed anything, they should ask Wangdu. Were there any questions?

'Yes,' said Aten. 'How long before we arrive in America?'

Captain Hank was vague. America, he said, was far away. The journey was difficult. They would not be going there immediately. Later perhaps. The decision was not his to make. He was obeying orders.

A truck was waiting. As the captain had said, the back was covered with canvas. They clambered inside. Sikh soldiers with rifles climbed in behind. Wangdu did not come with them. He said he would sit in front with the driver. If they wanted anything, they could tap on the back of the cabin. As for Captain Hank, he said he would be right behind. It wouldn't do, he said, for an American to be too closely associated with this little party. People would start asking questions and the last thing they wanted was for anyone to ask questions.

They set off. Heading south, according to Lotse who could see the position of the sun through a hole in the canvas. As before, the back flap was open so they could see the road behind. Captain Hank followed at a safe distance. Now and then he could be seen fingering his throat where Muja had tried to strangle him.

The soldiers chatted amongst themselves, rifles resting across their knees. They included two of the Sikhs who had pulled Muja off Captain Hank. Now and then they stared menacingly at Muja as if to say, 'Don't think that's all, you son of a whore. You've still got it coming to you yet.'

'They are not pretending,' Aten whispered to Ari. 'We *are* prisoners.'

Two things Ari would always remember about that journey. The heat and the people. There were parts of Tibet where a traveller could go for a week without seeing another human being. But in this strange land every road was a chaos of people. People on bicycles, in ox carts, or jam-packed into motor vehicles of every shape and size. People in every field, in every ditch, behind every tree. Old men with small bundles. Young men and women bearing loads great enough to crush them. Ancient grannies bent double. Small children looking after smaller children. People squatting, staring, hammering, selling, buying, spitting, pissing, repairing, cursing, begging. And, in the midst, an old man with a white beard, curled up on the pavement, asleep.

And the noise. Every bicycle had a bell that seemed to ring with every turn of the wheel. On every corner a radio blared. Dogs barked. Horns hooted. There was scarcely a moment in the whole journey when the driver of their truck was not sounding his horn. He hooted at cows and dogs that lay down in the road, at children who played hopscotch, at every bicycle, at every other vehicle. He hooted at everything that moved and many things that did not move. And nothing and no one took the blindest bit of notice.

The going down of the sun brought some relief from the oppressive heat. Unseen by the guards, Muja had managed to loosen one of the ropes binding the canvas to the truck. Cool air leaked in. They took turns to inhale.

Towards sunset the truck came to a halt. Through the gap in the canvas they could see that they had reached the bank of a river so wide that the opposite shore was invisible. At first, Ari thought that they had reached the sea. Phuntsog had once told him that there were oceans greater in area than the whole of Tibet. He had been sceptical, but had filed away the knowledge for future reference.

A jabbering mass of women and children selling mangoes, cigarettes, and sweetmeats of every description laid siege to the truck. The Sikh soldiers brushed them aside as though swatting flies.

Wangdu appeared and gave each of the Tibetans a mango, which they devoured gratefully. They had reached the Brahma-putra, he said: a great river that began its journey in Tibet. From here on they would travel by boat. The journey would take two nights and one day. For the time being the manacles would be necessary. He was sorry, but there was no alternative.

It was dark when they boarded. Until now Ari had never seen a boat bigger than the yak coracles they had used on their journey to Kalimpong. This boat was as big as the warehouse of Sonam's uncles. It had three decks, each ablaze with light. On top a funnel emitted a thin plume of smoke. On each side there were wheels higher than two men, half submerged in the water.

Like everything else in this country, the boat was crowded. Young men leaned over the railings, shouting messages to friends and relatives on the river bank. New travellers were arriving every minute on passenger bicycles laden with metal trunks, cases, and bundles. As each newcomer arrived, porters with red armbands fought one another for the privilege of carrying his luggage aboard. Arguments of great ferocity raged on every side. Everyone joined in. There were many opinions in this country. And all strongly held.

They were linked to one another by a long chain attached by a manacle at the wrist. Ari first, then Lotse, Aten, and Muja. One of the Sikhs held the keys. He grinned maliciously as he tightened the manacles on Muja's wrists. Wangdu spoke sharply to him and he reluctantly loosened it. Ari was pleased by this. It was the first sign that Wangdu was on their side.

They walked in single file, the chain hanging loose between them. Two of the Sikh soldiers went ahead to beat a path through the crowd, making liberal use of their rifle butts. There was a vigorous exchange of abuse.

On board it was the same. People pushing, shoving, shouting. Porters with huge boxes balanced on their heads. Families, who had staked a claim to a place on the deck by unravelling a square of bamboo matting, fought to repel intruders. And a boy led a blind beggar, a single coin rattling in an old tin.

There were stairways, up which people flowed and ebbed. The Sikhs forced a way. The chain made movement difficult. Wangdu trailed behind. Of Captain Hank there was no sign.

Bodies littered the upper decks. Men reclining on mats, heads at rest on their baggage, eyes closed. Oblivious to the mayhem. Eventually, a space was miraculously found. An air pocket of calm in the midst of madness. Bamboo mats were unrolled. Men stared. One of the Sikhs gestured that they should sit. They sat, chains clinking. Muja held out his wrists. The Sikhs ignored him. They sat clutching their rifles.

'Unlock,' said Muja.

'Later,' said Wangdu.

'There are too many people. This ship will sink.'

'Pray to the Buddha that it does not.'

The ship did not sink. It floated unsteadily, swaying and swirling in the strong current. The big wheels turned, the funnel belched thick smoke, there was a hiss of steam, a stench of shit.

There were stars, too, and a thin moon, which soon became invisible because the deck above afforded shelter. They would be grateful for that when the sun rose. The only sign of land was an occasional, distant light. They passed other boats, much smaller. Black shapes in the water. One or two burned oil lamps. Voices could be heard in the darkness.

Wangdu produced food. Rice and chicken wrapped in leaves. 'Leaves of palm tree,' said Wangdu. 'P-A A-R M,' he spelled it out. They were not interested. It was so long since they had slept.

Wangdu refused a request to remove the chain. 'Very sorry. I have orders.' Muja cursed loudly. Wangdu looked ashamed. 'My orders,' he kept repeating. The Sikhs laughed.

Ari slept in fits, awoken sometimes by one of the others tugging on the chain. Sometimes by Phuntsog's thighbone digging into his chest. Once during the night they stopped to take on more passengers. There was a babble of voices. Shouting. A horn hooting. Bare feet stepping cautiously among the bodies. Ari dozed, dreaming of a land of mountains and cool streams. A land without heat or people, but when he awoke the heat and the people were everywhere. His head ached.

They did not see the sun rise. It came from behind. The land was a thin strip on the horizon. They passed small boats with ragged sails, crammed with small brown children waving. They overtook a chain of barges loaded with timber. Men in white turbans squatted on the logs, staring sullenly. The body of an ox floated by. On its back. Legs stiffly pointing to the sky. Later they passed the body of a child. Later still, a woman, face downwards. Vultures hovered. This was a cruel country.

By dawn of the second day the river had narrowed. The houses were of brick and tile. Warehouses loomed, bigger than those of Sonam's uncles. They passed huge ships at anchor, piled high with grain, sand, bales of wool . . . and people. The sore on Ari's right arm was bleeding where the manacle rubbed. 'We arrive,' said Wangdu.

15

A NEW CHAOS awaited. A crush of people behind wooden barriers. Some pressed so close that they seemed about to suffocate. They were kept back by uniformed men with long sticks. Whenever one attempted to slip through the barrier, the men with the long sticks would lash out unmercifully. They reminded Ari of the bodyguard monks who protected the Abbot during public festivals.

The barrier broke. The uniformed men flailed uselessly. They had lost control. The mob laid siege to the boat. Even before the walkways were lowered, men were swarming aboard, offering porters, taxis, cyclos, hotels, brothels, fortune-tellers. Everyone had a deal to propose. Everyone offered the best price.

'Wait here,' said Wangdu and disappeared. They waited. The Sikhs lounged. The prisoners sat cross-legged in the shade, chains clinking. Ari licked the blood from the sore on his wrist. The heat was merciless. Muja had gone off the idea of going to America. 'I will go home,' he murmured.

'How?' asked Aten.

'I will find a way.'

In due course Wangdu reappeared. 'We go,' he said. The bedlam had subsided. Wangdu led the way across decks strewn with debris. They went down the stairs in single file. One of the Sikhs had hold of the chain. Now and then he pulled sharply to indicate that they should move faster.

Another truck awaited. The driver was also a Sikh. Muja's turban had unwound and trailed along the ground. Ari's almost covered his eyes. People stared.

They clambered aboard. Wangdu came too. They glimpsed Captain Hank. He did not even glance at them.

After they had driven a short distance, Wangdu ordered one of the Sikhs to remove the manacles. He did so sullenly. The chain fell clinking to the floor.

Muja said: 'Even the Han treat us better than this.'

Wangdu looked alarmed. 'Be patient,' he said. 'Everything will work out. You will see.'

No one believed him.

They drove through streets more crowded than ever and then into countryside. Even the countryside seemed crowded. After a while, they stopped. Aten had his eye pressed to a gap in the canvas. He could see a big fence, he said. Like the one surrounding the Han encampment at Litang.

They could hear voices. The driver was speaking to someone outside. They were moving again. 'We are inside the camp,' Aten reported.

'What is this place?' Lotse asked Wangdu.

'You will see,' was the best that Wangdu could offer. His credibility had reached a new low.

They passed iron birds in huge warehouses, a nose or a wing protruding. Men clambered on them. Humans looked small beside these huge machines. Aten said, 'Look, the iron birds have servants.'

They passed long houses, like those in which the Han soldiers had lived, except that these were made of wood, not stone. There were trees, too. With tall bare trunks. P-AA-RM trees, Wangdu had called them. In Tibet there were no such trees.

When at last they halted, it was by a house, a two-storey secluded house, surrounded by trees and hedges, well away from the long houses of the soldiers and the caverns inhabited by the iron birds. The house was made of stone and the walls were painted white, like the houses in Tibet. And there on the doorstep to greet them was Captain Hank.

'Er, gentlemen,' said the Captain.

'Brothers,' translated Wangdu.

'He is not my brother,' whispered Muja. 'I will kill him.'

'I, er, apologise for the inconvenience to which you have been subject.'

They were standing in the shade of the palm trees. The imprint of Muja's thumb still showed on Captain Hank's neck.

'I want you guys to make yourselves at home,' the Captain was saying. 'You will be here for a day or two before we commence the next stage of our journey.'

'To America?' asked Aten.

'Er, not exactly,' said the Captain.

'Where then?'

'That, gentlemen, I am not at liberty to disclose.'

The house was smaller than Sonam's, but inside the air was cool and fresh. As cool as the air in the mountains of Tibet. How could this be, when the air outside was so hot? The mystery was soon resolved.

'This, gentlemen, is an air conditioner.' Wangdu struggled with the translation. 'Air machine,' was the best he could offer.

Captain Hank tapped a box on the wall. It rattled. He turned a switch and the rattling increased. He turned it the other way. The rattling diminished. 'There is one of these in every room. If you don't like the noise, you can turn it off and use this.' He flicked a switch on the wall and the fan on the ceiling turned. 'And when you want light, you do this.' Captain Hank flicked another switch.

Electric light was not new to Ari and Aten. They had seen it at Sonam's house in Kalimpong, but for Lotse and Muja it was a miracle as great as any ever worked by the lamas.

Muja took one step towards the light switch. He moved with stealth, eyes fixed on his prey. He might have been hunting a fox. Suddenly he lunged at the switch and withdrew his hand as though bitten by a snake. Behold, there was light. He circled the lone bulb hanging from the ceiling. He tapped it cautiously. It swayed, causing shadows on the wall to leap. Muja reached again for the switch. This time his hand lingered. The light went off. On-off, on-off. Then Muja laughed, a loud raucous laugh. Lotse was laughing, too. Ari and Aten joined in. Everyone was laughing. Even Captain Hank.

Upstairs much sport was had in demonstrating the workings of the bathroom. Everyone had a turn at flushing the toilet. Wangdu gave a demonstration of the use to which soap should be put, but not before Muja had tried to eat a mouthful. The shower was demonstrated. Most American people, said Captain Hank, showered at least once a day. In hot countries like India and Pakistan, people sometimes showered two or three times a day. This was greeted with incredulity. Wangdu had to translate twice. In Litang, explained Aten, it was the habit to bathe only once a year, usually after harvest. Captain Hank just shook his head.

There were three other rooms. 'Bedrooms,' said the Captain. He put his hands together and made a little gesture to indicate sleeping. On each bed there was a clean set of clothes. Trousers, a shirt, and underpants. Underpants were an entirely new concept and had to be explained. It was not until, amid general hilarity, Captain Hank had lowered his trousers, that everyone understood.

In each room, by each bed, there was a pocket-sized picture of the Dalai Lama. Captain Hank had thought of everything.

Before he departed the Captain drew attention to the blinds that covered every window in the house. These, he said, were to stay down. They were free to amuse themselves in the house as they wished, but no one, repeat no one, was to set foot outside the door. Two Sikh soldiers would remain on guard outside to make sure these instructions were obeyed. Their presence in Pakistan was, he said, a secret. The Pakistan people were good friends of the United States, but they sure as hell did not want to be embarrassed. It was his job to make sure that the Pakistan people were not embarrassed. 'Otherwise,' he added, 'the big white chief at Langley would have my ass.'

Since there was no equivalent in the Tibetan language, Wangdu improvised, 'If anything went wrong, Captain Hank's superiors would cut off his bottom.'

They shook their heads in sympathy. Not even the lamas had devised a punishment so cruel.

As soon as Captain Hank was out of the door they tore off their turbans and Sikh pyjamas and took turns in using the shower. Lotse's scars were vivid. They lacerated his back down almost to his waist.

'What is that?' Ari pointed to the scars.

'A flogging.' Lotse beamed. He was proud.

'Why?'

'I went with the daughter of a Lhasa official,' Lotse laughed loudly at the memory. 'In a barley field at harvest time. She was very hot. Worth a flogging.'

Muja had discovered that the flow of water could be adjusted by turning a handle on the wall. He squirted water at anyone who so much as put his head around the door of the bathroom. There was a brief skirmish with Lotse when Muja refused to relinquish the hose. Wangdu was called and the matter was settled amicably. Water sprayed everywhere. It ran down the walls, dripped from the blinds that covered the window, and collected in puddles on the floor. Mostly it ran away down a drain in the corner. There was much puzzlement as to where the water came from and to where it was going. No one had seen a stream or a well. In the end they decided it was yet another miracle of the foreigners and did not allow the mystery to spoil their enjoyment. They splashed each other like children playing in a river. Ari covered himself in soap, as Captain Hank had advised, and watched as it was rinsed away. Afterwards he felt clean and cool. A strange sensation because he had never felt dirty.

Towards evening Captain Hank reappeared, exuding good will. He was carrying drinks in bottles. The bottles were cold. 'My,' he drawled, 'you boys are going to love this.' The Captain removed the tops with a little metal lever. They put the bottles to their lips and drank. It was unlike anything Ari had ever tasted before, cool and sweet. He decided that he liked it. Captain Hank watched them gulp it down. A satisfied smile on his face. 'I expect you boys would like to know what you have just been drinking?'

They nodded.

'Gentlemen,' said the Captain solemnly, 'I think I can safely say that you have just become the first persons in Teee-bet to drink Pepsi Cola. Congratulations.' He shook each of their hands in turn. They had made history.

'Are there yaks in America?' asked Lotse. They were eating rice and meat in metal dishes. It was brought by servants. Thin, brown, harassed men who served the food without speaking and scuttled away.

'Yaks? Not exactly, but we got something similar, I guess.'

In Tibet, explained Lotse, the yaks were looked after by nomad people. In the summer they took their herds up to the high pastures and in the winter they brought them down to the valleys. Were there any nomad people in America?

'Well,' said the Captain, 'that's a long story. Many years ago America was populated entirely by nomad people. They were called redskins. Come to think of it, they look a little like Tibetans. In fact the resemblance is remarkable. Quite remarkable.' He spoke slowly and glanced at each of them in turn.

'What happened to the redskins?'

'Well, then the white man came and he sort of pushed the redskins aside and settled their land. There are some redskins today, but not so many. Most of them live on special reservations. They got a raw deal. I guess you could say the white man more or less wiped them out . . .'

Wangdu's voice faded as he translated. It wasn't until the Captain reached the end that Wangdu's alarm registered. He did his best to repair the damage. 'I guess,' he added, 'that wasn't a very creditable episode in American history . . .'

But it was too late. 'You are saying,' said Ari quietly, 'that the white man stole the red man's land. Just like the Han is taking land from the Tibetans.'

'No,' said the Captain emphatically, 'that was not what he was saying. Well, not exactly.'

No more was said about redskins. The Captain gave a short discourse on the significance of Pepsi Cola to the American way of life and then announced he must be off. 'You boys ought to get an early night,' he advised, 'because tomorrow you're going for your first ride in an airplane.'

16

THE PLANE WAS the height of four men. Its wings cast long shadows. To each was attached two large blades, like the ceiling fans at Sonam's house in Kalimpong. A ladder led into the belly of the beast. 'Up,' said Wangdu, 'quickly.' Quickly, that was all Wangdu seemed able to say.

Ari was first inside. Aten followed, then Lotse. Muja hesitated. 'I'm not going,' he said. Muja, the bravest of them all. Wangdu spoke sharply to him and he ascended, sullenly.

'Be seated, gentlemen,' said Captain Hank.

They hesitated. 'Please, gentlemen.'

Ari sat by one of the portholes, with Lotse beside him, Aten and Muja behind. Wangdu and the captain were standing in the aisle.

They waited. It was very hot. The Captain looked anxiously at his watch. A minute passed. Then five. Outside another vehicle drew up. A door slammed. Voices. Two men appeared. Americans. Captain Hank introduced them. 'Gentlemen, this is Major Chuck,' he indicated a plump, perspiring man with black curly hair and glasses. Ari had seen glasses on sale in the bazaar at Litang. They were popular with aristocrats and lamas. 'And this,' Captain Hank indicated a younger man whose smile revealed gleaming white teeth, 'is Lieutenant Bob – of the United States Airforce. They are going to take us on a little trip.'

Captain Hank conferred briefly in a low voice with the two new arrivals. Then they turned and disappeared through a door at the front.

'So,' whispered Lotse, 'the iron bird cannot fly by itself.'

The plane sloped steeply upwards. Ari gripped the arms of his seat. His knuckles were white. Behind, he could hear Muja praying: '*Om mani padme hum. Om mani padme hum* . . .' Lotse's eyes were closed. A bead of sweat trickled down his forehead.

Cautiously, Ari eased back the blind. The earth was far below, parched and cracked, dissected by streams and small rivers, only half filled by water, weaving through an ocean of dry mud. There was a thin road, fringed by palm trees. People swarmed, like ants. Now and then a vehicle passed, the sun glinting in its wing mirrors.

So many rivers meandering, intersecting and, between them, islands of mud. Everything flat. Ari pulled the blind hard down and it retracted. Captain Hank did not seem to care. Behind him Muja did the same. Lotse had leant across to share the view. His long, matted hair brushed Ari's face.

They were heading south-east, half into the sun. The sky was blue and cloudless. It swallowed them. By now they were so high that it was no longer possible to distinguish individual human beings. The plane had levelled.

'So much water,' said Lotse. There was now more water than land. The only earth was the islands, hundreds of islands large and small and almost every one inhabited. A ragged handful of trees, patches of scrub, and rich brown soil recently vacated by water. Occasionally they passed over a patch of burnt green or a clutch of poor houses casting long shadows in the early morning light. Temporary settlements waiting to be swept away, when the water rose. The water, too, was mud-coloured. Small boats speckled the rivers, hardly moving in the calm.

At first the land was flat. Then a hill appeared. Then another and another. There were trails and small settlements. Now and then smoke spiralled upwards. As they headed east and the hills grew larger and greener. There were deep, uninhabited valleys with winding rivers. The lower parts of Tibet were like this, or so Ari had heard.

Captain Hank was on his feet. Wangdu had stood, too. 'Gentlemen, we are now over Burma,' he said. Burma, Burma. The name rang bells. Phuntsog had said there was a land of this name far to the south of Litang. According to Phuntsog, the people there were also Buddhists. Ari reached inside his shirt and touched the bone. Old Phuntsog had been so wise. If only he were here now.

'We are going to America?' asked Aten.

'Er, not precisely. No. As I have explained, gentlemen, I am not at liberty to disclose your destination.'

There was cloud now. Thin wisps far below, drifting between hills. It was strange to see cloud from above. It thickened until it formed an impenetrable luminous carpet. The ground became invisible.

They flew on. An hour passed, two, three. It was not like Tibet where distances were measured in days. Wangdu distributed mangoes. Ari sucked eagerly, juice dribbling down his chin.

The sun was behind them now. The cloud had evaporated. Below there was a vast expanse of blue. Was this the ocean of which Phuntsog had talked? Wangdu confirmed that it was. Once or twice they passed small islands. Now and then a boat. By and large, however, the ocean was as empty as the Chang Tang in winter.

The plane tilted forward. They were going down. Captain Hank was on his feet again. 'Gentlemen, we are about to land –'

'In Burma?'

'No, not Burma.'

'Where?'

'How many times must I tell you?' I am not at liberty . . .'

They descended rapidly. Lotse's eyes closed tight. Muja prayed aloud. Ari's ears ached. They were going to burst. He wanted to scream with pain. His stomach remained behind in the sky.

Fritz Neumann stood towards the rear of the reception committee watching the boys as they clambered unsteadily down to the tarmac. His first thought was that they could do with a haircut. All except one whose head was shaven closer than a US marine's. That must be the lama. Crocker had said to keep an eye out for him.

In preparation for this moment, Neumann had spent a month in the language labs at Langley, brushing up his Tibetan. No expense had been spared. Crocker had flown in a missionary who spoke the Kham dialect. By the end of four weeks Neumann figured he knew enough to get by.

'Remember, Fritz,' Crocker had said as he waved Neumann off at National, 'these boys have got to go home looking as though they've never been away. We don't want them acquiring any of our bad habits. No TV, no burgers, no baseball. Just train them up, kiss them goodbye, and send 'em home.'

'And above all, no names. If it all goes wrong,' Crocker had added with foresight, 'we don't want no comebacks.'

After the first day, they didn't see much of Captain Hank. There were new Americans in charge. One, a fair-haired man with blue eyes, spoke Tibetan. The Kham dialect. Not so good, but enough to be understood. Not bad considering that he claimed never to have set foot in Tibet. He had, however, spent a little time in Kalimpong. What did they think of Kalimpong? Wasn't that some crazy town? He had learned his Tibetan in America.

'How many Americans speak Tibetan?' Aten had asked on the second day.

'Four or five, maybe. As for the Kham dialect, I guess I'm the only one.'

The American said his name was Bill. When they got to know him better he revealed that he was originally from Germany, a country in Europe. Near Yingland? Aten had demanded. Yes, said Bill, he guessed it was.

One American was more important than the others. He had a stomach that bulged and small glasses that balanced on the end of his nose over which he looked like a hawk stalking prey. The other Americans called him 'the Colonel'. On the first day the Colonel made a little speech. The American and Tibetan peoples, said the Colonel, were close friends. Their governments had been good friends for many years (this was news to Ari, but then there were many things he did not know).

'Speaking personally,' said the Colonel, 'I have always had the greatest respect for His Holiness the Dalai Lama. And I know that the President shares my sentiments.' Who was this President? Later, Wangdu told them that the American President was the most important man in the world. Apart, of course, from the Dalai Lama. The President's picture hung in the hallway of their billet. Next to one of His Holiness.

'It is the President's intention,' the Colonel went on, 'to organise the moral forces of the world against the immoral. In particular against communists.' America would help to liberate Tibet. And not only Tibet – in due course they would liberate the whole of goddamn China. Liberate. The Han had used that word. They were going to liberate Tibet, too.

'Americans and Tibetans,' asserted the Colonel, 'are brothers. Our friendship will last, not for one or two years, but for many.' The Colonel made much of this. 'America does not enter lightly into alliances,' he said. 'We always stand by our friends.'

The Colonel peered at them over his glasses. His bald head was traversed by a single strand of black hair, which had its origins somewhere behind his left ear. He spoke of freedom, liberation, justice. The very words the Han had used when first they came to Litang. A tiny thought stirred in Ari's mind. It was of no importance, but he stored it away.

'You will be in this place for several months. There is much to learn. We will try to make your stay as comfortable as possible. If you need anything just ask Fritz here,' he indicated Bill. 'I am sorry there are no mountains, but we are working on that.'

On that mysterious note, the Colonel concluded. Were there any questions? Aten had one. 'Will we learn to make iron birds fly?'

The Colonel allowed himself a flicker of a smile. 'No, son, I am afraid not.'

Neumann watched and waited. Mike Silver was in charge of knocking the boys into shape. He gave them hell, shouting abuse that wasn't intelligible in English, never mind Tibetan. At first, poor Wangdu did his best to translate, but soon gave up. They started each day with a work-out followed by a couple of turns around the perimeter. By the time they finished the sun was coming up and the sweat just poured out of them. Only Ari had difficulty keeping up. The prayer hall in Litang had not prepared him for this. 'For Christ's sake, Mike, go easy on the boy,' said Neumann after watching Silver bawling out Ari for finishing well behind the rest of the field after one of the morning runs. 'These guys have never been below twelve thousand feet in their lives.'

That Mike, he was a monster. Already Muja was muttering dark threats against him. Ari complained to Bill.

It was all right for Lotse and Muja, and even Aten. They were nomads, used to a rough life. But as for Ari, he was a lama. He knew only how to pray and read holy books. Bill was sympathetic. From then on Mike eased up a little.

During the day they were not allowed out of the compound. The Colonel had given strict instructions. The compound was screened from the rest of the base by a thicket of bamboo. The only time they saw other people was on those early morning runs. There were many more Americans, soldiers. Also running. The Americans ran in formation, cursing and grunting. Another soldier ran behind, shouting abuse just like Mr Mike. Some of the soldiers were black. Ari stopped dead in his tracks the first time he saw a black man. Later, they asked Bill. Yes, he said, there were many black men in America.

'What did they eat?' asked Aten.

'The same as most Americans. Steak, french fries, ice cream.'

'Ice cream? What is that?'

'Jesus, you guys ask a lot of questions.'

Once, on one of their early-morning runs, they saw a group of small, yellow men exercising.

'Han?' asked Aten when they got back to their compound.

'Er, not exactly.' Bill was evasive.

'What then?'

'I don't think I ought to go into that. Right now we're running a number of small wars around these parts.'

Later, much later, when they had got to know him better, Bill was more forthcoming. 'You guys aren't the only ones on Uncle Sam's payroll. We've got all sorts here. Meo from Laos, Shan from Burma, Khmer . . . Why, we're even putting half a dozen White Russians into Vladivostok.' Who were these people? Where were these places? Bill did not say. After that he clammed up. 'If the Colonel knew I was telling you all this, he'd chew my balls off.'

From the first day, Bill seemed to take a particular interest in Ari. And for his part Ari took a shine to Bill. It wasn't just that he spoke their language. He seemed to care about them. He wanted to know about Litang. About Ari's family. How big was their house? About Sonam and Drolkar. About life in the lamasery. Ari told Bill how, in his previous incarnation, he had been a hermit in cave on the hill behind the lamasery. And how fortunate he was to have been given another life in which he did not have to live in a cave like the old hermit. Yeah, said Bill, that really was stroke of luck. There was no sense in being cooped up in a smelly old cave.

Bill asked about the Han. When had they arrived in Litang? How many were there? Ari told him in detail about the siege of the lamasery. Bill expressed surprise that the lamas carried guns. That was not unusual in Litang, explained Ari. Sometimes the big lamaseries even went to war with each other.

Ari told Bill how the lamas had held out against the Han until they brought up a plane to bomb the lamasery. He described how he and Aten had escaped to Kalimpong. Bill wrote it all down in a notebook he always carried. Bill was always making notes. Whenever one of them said something that interested him, out would come his notebook.

Bill told Ari a little about himself. There had been a big war in Europe, he said. His family had been on the losing side so, after the war, they had settled in America. He went to work for the American government. To help make people free. He had an aptitude for languages so, whenever the American government had a difficult case, they always sent for Bill. That was how come he had been assigned Tibet.

The routine was the same each day. Running, exercise, and – later – hand-to-hand combat at which Lotse and Muja excelled. Breakfast was butter, tea and *tsampa*. 'Uncle Sam likes his guests to feel at home,' explained Bill. (Who was this Uncle Sam? Ari concluded that it must be another name for the President.)

After breakfast, they were given lessons on how to operate radios like those of the Han. It was very complicated. There were many new words and symbols to be digested. Wavelengths, frequencies, call signs. Codes had to be learnt by heart. They learnt how to dismantle the machines, how to reassemble them. How to make repairs. Their teacher was yet another American, Frank. He was older than the others. His hair was turning grey. Usually Wangdu translated. Bill would stop by each day to see how they were getting on. Ari picked it up quickly but the others found the going hard. They had never even learnt to read or write. 'We came here to learn about killing Han,' moaned Lotse. 'Not to learn how to use their talking machines.'

There were courses on map-reading, starting with a little basic geography. They listened incredulously while Bill advanced the view that the world was round. In support of this proposition he produced what he called a globe and spent an afternoon showing them what was what. There were about one hundred and sixty countries in the world, he said. Ari counted up. He could only think of five, including Yingland and America. Six, if he counted Germany where Bill originated.

After about a week during which they struggled with radio work and map-reading, Bill decided to organise literacy classes for Aten, Lotse, and Muja. He and Wangdu took turns teaching. Ari helped out. The problem was there were no textbooks. Bill sent a cable to Kalimpong and after a couple of weeks a well-thumbed sheaf of hand-written prayers arrived. Bill just shook his head in amazement. 'Jesus, they must have dug these out of some museum.' For the future, he would see if the boys at the language labs at Langley could run him up a little basic textbook. In the meantime he would have to improvise.

Early on they had a visit from a doctor. Unlike the lama doctors in Litang, he muttered no prayers and offered no magic potions. He made them strip off and examined each in turn. He took a particular interest in Lotse's penis. Afterwards he pronounced them all fit except for Lotse whose backside he injected with a needle. This happened several times. The doctor said the needle contained a powerful medicine. The doctor told Lotse he was not to have any contact with women until his penis was cured. This made Lotse laugh. 'Where will I find a woman in this place?' he asked. The doctor and Bill laughed too.

The doctor also remarked on the scars on Lotse's back. Lotse explained, through Bill, about the Lhasa official's daughter and the flogging. The doctor shrugged and, according to Wangdu, said, 'Jesus, what kind of outfit are we bankrolling this time?'

*

'Who is this Jesus?' Ari asked Wangdu one evening.

Wangdu explained that he was a holy man who had died many years ago, not so long after the Buddha.

'Foreigners believe in him, like Tibetan people believe in Buddha.'

Later Ari took up the matter with Bill. 'Has he been reborn, like our Buddha?'

'I guess he was. According to some folks, anyway.'

'So where is he now?'

'Don't worry, son, wherever he is, he's on our side.'

In the third week another batch of Tibetans arrived. Six. Two from the Lhasa region, one from Phari, near the border, and the others from Kham. They had all been recruited in Kalimpong.

One of the Khambas was a monk from Litang. Like Aten he had been a servant. Ari did not recognise him, but Aten knew him well. After the siege, he told them, most of the lamas had been captured. Instead of killing them, as they had expected, the Han had merely given lectures on the benefits of liberation and sent them home to their villages. Most of the senior lamas, however, were still being held. The Abbot had been taken away. He did not know where. To China, it was rumoured.

The new arrivals were housed in another part of the same compound. Those who could read and write were immediately set to work on the radio and map-reading courses. The others joined Wangdu's literacy classes.

'We've almost got enough for a baseball team,' said Bill one evening.

Next day, Bill turned up with a baseball and bat. He gave a little demonstration out in the compound. They took turns with the bat. When Muja's turn came he hit the ball right out of the compound. Bill had to go and retrieve it. 'I think we'd better call it a day,' he said when he returned.

Later, however, they pressed him to let them play. Bill said he didn't see why not. He would have a word with the Colonel. When he returned he said: 'The Colonel has given his approval, but on one condition. When you guys go home he doesn't want you introducing baseball to Tibet. Otherwise people might start asking questions.'

From then on baseball became a regular part of the programme. Every evening after classes they played a few rounds. The Colonel had given permission for them to leave the compound and use one of the playing fields where, during their early-morning runs, they had seen American soldiers exercising. It seemed to have been placed off-limits to everyone else on the base because no one came near them.

Bill had also introduced them to American food. 'About time you guys put a little variety into your diet,' he said one evening. He brought them thick slices of meat between slabs of bread. 'Get your teeth into these,' he said. 'The kids back home go big on burgers.'

Burgers, supplemented by French fries and Pepsi Cola, became their staple diet for a while. Then one day they disappeared from the menu as suddenly as they had come.

'Colonel's orders,' said Bill. 'He says we don't want you guys taking American habits home to Tibet.' After that it was back to *tsampa* and dried meat. Bill occasionally threw in a few French fries. 'I don't see how the Colonel can complain about French fries,' he said. 'After all, you grow potatoes in Tibet.'

After two months Mike said he was going to arrange a little shooting practice. Lotse and Muja cheered up at this. They had been complaining for weeks about the lack of facilities for killing Han. They were taken by truck to a shooting range on the other side of the base. As before, the back of the truck was enclosed so that no one could see them. At the range there was no one else around.

The weapons were a disappointment. Mainly British .303s, and fifteen-year-old Japanese and Chinese pistols. Muja was angry. 'We have these in Litang,' he raged. 'They are no use for fighting Han. We need modern weapons, not this rubbish.' Mike was apologetic. The problem was, he explained, that the American government did not want the Han to know they were helping the Tibetans. If they gave them American weapons, the Han would soon realise. He was very sorry. If it were up to him, he would give them the most up-to-date equipment available. Unfortunately, it was in the hands of politicians and politics had never been his strong suit. Matter of fact, he was none too keen on politicians.

Muja said he didn't know what a politician was, but if he met one, he'd kill him.

From .303s they graduated to 55 mm mortars, hand grenades, and sub-machine-guns. One morning Bill appeared and said the time had come for them to learn about jumping from airplanes.

The first two mornings were spent making practice jumps from a wooden tower at the back of the compound, parachutes strapped to their backs. Captain Hank had made a brief reappearance and spent a morning showing them how to fall and how to land. One of the new arrivals broke his ankle and had to be excused, but the rest went up on schedule.

Aten was first out. He didn't bat an eyelid. Just fell forward and was gone. Poor Lotse was shaking like a leaf. Bill practically threw him out. When Ari's turn came he closed his eyes and rolled forward. He counted to five and spread his arms to slow his fall, just as Captain Hank had instructed. After what seemed an age, the chute opened automatically. Ari opened his eyes. Below to his left he could see Lotse's chute, then Aten's. There were two or three others in a trail above. In the distance to his right he could see the plane turning for a second pass.

Ari hit the ground feet first, falling backwards as he did so. As he fell he hit his head and lost consciousness. When he came round, Bill was standing over him. 'Boy, am I proud of you guys,' he was saying. They were all down safely.

That evening Bill turned up with a barrel of *chang*. 'I thought we might have ourselves a little celebration,' he said. 'You guys are going home.'

17

B Y THIS TIME tomorrow they would be back in the mountains of Kham. It took a moment for the news to sink in. The outward journey had taken five months of walking, two nights and a day on that stinking boat and many hours by plane. The return journey would take just seven hours.

Ari, Aten, Lotse, and Muja would be dropped into Batang, a couple of days from Muja's village. To enable them to keep in touch, they would be equipped with a radio receiver and transmitter. If all went well, supplies of arms and medicine would follow.

'When?' demanded Muja.

'When the time is right,' said the Colonel vaguely. He avoided their eyes.

The two Lhasa boys would be dropped near Lhasa. They were, as the Colonel put it, to be the Dalai Lama's link to Uncle Sam. Their mission was to establish contact with the Dalai Lama through his chamberlain, Thubten Woyden Phala. Phala was to be persuaded that the Dalai Lama should make an open appeal for American assistance. 'That way,' explained Bill on their last night together, 'our little operation can be legalised and we can go in big.' He warmed to his theme. 'Instead of those lousy old .303s, you boys will get the real stuff. M-14s, 105s, maybe something that will take care of those Han planes. Who knows, before too long we might be giving you some planes of your own? The Tibetan airforce. Now there's a thought. Those goddamn Han won't know what's hit 'em.' Lotse and Muja grinned broadly at Bill. He wasn't like the others. He was on their side.

By now they had made half-a-dozen drops. The final two in darkness. On the last occasion there had been a brief panic when a gust of wind had caused Lotse to drift outside the drop zone. He had come down in a rice field several miles away and been rescued by a family of farmers who were greatly excited by Lotse's sudden appearance in their midst. They gave him tea and jabbered away in a strange language. Despite his best efforts, Lotse was unable to establish what country he was in before Bill arrived and whisked him away.

There were many hours of briefings. Repeatedly it was impressed upon them that, when they returned to Tibet, they were to say nothing of where they had been and what they had learnt. Under no circumstances were they to disclose their contact with America. Not to anyone, friend or foe. They were to hide their maps and radios and use them only when alone. If anyone discovered their equipment, they were to say they had purchased it in India. For this reason they would be given only out-of-date equipment of the sort available in India. The radio was Japanese, left over from World War Two. It had to be wound up by hand. Lotse was disgusted. By now he knew enough about radios to realise that even the Han were better equipped than this.

'We were told American would help us. What use is this against the Han?' He gave the radio a kick.

Bill explained patiently. 'If the Han find out that America is helping you, they will tell the Indian government. The Indians will then kick all Americans and Tibetans out of India and make it impossible for us to help you. At the moment India and China are friends. In future it may be different. We are working on that. For the time being, however, we must be careful not to upset the Indians.'

On that last evening Neumann spent five minutes on the scrambled line to Langley. 'Harvey, how many times do we have to go over this? He's the only one. The others are all country boys. Okay for the rough stuff, but useless for what we have in mind.'

'What about the Lhasa boys?'

'We need them to talk to Phala. He's an aristocrat. He ain't going to deal with hicks from the outback.'

There was silence punctuated by a crackle of static. This was the moment. If they didn't do it now, they never would. No doubt Crocker was thinking that he should have come out and taken personal charge of the selection, but it was too late for that. Finally, Crocker pronounced. 'Okay, Fritz, bring the boy in.'

Two hours before they were due to depart Bill came to see Ari. It was already dark. They had just finished eating. Steaks and Pepsi Cola smuggled past the Colonel as a farewell gesture.

Bill wanted a quiet word. It would be better, he said, if they went outside. In the compound the air was cool. The trees hummed with unidentified insects. There had been a change of plan, said Bill. Ari would not be going home after all. At least, not immediately. Instead he was going to America. They had something else in mind for him. Another mission. He could not go into details. It was a secret.

Ari protested vigorously. 'America, after all this time. That is what they told us in Kalimpong. Instead you bring us to this place and you do not even tell us where we are. I want to go back to my country to fight the Han.' He was almost shouting. Bill asked him to keep his voice down, otherwise he would disturb the others. If he insisted on returning to Tibet immediately that was okay, but he would be passing up a unique opportunity to serve his country.

'Why not someone else? There are others you can choose.'

'Ari,' he touched the boy's forearm, 'we have been watching you closely over the last four months. You are the one we want. It is a great honour. A chance to save Tibet and, maybe,' he added, 'even to alter the course of world history.'

If anyone but Bill had asked, Ari would flatly have refused. For some time he had noticed that, as with the Han, there was a gap between what the Americans promised and what they delivered. Bill, however, seemed different. He had been on the side of the Tibetans since they had first arrived at this unknown place. He had taken the trouble to learn their language. And wasn't it he who had smuggled through the steaks and the Pepsi Cola in defiance of the Colonel's express instructions?

The other Americans just seemed to be doing a job, but Bill seemed really to believe in Tibet. He even had a small picture of His Holiness above the mirror in his jeep. 'I reckon you Tibetans could teach us Americans a thing or two about civilised living,' he had once confided to Ari. 'One day, when I get some time off, I might just devote a while to studying the teachings of the Buddha.'

So when Bill persisted, Ari reluctantly agreed. 'I'll tell the others that I won't be coming.'

'No,' said Bill, 'that wouldn't be a good idea.' Instead, he said, there would be a last minute medical inspection. The doctor would find that Ari was unfit to travel. The others would be told that he would be following with the next batch.

At around midnight they were assembled outside in the compound. Ari, Aten, Lotse, Muja, and the two boys from Lhasa. They were dressed in woollen *chubas* and boots, the clothes in which they had left Kalimpong. Their equipment was spread out on the ground before them. The compound was lit by floodlights.

Each man had a pistol, a light machine-gun, and a wad of Tibetan currency specially shipped in from the bazaar in Kalimpong. They had a week's supply of *tsampa* and dried meat and a modest medicine pack containing bandages, penicillin, and assorted stomach tablets (their training had included a course in first aid). The supplies had been purchased in India and bore appropriate labels. The radios were elderly models left behind in Burma by retreating Japanese. The Lhasa boys had custody of one. Aten was in charge of the other. Once he had graduated from his literacy course, Aten had thrown himself wholeheartedly into mastering the radio and emerged top of the class. He was proud of his achievement. Lotse and Muja were duly deferential.

Finally, they had each been issued with a phial of poison with instructions to tape it to their bodies and swallow it in the event of capture. Muja took his with a contemptuous snort. He had no intention of falling alive into the hands of the Han. He would die fighting.

Bill and Mike insisted on a thorough search. They wanted to make sure that no one was carrying anything that would link them to the Americans. They inspected every item in the baggage, even the labels on the medicine bottles. In Lotse's rucksack they found the metal cap from a Pepsi Cola bottle.

'What's this, asshole?' Mike held the bottle top about an inch from Lotse's nose. Lotse just grinned at him.

'Souvenir,' he said.

Mike was furious. 'How many times do I have to tell you?'

Lotse just carried on beaming.

Then came the medical inspection. 'We had one yesterday,' protested Aten.

'Can't take no chances,' said Bill. 'We want you boys in tip-top shape.'

The doctor went through the motions. He had them open their mouths and peered down their throats with a little torch.

Then he asked them to open their shirts and *chubas* and listened to their chests through a piece of metal on the end of a rubber tube. It was a routine they had been through many times before. Ari was last in line. He was shaking when the doctor reached him. This was deception. Phuntsog had taught him never to tell lies. It was one thing to deceive the Han, but these were his best friends. He put a finger beneath his *chuba* and touched his relic of Phuntsog. What would the old lama have said?

When Ari's turn came he opened his shirt slowly. The doctor made a little show of listening through his rubber tube. Then he frowned and shook his head. The others were looking at Ari. What had gone wrong? The doctor said something to Bill. Bill affected concern. 'I am afraid,' he said slowly, 'Ari has a chest infection. The doctor says he cannot go.' Bill sounded as if he had been struck by a thunderbolt. The Colonel, too, looked grave. So did Mike. These Americans were so clever at deception. Almost as clever as the Han. The Colonel and Bill made a little show of consulting with the doctor. 'He says you may be well enough to go in with the next batch in a week or so.'

Ari looked miserable. He didn't have to pretend.

Aten said, 'None of us will go. We will all wait until Ari is well again.' This was an unforeseen development.

'I am afraid that won't be possible. Arrangements have been made.' There was a trace of panic in Bill's voice.

Aten said: 'We came together. We will leave together.'

'Right,' said Lotse. Muja nodded.

Bill asked if he could have a private word with Ari. They walked a few paces into the shadows. 'Tell them they must go,' said Bill.

'You must persuade them, otherwise the whole operation will be aborted.'

'What can I say?'

'Tell them that you will catch up next week. That we will drop you in the same area.'

'That's not true, is it?'

Bill did not reply. Ari shook his head. These Americans had turned him into a liar.

It took the best part of an hour to persuade the others that they had to go. Bill and the Colonel were pacing up and down in the shadows, looking anxiously at their watches.

Eventually Ari came over. 'Okay,' he said, 'they will go.' He could not bring himself to look Bill in the eyes. He was ashamed. Bill patted him on the shoulder.

The truck was waiting. They climbed aboard, all carrying rucksacks, Aten and one of the Lhasa boys each with his radio neatly packed away. The radios were heavy. Ari climbed up after them.

'Not you, Ari.' It was Bill.

'I will see them go.'

Bill did not argue. He just climbed up after them and fastened the back flaps. They sat silently in the darkness while the truck bumped across the base. Behind they could hear the Colonel, Mike, and Wangdu following in the jeep. Ari was sitting next to Aten, who was lightly holding his hand.

'I don't think we will meet again in this life, Rimpoche,' he whispered.

'Of course we will.'

'I don't think so, Rimpoche.'

The truck came to a halt in a dark place near the edge of the base. They could see the perimeter fence and the black shape of a plane. There was no moon, but the stars were bright. Bill produced a torch and led them to the steps leading up into the plane. As they moved closer, they could see that it had no markings. No yellow star, no lettering. When they were up near they could see that it was painted entirely black although, on close inspection, it was

123

possible to make out letters and symbols underneath the black paint which had recently been obliterated. In the cockpit there was a solitary light and two faces peering from the window. One of the men inside waved to Bill. He, too, was an American.

The five Tibetans lined up at the foot of the steps, equipment strapped to their backs. Pistols holstered to their belts. Sub-machine-guns hanging from shoulder straps.

The Colonel shook hands with each one in turn and mumbled something about a historic mission. Bill followed suit. Wangdu embraced each one. Then it was Ari's turn. He started by embracing Lotse, then Muja and the Lhasa boys and, finally, Aten.

Lotse said nothing. Nor did the Lhasa boys. Muja said: 'I will kill a Han for you.'

Aten said, 'See you, Rimpoche, in another life.' The tears in his eyes glinted in the light from Bill's torch.

Ari watched his friends disappear one by one into the belly of the plane. Mike climbed up behind. He would be the last American they would ever see as they plunged into the darkness. Unseen hands drew in the steps. The heavy door swung shut and was locked from inside. The engine was running. Ari glimpsed Muja's face at one of the portholes. There were red lights on the wing tips and under the belly.

Bill, the Colonel, and Wangdu walked back towards the truck. Ari followed a few paces behind. The plane's engines screamed. They put their hands to their ears and turned to watch as it accelerated into the night. Ari watched the red tail-light rise and disappear towards the west, carrying with it the best friends he had ever had. And leaving him alone with these deceitful Americans.

18

'OKAY, ARI, NOW it's our turn,' said Bill. They were in the back of the Colonel's jeep. Wangdu was sitting quietly in the corner. The Colonel was driving. He was smoking a fat cigarette. The empty truck was following.

'Our turn?'

'To take a trip.'

'A trip?'

'To America. Like I told you.'

'Now?'

'Yes, now. Our plane is waiting.'

There was, said Bill, no need to go back to the house. Wangdu would go collect his clothes. He could change out of his *chuba* in the back of the jeep. As for his equipment – the food, medicine, and guns – he would not be needing that. At least, not for the time being.

'What will you tell the others?' By now there were about twenty Tibetans living in the compound.

'We won't tell them anything, except that you all got off on schedule. As far as they are concerned you have returned to Tibet.'

'Who knows about this?'

'Only me and the Colonel. Oh yeah, and Wangdu.'

'And Mike?'

'No, he does not know.'

These Americans, they even deceived each other.

They parked behind some trees near the entrance to the compound. Wangdu was gone about five minutes before he came back with Ari's American clothes – a couple of shirts, trousers, underpants in an old rucksack. There was no sign of the guns, money, or medicine, but Wangdu did bring with him the week's supply of *tsampa* and dried meat. 'To eat on the plane,' he said. 'The journey is very long.' Wangdu, it seemed, had been to America. He knew so many things.

Ari changed into his American clothes while Bill paced up and down outside the jeep, conferring urgently with the Colonel. Then Wangdu reappeared, extending his hand through the back of the jeep. 'I wish you good luck.'

Ari was surprised. 'You aren't coming?'

'No, Bill will take care of you. I stay here.'

Ari was siezed with panic. 'Why are they taking me to America?'

'I don't know.'

'Are you sure?'

'Yes, they tell me nothing, except that your mission is a big secret and very important.'

It was impossible to tell if Wangdu was lying. His eyes were hidden by the dark. Also, he was from Lhasa and it was a well-known fact that Lhasa people were tricky. Quite apart from which, Wangdu was educated and, as Ari was coming to realise, educated people seemed to find lying easy.

Another plane was waiting. This one bigger. It had not been blacked out. The star of the United States Air Force showed clearly. This plane did not seem to be a secret. It was parked openly, near buildings with a forest of masts and aerials. There were floodlights and men loading boxes through a door in the underbelly.

They drove up to the steps. The Colonel extended his hand. A fat cigarette still clamped in the corner of his mouth. 'So long, son, and good luck.'

'He is not coming with us?'

'No.'

'Who is?'

'Just you, me, and the crew.' For the first time Ari noticed that Bill was carrying a small black case. They travelled light, these Americans. In Tibet an official of Bill's rank would merit at least one servant and three baggage mules.

'Only two people, and the airplane is so big?'

'You are a very important passenger.'

*

They flew east into the dawn. Bill announced that it was still yesterday in America. Daytime in America was night-time in Tibet, he said. He explained this many times but it did not make sense.

Daylight revealed that they were flying across limitless ocean. The sun glinted on waves.

'There are no yaks in America?'

'I have told you before. No. Except maybe in the zoo.'

'Zoo?'

Bill sighed deeply and explained that it was a place where people went to look at animals.

'Like a market?'

'Not exactly, no.'

Like so much else it made no sense.

'If there are no yaks, then how do the farmers plough their fields?'

'With iron horses.'

'Like the Colonel's jeep?' Surely not.

'No, with a tractor, a special type of iron horse made for farmers.' There were, Bill explained, many types of iron horse in America. Nearly every family owned one. Some families owned two or three.

Ari considered this information carefully. At length he said: 'American people, they are very rich?'

'Compared with Tibetans, I guess.'

'Maybe Americans have been so good in their early lives that the Buddha rewards them with iron horses and Pepsi Cola.'

Bill just smiled. That, he said, was one possibility he hadn't thought of.

Bill dozed. Ari was too excited to sleep. He was thinking about America and about Aten who would soon be home in Tibet. Ari wished he was with Aten. America was no place to be alone.

The sun was high now. The ocean had disappeared under a thick blanket of cloud. The cloud lasted for hours and when it had gone there was still the ocean.

They landed once. To take on gas, said Bill. Ari had learned early on that gas was what made planes fly. He watched through a

127

porthole as men in peaked caps pumped gas into the wings of their plane. 'Where is this place?'

Bill was as vague as ever. 'Just another airbase.'

It looked much the same as every place Ari had ever seen in the world outside Tibet. A high wire fence, watch towers, a cluster of white buildings covered in radar antennae, long houses where soldiers lived, warehouses, and wide, empty roads for the planes. 'America has airbases everywhere?'

'Just about every place in the Free World.'

The Free World, as Bill had several times explained, was every-where there were no communists. Once communists took over a country, it stopped being free. Take China, for example, that had been a fully paid-up member of the Free World until those goddamn communists showed up. The loss of China had been a serious blow to the Free World, but Uncle Sam was working hard to get China back. That was where Tibet came in.

'When Tibet is free, will we have American bases?'

Bill gave the proposition due consideration. 'Yes,' he said at length, 'I guess you will.'

At last Ari slept. When he awoke it was dark and there was land below.

'America,' said Bill.

A forest of lights. They stretched for ever, illuminating great highways along which flowed a continuous chain of vehicles, blurring into one long procession of light.

'Los Angeles,' said Bill. 'More people in that city than in the whole of Tibet.'

It was too great a thought for Ari to absorb. 'We are stopping here?'

'No.'

'Where then?'

'You will see.'

Gradually, the lights thinned, giving way to total darkness. Now and then they passed a lone light flickering along an invisible highway. America, too, was an empty country.

Dawn came. The second dawn of that long day. And with the dawn came mountains with snow and deep valleys filled with pine forests. The plane was sloping forward. They were going down. Its shadow skimmed the mountain tops. The snow was pink with the rising sun. Where was this place? Perhaps, after all, they had brought him back to Tibet.

But no. Here was the familiar high wire, here were the watch towers, the white buildings crammed with antennae, the wide road of the airplanes. Another airbase. This one smaller than the others. The pine forests came almost to the wire. The mountains towered. Ari's spirit soared. It was good to see mountains again. Outside, the air was cool. Not since Kalimpong had breathing seemed so worth while.

There was a man waiting. An American. He shook Bill's hand vigorously and slapped his back. He seemed very happy to see them.

'Call me John.' The man extended his hand and beamed at Ari. He was not fat, but he looked as though he might be one day. The flesh on his face was just beginning to lose track of his cheekbones. He wore a hat that concealed most of his hair. Ari would always remember that hat because at no time, day or night, indoors or out, did he ever see this man not wearing his hat.

'My pleasure,' said John. 'My very great pleasure.' He said it several times over. He was an extremely happy man.

In particular he seemed happy with Bill, whom he referred to by another name. At first it was hard for Ari to understand. Later he concluded it was Frit or Frits. Ari remembered once hearing the Colonel refer to Bill that way.

Ari soon realised that John also had another name, by which Bill addressed him when they talked among themselves. He seemed to be known as John only for the purpose of conversations in which Ari was involved. It was not a matter upon which Ari dwelt. He simply filed it away in his store of secret knowledge. There would be time enough to contemplate such mysteries in the years ahead.

19

O N THE FIRST day they took Ari for a run in the mountains.
He had been given new clothes for the occasion. Blue trousers
with a white stripe up the side and a matching top, which pulled on
over his head. Bill and John were wearing identical outfits, John
still in his hat.

They set off up the mountain in a jeep. John was driving, a
cigarette hanging loosely from a corner of his mouth. As ever, Ari
sat in the back with the flaps down. Ari asked for them to be turned
back but his objection was over-ruled. 'Sorry,' said Bill, 'but that's
how it is. You should know that by now.'

They did not go far. The jeep bumped to a halt up a forest trail.
The trees were tall, straight, and dense, like those in the lower
valleys of Tibet. John parked in a clearing. On one side the trail fell
away into a deep valley. There was a view of snow mountains.
'You guys take a little run and I'll just sit here and think,' said John.
Ash fell from the end of his cigarette.

Ari and Bill jogged off up the trail. Before long they had left the
trees. In places there were shallow snow drifts. It was the first time
since Tibet that Ari had been close enough to touch snow.
Reaching down he scooped up a handful. He let out a whoop of
joy.

'Anyone would think you had never seen snow before,' said Bill.
They had come to a halt, panting. Their breath formed little
clouds.

'You have snow.'

'In America, son, we got everything.'

Whe they got back to the clearing, John was sitting on a log,
admiring the view. The cigarette had gone. Instead he was chewing
rhythmically. 'Ari,' he said, 'how many of your people know you
are with us?'

'My people?'

'Tibetans.'

Ari counted on his fingers. There was Sonam, Drolkar, and the servant girl, Rinchen.

'Where are they?'

'In Kalimpong.'

John looked worried and said something would have to be done about them. Bill said they had already been taken care of.

'What about the rest of your family?'

'They think I am in India – unless Sonam told them.'

'How could he, if they are in Litang and Sonam is in India?'

'Some people go – traders maybe.'

'Forget it, Harvey, that end's watertight,' said Bill.

'Who else knows?'

'Wangdu.'

John looked blank.

'You know,' said Bill, 'the guy we used at Clark to help us train these fellows. He's a hundred per cent.'

John looked sceptical. 'Does he know our boy's over here?'

'Yes.'

'Does he know why?'

'No one does, except you, me, and Kumiskey.'

How well did Ari speak the Lhasa language, demanded John, one morning. A little, said Ari. Some he had been taught by Phuntsog. Some he had picked it up from Wangdu. 'Fine,' said John, 'just fine.'

Why did he he want to know?

'Be patient, son, you'll soon find out.'

Two hours every afternoon were given over to pistol practice. To begin with, there was a wide choice of guns. Chinese, Russian, Japanese, and some from countries of which Ari had never heard, but never American.

They tried him indoors and out in the forest. The indoor targets were life-sized cardboard cuts-outs, their features unmistakably Han. Sometimes the targets were moving, sometimes still.

Sometimes spaced apart, sometimes bunched close together. Sometimes he would be told to select one cut-out target from a group.

He was good. By the end of the second week he could put a bullet between the eyes of a moving target at thirty paces. John said he was very proud of Ari.

They taught him how to shoot with his arms outstretched, using one hand to steady the other. How to shoot standing up, sitting down, with the gun concealed in his *chuba*. They showed him how to use a silencer. How to walk with a gun strapped to the inside of his leg. They showed him different types of ammunition. Bullets that entered the human body making scarcely a mark. Bullets that exploded only after they had penetrated the target. They told him he must always shoot to kill, never to wound, and they showed him which parts of the human body would, if penetrated, result instantly in death.

They were lining him up to kill someone. And not just anybody, but some particular person. In due course, he supposed, they would tell him who.

There were courses in what John liked to call 'motivation'. There was no equivalent in the Tibetan language. Bill just said it meant doing a good job. They taught Ari about communism. How it was a world conspiracy that had begun in Moscow forty years ago and was spreading like wildfire. It wasn't just Tibet that had been invaded by communists. There was Korea as well and some parts of Europe. Ever since Bill had turned up with that globe, back in the other training place, Ari had a rough idea where these places were.

Ari was pleased to learn that Tibet was not the only country threatened by a communist takeover. This meant that Tibet was not alone. In fact, according to Bill, just about everywhere was threatened, America included.

America, he said, was the ultimate goal of the communists. If they could take America, that would be it. They would control the whole world. An investigation a few years back had revealed that there were communists all over America, even inside the government. Fortunately, the rot had now been stopped, but you could never be too sure. These communists were clever bastards. They were also very mean. It was not unknown for them to rape and murder women and children.

Ari said that, for all their trickery, the Han communists whom he had seen had never done such things. Which was more than could be said for the Han who had come to Tibet in the old days who – according to John – were Free Chinese.

For a moment John looked black. He was about to say something angry but stopped himself. In the end he forced a little smile and changed the subject.

The days passed slowly. Every day he thought of Aten, Lotse, and Muja in the mountains of Kham. Were they home? Ari asked after about a week. On that very morning, said Bill, there had been a cable from Pakistan to say the boys were down safely. Ari was relieved. He wished he were with them. It was lonely in this place.

They kept him in a little house. Bill and John lived there too. Usually the three of them ate together. Bill did the cooking. Ari ate the same as they did. At breakfast they had fried eggs, bacon, and tomatoes. Dinner was usually a stew or a steak with rice and French fries. John complained a lot about the food, but Ari was happy enough. These Americans lived well.

They taught him to play a game with cards. It was the first time Ari had heard of such a thing, but he caught on quickly. In Litang the traders gambled with dice carved from small animal bones. Even some lamas played dice. Bill and John played poker. At first they played for match-sticks, but John said that wasn't much fun so they played for cigarettes. That wasn't any good either because only John smoked. Until Ari tried one of John's cigarettes and decided that he liked it. Bill didn't think it was a good idea. 'Harvey, I don't think we ought to be teaching this boy your bad habits.'

John was scornful. 'Aw, Fritz, forget it. A couple of cigs a day won't do the boy no harm.'

Ari turned out to be very good at poker and before long he had cleaned John out of cigarettes. They switched to ten-cent coins instead. Ari cleaned those up, too.

'This boy's sure got a lucky streak,' said John as Ari cleaned up for the third night running.

'He's going to need it, where he's going,' said Bill.

Ari just grinned at them, his half tooth exposed.

One morning, after their run in the mountains, John turned up with a pile of photographs and a chart which he unrolled and hung on the wall. 'The Communist Party of China,' he said. 'I'm going to teach you about it.'

First he got out the photographs and spread them on the table. 'Do you recognise this guy?' John pointed to a picture of the moonfaced Han whose likeness had first begun to appear in Litang at about the time the road was opened. 'That's Chairman Mao,' said John without waiting for Ari to reply. 'Number one son of a bitch. And this . . .' He held up a picture of a man whom Ari had never seen before. Ari shook his head. '. . . Chou En-lai. Number two. A very smart cookie.'

They went through the pictures one by one . . . Liu Shao-ch'i, Chu Teh, Chen Yi, Teng Hsiao-ping . . . With the exception of Chairman Mao, none of the names meant anything to Ari. Why were they showing him these pictures? It did not make sense.

'Point one,' said John, 'all these guys are primarily agents of Moscow.' Ari knew about Moscow now. They had shown him the Soviet Union on Bill's globe. Bigger than China and America added together. Thick red arrows pointing out of Russia into China and from China into Tibet. 'Lenin gave these guys the Chinese franchise, just like he gave Ho Chi Minh the franchise on Vietnam.' Vietnam, Ari gathered, was a country further east than Tibet that was also threatened. As for Lenin and Ho Chi Minh, he had no idea who or what they were and John did not explain.

'Point two, these guys are ruthless as hell. Once they start something they never give up. And, let's face it,' John took a drag on his cigarette, 'they have been very successful in a relatively short time.'

John had been looking grave. Suddenly he cheered up. 'We think, however, that they can be stopped in Tibet.'

Ari was relieved to hear that.

They turned to the wall chart. It was a diagram showing the structure of the Chinese Communist Party from the street committees to the Politburo. There were district committees, county committees, provincial committees, autonomous regions, a central committee, and every one had its own congress. It was very confusing. 'I expect you are wondering why we are telling you all this?'

Ari said he was.

'Well son, we – that is, Fri . . . , er, Bill, and I – were wondering if, when you get home, you might like to sign up with the Communist Party.'

Ari was dumbstruck. So this was it. They were not teaching him to fight the Han. They were asking him to join them.

'If we're going to free Tibet, we need all the help we can get. In particular we need people on the inside.'

Bill explained that he and John had been asked by the President (he glanced reverentially at the portrait of the elderly, bald man with big ears, which hung above the fireplace next to the Dalai Lama) to find a Tibetan capable of carrying out a mission so secret and so important that the future of the Free World depended upon it. They had looked carefully at all the Tibetans who had come out for training and decided that Ari was the one.

'What mission?' Ari had found his voice again.

'Er, well, we'd rather not go into that right now,' said John. 'It's kinda special.'

'You can say that again,' added Bill.

Every day, after they returned from their run on the mountain, there was a session with the photos and the wall chart. By the end of a week Ari could identify every one of the big Han. They brought him other pictures of the same men in different locations. Sometimes there were several in the same picture. Once or twice they threw in a few new guys. Later they showed him movie film of Chairman Mao waving to millions of people. It was the first movie Ari had seen, although he knew of such wonders from those who had been entertained at the Han encampment.

In the afternoons they continued with target practice. By now they had narrowed down the type of pistol with which he best performed to one of two: a Japanese Nambu and a Browning GP 35. They tried him out with rifles, too, but gave up after a few days.

He wondered why they were so keen that he should learn to shoot, if he was going to spy on the Han instead of fighting them. A dark thought flashed through his mind, but he dismissed it.

One evening, instead of the usual game of poker, Bill turned up with a pile of paper, every page covered in Tibetan characters written like a child's handwriting.

'All my own work,' said Bill. He was pleased with himself. 'Well, to be strictly accurate, me and Mickey Spillane.'

'Spill-ane? Who is this man?'

'Probably the most widely read man in the whole of America, if not the entire world. I've translated him into Tibetan for you. Well, not exactly for you. It was a little exercise I did when I was learning your language. A sort of master's degree, I guess.'

Ari leafed through the pages. The sentences were short. Easy reading except that Bill's Tibetan left a certain amount to be desired.

'Figured you might like a read. Must get a bit boring here without any of your own people to keep you company.'

Ari read with incredulity. The only books in Tibet were written by lamas and they were about the Buddha and his works. So far as he knew there were no books on any other subject. In his lessons with Phuntsog, he had been made to read books like Sakyapa's *Knowing All*, and the Kangso on the worshipping of deities. But Mickey Spillane, that was something else entirely.

One evening, after a couple of weeks had passed, John and Bill said they had something important to discuss. They looked very grave so Ari guessed it concerned his mission. They had finished eating and Bill had cleared away the plates. A log fire blazed in the hearth. John was smoking a pipe as he sometimes did in the evenings.

'Listen, son, in a couple of weeks we'll be sending you back to Tibet.'

Two weeks. Ari's heart leapt.

'We're going to drop you in near Lhasa. We want you to make your way there and stay put. Lhasa's going to be your home from now on. There are a lot of Kham people camped out there right now, so you shouldn't have much trouble finding your way around.'

'What about my family? My mother, my sisters. They are in Litang.'

'We don't want you going back to Litang. You're known there. Someone's bound to point you out. If the Han know that you were in the lamasery, they'll arrest you and your cover will be blown. We don't want people asking questions. You're starting life again. That's the whole point of this exercise.'

'And Sonam?'

John looked uneasy. 'He's been told that you're dead. That you died of tuberculosis – that's a breathing disease – a month after leaving Kalimpong. No doubt he will get word to your family . . . I'm sorry. We had no choice.'

Ari was staring blankly at the floor. So, he was dead. That's what they had told Sonam. That's what Sonam would tell his poor mother. She would be out of her mind with grief when she heard this news. And his sisters, his beautiful sisters. He would never see them again. These Americans, they were as cruel as the Han.

'*No*. No more. Nothing. I will go home.' Ari was on his feet. He was shouting – like Muja when he had attacked Captain Hank.

'Now, hang on a minute, son.'

'Take me back to Kalimpong. I don't want any more of this.'

Bill was standing, too, his arm round Ari's shoulder. 'Okay, Ari,' he said quietly. 'If that's what you want, we'll take you back to Kalimpong. But first, don't you want to know what we have in mind for you?'

'What?' Ari's tone was sullen. He no longer cared.

Bill spoke slowly. John was quietly puffing at his pipe.

'We want you to kill Chairman Mao.'

Ari sat down. So this was it. They must be mad.

'You joke with me?'

'Ari,' said Bill quietly, 'we don't make jokes about a thing like that.'

That they wanted him to kill was no surprise. Why else had they taken such interest in his prowess with a pistol? But to kill Chairman Mao, the Han God. How was that possible?

What they had in mind, said Bill, was that he should go to Lhasa, where he was not known. Find a job with Han. Any job. They were always on the look-out for friendly Tibetans. He should try to pick up a bit of the Han language. Be polite and friendly. Make out like he believed their propaganda. Sooner or later he would be asked if he wanted to join the party. He should do so at once, but he should not volunteer. Wait to be asked.

'And if they don't ask?'

'They will. Right now the Chinese need all the friends they can get in Tibet.'

'Then what?'

'At first, nothing. Join the party. Keep your head down. Learn their slogans. Do what they tell you.'

'It's like this, Ari,' said John. 'We think of you as a long-term investment, huh, operation. It may take five, ten, maybe even twenty years. We want you to work your way up the Tibetan party to the point where they introduce you to the Chairman. It's bound to happen sooner or later. Right now, there ain't too many Tibetans queuing up to shake hands with Chairman Mao.'

'And then?'

'You kill him.' Just like that. They made it sound so simple. 'We'll give you a couple of guns. All you have to do is keep them oiled and hidden and bide your time.'

So, it was exactly as Phuntsog had prophesied. Ari was the chosen one. In his last life he was a holy hermit living in a sealed cave. In this life he was to be an assassin. Had the idea come from Buddha? Or from the Americans?

John said Ari should take a day or two to think about it. They would not press him. If he insisted, they would abort the operation and send him back to Kalimpong. They hinted, however, that were he to reject their proposal, he would be letting down his country in a big way. He had been chosen because he was the best – in fact the only – Tibetan to come out so far capable of taking on a mission of this importance. The sudden death of Chairman Mao could lead to the disintegration of the Chinese Communist Party. At the very least, it would send the Han reeling. That would be the moment to launch a counter-offensive. Plans for that were already in hand, Bill implied. As for Ari, he would be a hero of his people for all time.

'I will be dead,' said Ari.

'I thought you guys believed in reincarnation,' said John. Bill did not translate.

'You will be provided with a painless means of taking your own life, in the, er, unhappy event that you are unable to effect your escape.' John was having trouble looking Ari in the eye.

For two nights Ari hardly slept. It was not the prospect of death that worried him: it was the prospect of having to spend the rest of his life pretending to be a traitor to his people. He remembered the contempt with which people in Litang regarded Tibetans who worked for the Han. The curses heaped upon their heads. How even their children were shunned. He remembered that first day he had set eyes on a Red Han, when the soldiers had come to tell the Abbot that Litang had been liberated. The little Tibetan interpreter had scuttled along after the Han, knowing the fate that awaited him should he be left behind. To endure that, when all the time he would be working for his people. That was almost too much to bear.

Over and over again the words of Phuntsog came back to him: *There are many ways of achieving nirvana. For you the Lord Buddha has reserved a special mission.*

When he rose on the morning of the third day, Ari had made up his mind. He told them he would do it.

20

JOHN WAS HAPPY again. A great burden had been lifted from his shoulders. He shook Ari's hand as warmly as on the day they had first met. Over again he kept saying, 'One day, son, your country will be proud of you.'

They gave him more parachute practice. Five drops. The last two at night. The drops went smoothly. Jumping from iron birds held no terrors for Ari.

They fitted him up with what John called a cover. Sooner or later, he said, the Han would ask Ari to write down the story of his life. It was essential that he should tell a tale that did not arouse suspicion. The key to a good cover story, said Bill, was to tell as much of the truth as possible. He spoke as though his life were dedicated to the truth.

Work on Ari's cover began at once. There were sessions every afternoon and evening, sometimes lasting into the early hours. John and Bill wrote everything down in notebooks. They argued over what was plausible and what was not. Could they disguise his trip to Kalimpong? It was well known that Kalimpong was crawling with Han agents. It wouldn't take them long to discover Ari's relationship to Sonam and the fact that he had mysteriously disappeared.

At one point they seemed to favour giving Ari an entirely new identity. That way, said John, they could keep him out of India altogether. Once the Han discovered he had been in India they would never trust him. The Han didn't trust anyone who had contact with foreigners.

They tried that out, but didn't get far. Tibet, said Bill, was not like America. Here you could set up a new identity for someone and provide him with all the appropriate documentation: passport, birth certificate, driver's licence, a Medicare number. There was no problem finding people to vouch for whatever version of events was on offer. But in Tibet that was not possible. The Company had no presence on the ground. No influence in the bureaucracy. Besides, you didn't need a licence to drive a yak. Not yet, anyway.

In the end they opted to do the best they could with Ari's existing identity. It was, said John, the option that entailed least risk. Communications in Tibet were none too good and he guessed it would be a while before the Han had everyone logged on computers.

Ari, they decided, could admit to being born in Litang. He could admit to being an incarnate lama. He could even own up to being in the lamasery throughout the siege – and to his escape. (Although, said John with a thin smile, it would not be advisable to mention killing the Han soldier.)

He could even own up to setting out for Kalimpong to stay with his brother-in-law until the troubles in Litang blew over. He should say that was his mother's idea. That much, at least, was true. At this point, however, a significant gap occurred. Ari should own up only to reaching Lhasa and not a step further. He should blot Kalimpong and everything that followed entirely from his mind. Forget the training camps, the airplanes, Pepsi Cola, burgers, baseball, Mickey Spillane, poker, and – above all – he should forget that he had ever met an American, let alone that he had set foot on American soil.

The gap that had to be accounted for was about three months. In Tibet three months was not a long time. He could lose a month or so by stretching out the journey from Litang to Lhasa. He could claim to have spent the missing two months touring the holy places around Lhasa. Goodness knows, there were enough of them. A week or two in the Drepung lamasery, then on to Sera and Ganden. Ganden was a fair way out of town. There was a great deal of coming and going. Ari's alibi was uncheckable, but not unreasonable. To make his account credible, Bill suggested that Ari undertake just such a pilgrimage as soon as possible after he got back to Lhasa.

'What do I tell them about Aten?'

'Nothing, unless they ask.'

'And if they do?'

'Tell them that you lost track of him in Lhasa. That when you last saw him, he was talking of heading back to Litang.'

'Supposing the Han discover I was in Kalimpong with Sonam?'

'Why should they?'

'The Han have many spies in Kalimpong. You said that yourself.'

'Even if they find out what Sonam's been up to, they won't necessarily link you with him.'

'But if they do?'

John took a puff on his cigarette. He pushed his hat to the back of his head. 'In that case, son, we're all up to our necks in yak dung.'

When Ari's cover was agreed, they made him write it out. Once, twice, three times. They looked for loopholes. They asked questions the Han might ask. Sometimes they fired questions without waiting for replies. They manoeuvred him into positions where he had no choice but to lie. Then they cursed him for lying. 'Never tell a lie unless you have to,' Bill insisted. They drummed that lesson into him.

At last, Ari could repeat his story word perfectly and answer every question without hesitation. Then and only then were they satisfied.

One night, without warning, Ari was bundled into a plane and flown halfway around the world. John and Bill travelled with him.

They came down in a place of awful heat. Ari recognised it at once as the airbase to which he had been brought with Aten, Lotse, and Muja after their long boat ride across East Pakistan.

He was installed in the same house with blinds over the windows and cool air machines in each room. As before, they gave orders that he should not set foot outside and, to make sure that he did not, the same arrogant Sikhs stood guard. Of Captain Hank there was no sign.

They returned his Tibetan clothes, shirt, *chuba*, boots, knife. It felt strange to wear Tibetan clothes again after so long. They kitted him out with a bag of *tsampa* and a pack of dried meat.

He received two pistols. The Nambu and the Browning – both of World War Two vintage and both fitted with silencers. There were also about a hundred rounds of ammunition. No sense in giving more, said John, he was unlikely to get an opportunity for more than two shots. The rest was for practice, should the opportunity arise. He should try to keep his hand in. For maintenance purposes, they provided a little kit of flannelette and oil, a cleaning rod and small brush. To store the weapons he was given a couple of yak-hair bags. He should bury the guns in a secure location at the earliest opportunity. Ideally, they should be disinterred, oiled, and tested at least once a year.

He would not be given a radio. That would be an unnecessary encumbrance. They did not expect to hear from Ari again, said John. In case that sounded a little harsh, he added that Ari enjoyed their complete confidence. 'We know we can count on you, son,' he said, patting Ari's shoulder.

The modest contents of his backpack were spread out on the floor. Bill checked each item, ticking it off on a printed list. They gave him a wad of Tibetan money and a couple of silver bars, hallmarked in Chamdo. 'For emergencies,' said John.

Finally, Bill produced a tiny metal case containing a small phial of clear liquid. When the time came it would fit neatly under the tongue. Its purpose had been explained. There was no need to dwell.

On the last evening John became emotional. He turned up with three small glasses and a bottle of the yellow liquid that Ari had last seen in Sonam's house. Bill remonstrated, but John said that a glass or two would do no one any harm. After all, it wasn't every day you kissed goodbye to an agent of Ari's potential.

In the event they had more than a glass or two. By the time Ari went to bed the bottle was all but empty. John kept saying what a privilege it was to have served with Ari. How honoured he was to meet someone who cared so much for his country. How he wished American youth had the sort of guts that young Tibetans like Ari were showing. 'The trouble with kids today,' said John, 'is that they've had it too soft for too long.' Bill didn't bother translating. He just looked embarrassed. As for Ari, he sat there, grinning. When he went to bed, the world was spinning.

Next night, after two hours of darkness, they put him in a covered jeep and drove him to a dark corner of the airbase, where a plane was parked. Jet black, like the one that had carried away Aten and the others. There were no lights, save the beam of a torch held by Bill.

The seats ran along the inside wall. John and Bill strapped themselves one on either side of Ari. He sat with his backpack on his knees. The parachute was already on his back.

They flew north. Bill insisted on keeping the windows covered. Ari could think of nothing, except that he was going home. John seemed more afraid than Ari. He puffed nervously at one cigarette after another. The smoke spiralled upwards in the beam of the dim light.

'Don't forget, bury your chute as soon as you land.' John was full of last-minute advice.

'Cut it out, Harvey, you're making the boy nervous.'

They flew on in silence. The journey was not long. 'We are now over Tibet,' said an unseen voice on an intercom. John nearly leapt out of his chair with fright.

Bill took a little walk, making sure the blinds were secured over all the portholes.

'Drop zone approaching, open rear hatch,' said the unseen voice. The plane was losing height.

Bill disappeared. There was a sudden inrush of cold air. The rear hatch was open. This was it. Ari stood up. He put his hand inside his shirt and touched his relic of Phuntsog. Now he would be safe. The backpack was secured. Bill checked his chute. 'Pull yourself together, Harvey,' he said. John looked as pale as death.

'Two minutes from drop zone,' said the unseen voice. John staged a sudden recovery. He was on his feet and had grabbed Ari's hand, mumbling something about honour and privilege. 'He wishes you good luck,' said Bill, steering Ari towards the rear of the plane.

Ari crouched by the hatch, gripping the handles on each side. The freezing air of Tibet numbed his face.

'Ten, nine, eight . . .' said the unseen voice.

In a few minutes he would be home. It did not seem possible.

'Seven, six, five . . .'

'*Tashi deleg*,' whispered Bill. So far as Ari knew, these would be the last words he would ever hear spoken by an American.

'Four, three, two . . .'

'GO.'

Bill's hand pushed between his shoulder blades. Ari was falling.

The parachute opened exactly on cue. It billowed above, huge and white. It must have been visible for miles. No one had thought of that. Anyway, it was too late now.

Somewhere above he could hear the drone of the plane. It was turning. Surely someone would hear. He peered down into the darkness. There was no light. No sign of life. Not even a nomad's campfire.

The earth appeared suddenly, as if from nowhere. There was a sudden bump and he was down. Parachute spread out behind like the cloak of a high lama. He lay dazed, half expecting a Han soldier to emerge from the darkness and arrest him, but no one came. There was no sound except for the distant hum of the plane and that faded rapidly, leaving him alone in the silence.

Ari was safely home.

PART THREE

===

July 1971
Tibetan Year of the Iron Boar

21

H ENRY KISSINGER ROSE early for what was to be the most momentous day of his life. He had not slept well. It was the only sleepless night of his career.

Kissinger breakfasted on black coffee and papaya and, by four o'clock, he was being driven through empty streets to Islamabad's Chaklala airport in a convoy of military vehicles. His escorts included the foreign minister of Pakistan, Sultan Khan, three assistants, and two secret-service agents. His destination was America's best-kept secret. Not even the agents in Kissinger's party knew where they were headed.

By four-thirty the Americans were airborne in a Pakistan International Airlines Boeing. The plane headed north-east, towards the Karakoram mountains. The Pakistan president's personal pilot was at the controls.

Kissinger's plane remained on the tarmac at Chaklala, parked in full view of the civilian passenger terminal. Evidence, for anyone who cared to look, that he was still in Islamabad. Inquirers would be told that the National Security Adviser had developed a stomach ache and retired for two days to the Pakistani President's guest house in the hills above Murree. To complete the deception, a dummy motorcade would set off later that morning to make the fifty-mile journey from Islamabad to the guest house.

By sunrise Kissinger was crossing the Karakorams. Jagged peaks ranged as far as the eye could see, glowing pink in the first rays of dawn. K2 towered. Glaciers glinted.

Suddenly the mountains fell away. They dropped without warning, down, down, down to a barren desert. The plane veered eastwards. Looking back, Kissinger could still see the mountains shimmering in the distance. The vision persisted for twenty minutes and then evaporated. He had disappeared over the edge of the earth.

*

Four days from now the whole world would know that America and China were friends again. In six months Richard Nixon, that old red-baiter, would be going in person to Peking to shake hands with Chairman Mao. Of course, there was a price to pay. Nothing was for nothing. One or two old allies would have to be quietly junked in the interests of global strategy. Little matters like Korea and Taiwan would have to be put tactfully on the back-burner. Kissinger would have his work cut out over the next few months explaining the sudden change of line to allies in Seoul, Taipei, Manila, Bangkok, Saigon, and Singapore. It was not a prospect he relished.

Still, he consoled himself with the knowledge that it wasn't only the Americans who would have some explaining to do. Chairman Mao would have to break to his people the news that, after two decades of denunciation, the American imperialists and their running dogs were now to be greeted as friends. Any student of communist China would testify that the Chairman and his colleagues had carried through some spectacular policy shifts in their time, but this one must have gone down like a lead balloon with some of those old Long Marchers in the Politburo. You had to hand it to the old fox. He certainly thought big.

No doubt the Chinese would also have difficulty explaining to their friends in Vietnam why Nixon was being fêted in Peking even as his B-52s were pounding the hell out of Hanoi and Haiphong. Kissinger smiled to himself as he considered the prospect.

As for Tibet, no one would even be indiscreet enough to mention the subject. It didn't even figure on the ratings.

At least it might not have done, but for Harvey Crocker. He knew what the National Security Adviser did not know. That somewhere down among those endless mountain ranges, between the Karakoram and the Himalaya, there lurked a boy – he'd be a man now – who was not party to the grand designs of statesmen in Peking and Washington. A remnant from a bygone era. A left-over from an operation that could not simply be switched off now that the line had changed. A boy who was beyond the reach of memoranda from Langley and the White House.

The chances were, of course, that the boy was burned out long ago. He might even be dead, for all that Crocker knew. Most of the boys dispatched from Camp Hale had either reappeared soon afterwards in Kalimpong or come to a sticky end at the hands of the Han. Of all the disastrous operations with which Crocker had been associated in his long career, Tibet was nearest to an un-mitigated failure. In the end the Company had cut its losses and handed the operation over to New Delhi. The Indians were now running a little exile army holed up in the Mustang valley in Nepal. It was a miracle no one had tumbled to it. From what Crocker had heard, the Tibetan resistance these days was more into banditry than fighting Han. They had become an embarrassment to every-one. The Indians and the Nepalese were trying to work out how to flush them out of Mustang without a fuss. As yet, no one had thought of a way. Mustang was off the beaten track and access was, to put it mildly, difficult.

As for Ari, he had not been seen or heard of since that night when Crocker and Neumann had dropped him back into the darkness above Tibet. From time to time they had made inquiries, but no one knew what had become of him. That was hardly surprising, considering how carefully the boy had been coached to stay away from his old haunts. As the years passed, Crocker had several times found himself thinking of the boy. Those evenings playing poker around the fire at Camp Hale. How he used to sit grinning innocently at them, not understanding a word they were saying. That last handshake before the final plunge. It was not like Crocker to get sentimental about an operation, but this one was different. It had been his baby from beginning to end.

Nixon had announced that he was going to China the day before Crocker's retirement party. It had come like a bolt out of the blue. A parting gift from the President. A repudiation of everything for which Crocker had ever worked. Just as well he was retiring. The world was getting to be a mite confusing.

Crocker couldn't sleep for thinking about that boy. Not after Neumman had raised the subject that night in the pizza parlour. Suppose the boy had done what they asked of him. And suppose, just suppose, he had manoeuvred himself into a position where he might be able to take a shot at the Chairman. And what if he got caught and the Chinese followed the trail back to Langley? Now that wouldn't look too good on the eve of the President's visit, would it?

Crocker wrestled with the problem for the first three days of his retirement. Then he called on Neumann for a consultation. Although he spent most of his time at his condo in Miami, Neumann still kept on his apartment in Washington. Sooner or later he would get round to selling it. Meantime, it was useful for coming up to town and looking out a few old buddies.

Neumann fixed them both a whisky and they got down to business. He was characteristically methodical. 'Who, besides ourselves, knows about Fire Monkey?'

'Only Kumiskey knew the full story and he's dead.'

'And the authorisation didn't go any higher?'

'Nope,' said Crocker. 'Kumiskey told me he wasn't letting those bastards on the seventh floor in on the deal. He wanted Fire Monkey to be his personal contribution to world history.'

Neumann smiled. That was just like old Stan.

'Of course,' said Crocker, 'there were others who had a part of the big picture. Hank Stone brought the boy out. Hank's been retired for years.'

'Where's he now?'

'Last I heard he was running fishing trips on the Colorado River. Anyway,' added Crocker, 'as far as he's concerned, the boy went back in with the others.'

'What about Mike Silver? He was with me at Clark the night we separated Ari from the rest.'

'Dead,' said Crocker. 'Chopper crash in Nam five years back.'

'What's on the files?'

'Kumiskey had me reclassify the papers. Under mineral rights in central Java, if I rightly recall. He figured he might one day have to be in a position to deny plausibly. That was his way of covering ass.'

'So, it looks like just you and me. And we're reliable, aren't we?'

Harvey offered no opinion. He merely said he could use another whisky. Ice, no water. Neumann went off to fix it. When he came back, Crocker had thought of something else.

'The point is, Fritz, it's not just us. Not now. Is it?'

'How do you mean?'

'There's Gerry Bannister and Cy Corrigan and, for all we know, that Italian friend of yours who runs that pizza house by the canal. Not to mention anyone else who happened to be within earshot. I mean we weren't exactly keeping our voices down, were we? We told them all about Fire Monkey. The other night, after the party, don't you remember?'

Fritz Neumann didn't reply. He just went as white as the Himalayan snows.

There and then Crocker put through a call to Langley. Director East Asia was friendly enough – to begin with, anyway. 'Hi, Harvey, didn't expect to hear from you again so soon. Gotten over your hangover yet? That was one hell of a party. Can't remember anyone else getting a send-off like that. Not in my time.'

Crocker told him there was a little problem. Some unfinished business. Probably nothing to worry about, but just as well to play safe.

'Sure, Harvey, just go right ahead and tell me. Nothing to do with your pension, is it? Those guys in pensions always need chasing.'

Crocker said no, his pension was just fine. The matter was, how should he put it, delicate. It would be better if they had a person-to-person. Perhaps Fritz Neumann could come in, too, because he was party to this little secret.

The director's goodwill went down a notch. 'Will it keep, Harvey? I'm fairly tied up right now, what with the President going to China and all that.'

'Now that you mention it, Melvin, what Fritz and I have to say has to do with the President's visit to China.'

Director East Asia said they'd better get over right away.

They sat in a suite of easy chairs in the Director's office. He told his secretary he didn't want any calls put through and apologised for having them brought up the fire escape to avoid the general office. 'It's just that we don't want any gossip.'

Crocker said he quite understood.

'Now what can I do for you boys?' It bugged Crocker to hear Director East Asia talk as though he, the Director, was one of them. He was hardly a day over forty, with a degree from Harvard and the barest minimum of field experience. Still, that was the way things were these days.

Crocker explained about Fire Monkey. Every so often Neumann chipped in with a detail that he had omitted. Director East Asia heard them out in stony silence. When – at last – he spoke, it was apparent that the icy self-control that had been with him since Harvard was on the point of deserting him.

'That's all I frigging need. You mean to tell me there's some little guy out there waiting to take out Chairman Mao and that we don't have any control over him and no way even of reaching him? Do you mean to tell me that we just wound him up and pointed him in the right direction and now we just have to sit back and keep our fingers crossed?'

Crocker shrugged as if to say, 'That was how it was in those days.'

'What the hell am I going to tell the White House?'

'Do you have to tell them anything?' asked Neumann innocently. 'I mean, the chances are that our guy dropped out years ago.'

'Listen, Fritz, it ain't like it was in your day. People don't run around concocting plans for taking out foreign heads of state – at least not without clearance at the highest level.' That very morning, explained the director, he had received as 'Eyes Only' from the National Security Adviser demanding a list of all current operations inside and around the Chinese mainland. The request was accompanied by a memorandum from the White House making clear that all China operations were being reviewed in the light of the President's forthcoming visit. The memorandum had concluded ominously: *The President does not wish to be embarrassed by activities undertaken either in the past or in the future by any agency of the American government. He wishes it to be known that he will view with extreme disfavour any act or statement by any servant of the Administration which places in jeopardy the success of his historic mission.*

Crocker said he was sorry. It had seemed like a good idea at the time. Who in the frenzied atmosphere of the Fifties could have predicted that America would be cuddling up to the Reds in China? And who would have thought that Nixon would be the one to do the cuddling?

Director East Asia soon calmed down. The thought occurred to him that these guys could do far more harm to his career than he could do to theirs. The same thought occurred to Crocker, too, although his small reserve of untapped decency prevented him from saying so. As the realisation dawned, the director's tone became conciliatory. He questioned them courteously about who else knew. Crocker and Neumann weren't entirely frank on this point. They kept quiet about Gerry Bannister, Cy Corrigan, and anyone else who happened to be in that pizza parlour.

The director said that, for the time being, he wasn't planning to tell the National Security Adviser or the White House or indeed anyone about Fire Monkey. There and then he had the file on mineral rights in central Java brought up from the basement and deposited in his office safe. He personally saw them off the premises. Again they left by the fire escape. 'Remember, boys,' he said as he waved them into Neumann's car, 'not a word to anyone.'

It was a couple of months before they heard any more. Crocker spent a lazy four weeks with Neumann in Miami, trying out the new golf clubs – his farewell present from the boys and girls at Langley.

It seemed that not everyone in China was keen on a visit from Richard Nixon. There were reports of a plane crash in Mongolia. The plane was rumoured to have been carrying a marshal of the People's Liberation Army. There was talk that he had been mixed up in an attempt to assassinate Chairman Mao. 'Just goes to show we aren't the only ones,' said Crocker cheerfully, as they sat with their feet up in front of the television, sipping Budweiser.

By the time Director East Asia did make contact, Crocker was back in Washington. 'Shall I come into Langley?' asked Crocker, trying to sound helpful.

'No, no, no, Harvey. I don't think that would be a good idea. I'll come to you. Tomorrow morning, at nine.'

After he had rung off, Crocker put in a call to Neumann. 'I think we got trouble,' he said. 'You'd better get your ass down here right away.' Neumann came over on the next plane.

Director East Asia rang Crocker's doorbell on the dot of nine. There was no exchange of pleasantries. No remarking on Crocker's newly acquired sun tan. He got straight down to business. 'We found your guy.'

'Praise be,' said Crocker, who was not much given to invoking the name of the Almighty.

'Amen,' said Neumann, which was about as high as he ever registered on the Richter scale of emotion.

Crocker had paused *en route* to the drinks cabinet where he was proposing to fix his first whisky of the day. Neumann was lounging on a chesterfield of dark-red leather, one of the first fruits of Crocker's retirement gratuity and a monument to his utter lack of taste. Director East Asia had seated himself on a well-worn armchair, pausing only to brush cigarette ash from the armrest. He was still wearing his coat.

'It wasn't easy. We had to use traders in Kathmandu. The only people going in these days. Kinda delicate. A lot of people are very touchy. Don't want to be seen talking to us.'

'You're keeping us in suspense, Melvin.' Crocker's hand hovered over a bottle of Johnnie Walker.

'He's a high-school teacher. In Lhasa.'

'Pull the other one, Melvin. This guy's a country boy. He couldn't teach to save his life.' Crocker poured himself a strong one and flourished the bottle in the general direction of Neumann, who did not react.

'And that's not all. He's done exactly what we asked. That is to say, what you guys asked.'

Neumann shifted uncomfortably.

'He's joined the party.'

'So, just because he's joined the party that doesn't mean he's going to shoot the Chairman for heaven's sake.' Crocker, bottle in hand, was making his way towards the one vacant armchair. 'In any case, how do you know you've got the right guy?'

Director East Asia's voice hardened. 'Point one: we've got it on two sources. Point two: he's not only joined the party, he's a big wheel on the Lhasa district committee.'

Crocker had settled into the armchair, whisky bottle on the floor by his right foot. An insolent grin had overtaken his bloated features. 'Okay, so he's a teacher. So he's a member of the party. So he's on the district committee. That doesn't mean he's going to take out Chairman Mao. For all we know he might have settled down with a wife and half-a-dozen kids and spends his weekends growing chrysanthemums.'

'He might have done, but he ain't.'

'Oh?'

Director East Asia was practically in tears. From the corner of his eye he caught sight of the medallion, embossed with the legend 'FOR CAREER ACHIEVEMENT', presented to Crocker on his retirement. It was draped around the neck of a bronze Buddha that had no doubt been looted from one of the civilisations that Crocker had been sent by the United States government to protect. At that moment Director East Asia would happily have stuffed the medal down Crocker's throat, but wiser counsel prevailed. 'Yesterday,' he said quietly, 'your Tibetan was appointed a delegate to the National People's Congress which opens in Peking this Fall. There, for the first time in his life, he will come within pistol range of Mao Tse-tung.'

The information was digested in silence. The insolent smile disappeared from Crocker's face as though someone had flicked a switch. Neumann was staring at the carpet. 'How do you know that, Melvin?' whispered Crocker.

'*Because his name has just been read out on the effing radio.*'

22

ARI RECEIVED THE news with a mixture of joy and foreboding. The moment had come. A chance to avenge his people for all the pain and humiliation they had suffered at the hands of the Han. Would he be equal to the task? The Buddha would give him strength.

For years he had been forced to suffer in silence as the Han colonised and destroyed his country. After the uprising he had watched as Han soldiers went from house to house rounding up males aged over fourteen. He had watched the convoys of trucks shipping them out to the labour camps. Worst of all was the knowledge that he was immune from the arrests, the interrogations, the beatings. Immune because he was one of that small élite of Tibetans who had crossed over. At times he wanted to shout, 'Take me too, I am one of them.' Only the knowledge that he had been reserved for a higher task kept him from fleeing. In the early days, before the final clamp-down, many people were leaving for India. Whole families would disappear in the night. All that stopped Ari joining them was the knowledge that he had a mission. One which he alone was equipped to carry out.

But it was hard. There were many moments when he might have given in. Then he prayed to the Buddha to give him strength. The worst was not the humiliations inflicted by the Han, but the jibes of his own people. The curses hissed at him in the bazaars when they saw him in his grey Han tunic: 'Han lover'. 'Son of the five-headed she devil', 'Betrayer.' Children threw stones at him and scuttled away down back alleys. Old ladies turned their backs when he passed them on the Barkhor.

Nowadays it was not so bad. The Great Proletarian Cultural Revolution had knocked out of most people whatever spirit had survived the torments of the early years. Older folk went about with their heads down, shoulders stooped, not wishing to see evidence of their country's degradation.

For those who wished to see, the evidence was everywhere. The padlocked metal gates that barred the entrance to the Jokhang, the holiest shrine in Tibet – Han soldiers had kept their pigs there during the Cultural Revolution. Not a word of Tibetan to be seen in public places. Even the street signs were in the Han language. After a decade of Han occupation, the *Thoughts of Chairman Mao* represented the sum total of available literature in the Tibetan language. It didn't matter that most Tibetans could neither read nor write. They all shared the humiliation.

So much bitterness had been seared into Ari's soul during that long night that the lowest point was impossible to identify. Was it the *thamzings* in the early days, the speak-bitterness campaigns where, each evening, the people had been ordered to assemble in some cobbled square to denounce some alleged exploiter? The victim, perhaps an incarnate lama like Ari, would have his arms twisted behind him until he was bent double while abuse and worse were showered upon him. How angry the Han had become when people refused to denounce with sufficient sincerity. Anyone speaking up for the victim would be dragged away to undergo a *thamzing* of his own. The cunning Han would place their agents in the crowds with carefully prepared denunciations designed to incite people against the victim.

Once Ari had been called upon to make a fraudulent denunciation of an old lama from Drepung who had been labelled a green-brain. That was the closest he had come to running away. In the end he had stayed and compiled a speech containing what he judged to be the barest minimum of falsehood and invective acceptable to the Han while at the same time letting the old lama off fairly lightly. It was not well received. He could feel the hatred of the crowd towards him, even as he delivered his speech. And it did not satisfy the Han either. Later, a Han cadre had scolded him: 'You will have to do better than that,' he said, 'if you want to be a good communist.'

*

A year after the uprising, he had been assigned to the labour camp at Nachin, half an hour by truck from Lhasa. By then Ari had taught himself enough of the Han language to make himself useful as an interpreter. There was a shortage of Tibetans willing or able to work for the Han.

At Nachin they had ordered all the prisoners to tell their life stories. They wanted every detail. Place of birth. Names of parents, brothers, sisters, uncles, aunts. Everyone had to account for each year of his or her life since birth. Since most of the prisoners could not read or write they had to dictate their statements. An interpreter would translate and a Han cadre would take notes. It was a laborious process made more so by the fact that extraction of even the simplest detail required careful cross-examination. The Han were obsessed with dates and numbers. Things which meant nothing to Tibetans.

The prisoners were being used to construct a station for making light. The Han claimed that their station would produce enough light for the whole of Lhasa and be of great benefit for the people of Tibet, but no one believed this. Most Tibetans had long ago observed that only the Han seemed to benefit from such projects.

The prisoners were camped in long rows of canvas tents. They worked for up to twelve hours a day with one or two days' rest each month. Each evening there were meetings at which the Han advised them of the error of their ways and of the path to righteousness. The Han called the process 'reform through labour'. The prisoners called it serfdom, worse than anything the lamas had dreamed up.

They were divided into work units. Each unit had as its head a prisoner who was judged to have made more progress than the others. He was chosen by his colleagues, often on the advice of a Han cadre, and was expected to submit reports on his fellow prisoners. Work units were encouraged to compete with each other and there were rewards for those who performed best. What struck Ari at once was that the entire system was managed by Tibetans. The Han had taught the Tibetans to police themselves. They were so clever.

*

It was winter. The mountains around Lhasa were powdered with snow. Icicles dripped from overhanging roofs. The Han went about in great coats and fur hats with flaps that covered their ears, bodies hunched against the cold wind.

Ari had been at Nachin for about a week. One afternoon he was warming his hands around a brazier, waiting for a truck to take him back into town, when he heard a familiar voice.

'Rimpoche.'

The voice come from behind. Ari hardly dared turn round.

'Rimpoche.'

He half turned and there, not ten paces away, was Aten. Aten. What was he doing here? He should be in Kham? How had he been captured? Did they know about the Americans? Did they know who had gone with him? No, Aten would never tell.

The sparkle had gone from Aten's eyes. His cheeks were more hollow than they had been after the siege of the lamasery, and his clothes were tattered. He was squatting among a group of prisoners awaiting transfer. Maybe to one of the camps on the Chang Tang, the desert of ice from which no one ever came back.

Each prisoner carried a blanket and a tiny bundle of possessions. Two Han soldiers stood guard.

'They are taking me away, Rimpoche . . .'

One of the guards spoke sharply to Aten, and Ari looked quickly away. He prayed that his face had betrayed no hint of recognition. He held his breath. The soldier was approaching. 'What did that man say to you?'

Ari did not reply.

'What did he say?' The soldier's tone was menacing.

'He asked for a cigarette.'

The soldier said nothing. He walked away, pausing only to aim a kick at Aten. The blow was not hard. It glanced off his leg. Aten wobbled, but did not lose his balance.

Ari did not look back until he was aboard the truck. As it pulled away he found himself looking straight into Aten's eyes. Aten was still squatting patiently by the track. A single tear welled in his left eye and trickled down his face, carving a path through the ingrained dirt. It fell with a splash into the dust.

Ari held Aten's stare until he was out of sight. What was his old friend thinking as the tear rolled down his face? That Ari had crossed over to the Han? That he had betrayed Tibet?

23

AFTER A YEAR at Nachin, Ari's performance was judged sufficient to qualify him for further advancement. 'You have been awarded a place at the South West School for National Minorities,' said the humourless Han who was in charge of Ari's work unit. 'It is a great honour.'

Ari made a little show of being suitably moved.

The School for Minorities was in Chengtu – a great city in the Szechwan province of China. In the old days a journey to Chengtu would have taken many months. Now there was a road and on that road a bus. Even allowing for landslides and other natural disasters, the journey took less than two weeks. Ari travelled with the other chosen Tibetans. They sang, drank *chang*, and laughed a lot, which did not please the Han in charge of them. 'You have much to learn,' he told them, 'before you can obtain a correct attitude.'

The journey to Chengtu did not take them through Litang. Instead, they took the northern route through Kantze. Ari was both disappointed and relieved. He was, after all, supposed to be dead.

Scarcely a day had passed when he had not thought of his mother and sisters. Had Dechen and Nyima found husbands? He hoped they were taking good care of their mother. She had looked so old and tired when he had last seen her. Little news reached Lhasa from Litang. The new road was supposed to have made travel easier, but the flow of pilgrims from the east had all but dried up. Only those on official business were permitted to travel.

Chengtu was the largest city Ari had ever seen, unless, of course, he counted his brief glimpses of Dacca and Los Angeles, which Ari was not in the least inclined to do. He had wiped those places from his memory. Even to dream of them was dangerous. He feared what he might say in his sleep.

Beside Chengtu, Lhasa was a village. Chengtu was bursting at the seams. There were so many people that they overflowed the houses, tea houses, and cinemas, and flooded the streets for every minute of the day and for much of the night. It was a relief to see that most Han were not at all like those in Tibet. They laughed, loved, and cried like Tibetans. They enjoyed picnics and worshipped gods.

There were about three thousand students at the School for Minorities. For reasons never explained, many were Han. Presumably the authorities believed that daily contact with so many young Han would have a civilising influence on the barbarian minority races.

About a third of the students were Tibetan. There were also many Lolo from the border region of Tibet and China. The Lolo were fiercely proud of their independence and not shy of saying so. Rumour had it they were still at war with the Han. Fights sometimes broke out between Lolo and Han students.

The regime was vigorous. Up at five. Callisthenics from six to eight. Classes on the Chinese constitution and on the history of the great and glorious Communist Party, from eight until five with an interval of an hour for lunch. In the evening an hour of basketball or table tennis. Like so much else, sport was obligatory. Ari soon learnt that there were few choices in liberated China. Supper (invariably Han food) was followed by two hours of classes in the Han language. By comparison, the routine at Camp Hale had been relaxed.

Each Wednesday there was a meeting of the whole school at which the students were variously exhorted to save grain, kill flies, destroy sparrows, resist imperialism, and learn the correct handling of contradictions among the people.

There was a course of lessons entitled 'The Great Motherland'. It was delivered by a bullet-headed little man called Comrade Kao who gave the impression of reciting facts and slogans that he had been made to learn by heart. He could be derailed by the simplest question. Although Comrade Kao was virulent in his denunciation of capitalism it did not escape the notice of his students that his two most prized possessions were a Parker pen and Rolex watch.

With one or two significant omissions, Comrade Kao's lessons bore a remarkable resemblance to those of John at Camp Hale. Communism, explained Comrade Kao, had begun in the Soviet Union and soon after had been introduced into China by Comrade Mao Tse-tung. He pronounced the Chairman's name with the reverence of a lama invoking the name of the Buddha. Between them, Kao continued, the Soviet Union and China had liberated most of the world's people. It was only – Comrade Kao did not bother to hide his disdain – stupid and backward people such as Tibetans and Lolos who had failed to welcome communism with flowers and open arms.

It surprised Ari to learn that communism was a foreign ideology. At least as foreign as all the other ideologies that the Han so roundly deprecated. The more he learnt about the Soviet system, the more Ari realised that the system the Han were so busily introducing into their own country was an almost perfect replica. From the Politburo to the street committees, the structure was the same.

From time to time mention was made of a distant and insignificant country called America. This country, said Comrade Kao, had supported the corrupt and parasitical Nationalist bandit regime, but the help of America had not proved sufficient. Thanks to the wise leadership of Chairman Mao and the party, the Nationalist bandit regime had been swept away. Chairman Mao had recently expressed the view that America was a paper tiger and a little song had been composed in support of that proposition. They were exhorted to learn the song by heart.

Comrade Kao's version of events did not always go unchallenged.

'If America is a small and distant country, why are the markets in Chengtu so full of American goods?' asked one of the Lolos.

Comrade Kao clutched uneasily at the Parker pen protruding from the top pocket of his tunic. 'These things are left over from the anti-Japanese war. At that time there were many American imperialists in our country.'

'Excuse me, Comrade. But your pen is not left over from the war. It is brand new and costs more than one month's salary.'

Comrade Kao's reply was drowned amid hoots of derision.

*

It was three years before Ari returned to Lhasa. By then he had learnt that religion is poison (Chairman Mao himself had said so), that the Communist Party of China was always right, and that the Tibetan people were only a tiny minority in the Great Family of the Motherland.

There were now more Han soldiers than ever in Tibet. While Ari had been away there had been a war with India and the border was closed. Trade had ceased. All roads now led to China. Contact with the world beyond was forbidden. The Democratic Reforms that had sparked the revolt in Litang had now been introduced all over Tibet. All the younger lamas were gone from the lamaseries. Many had returned to their villages and married. Others had fled to India. Some were in labour camps. Those who remained were denounced as greenbrains and were mostly elderly. Children were encouraged to mock them as they scuttled through the streets.

Ari was put to work at the Lhasa Number One Secondary School. At that time it was also the only secondary school in Lhasa. About half the students were children of Han cadres and the remainder were children of Tibetan cadres. Although he was called a teacher, Ari was little more than an interpreter for the teacher who, like all the teachers, was a Han and who, like most Han, spoke not a word of Tibetan and showed not the slightest interest in learning.

Ari was given a room in a compound with other progressive Tibetans. The bolder ones set up little altars in their room with butter lamps and pictures of the Dalai Lama. Ari did not dare do this for fear of drawing attention to himself. The only decoration in his room was a poster depicting Chairman Mao as the father of all races. At his feet were assembled people of all colours. There was even a Tibetan. The slogan on the poster said: 'PEOPLES OF THE WORLD, UNITE'.

Ari's only concession to the old world was his relic of Phuntsog. He wore it still under his grey tunic and hoped that no one would notice.

A Han soldier stood guard at the gate of the compound where the Tibetan teachers lived. His job was to keep out bad elements. This was necessary because bad elements had several times set fire to the homes of the Han and their collaborators.

*

After he had been home from Chengtu for about half a year, Ari went on a short journey. He waited until the week of the Tibetan New Year when the Han control over people's movement relaxed and then he set off along the road leading south out of Lhasa. After he had walked for about two hours he paused to see if anyone else was about and, having satisfied himself that he was alone, turned off up a narrow track.

He followed the trail over a barren hill to a point where he could no longer be seen from the road, and then slithered into a deep gully, dislodging small stones as he went. The bottom of the gully was filled with boulders. It was a place where evil spirits dwelt and where no sensible Tibetan would ever set foot.

Ari wondered if he could still find the place after so long, but he need not have worried. The stones were exactly as he had left them. He removed the largest and then the smaller ones. Then he scrabbled in the dirt with his pen-knife. He dug down about three inches before he came to the yak-skin bags. They were intact.

His hands trembled as he removed the bags and reached inside. They were there. Both guns. The ammunition and the phial of poison. He drew out the Browning, caressing the barrel as though it were a baby's cheek. He removed the safety catch, cocked the hammer, and pulled the trigger. It surrendered to only the slightest pressure. It was as good as new.

He tried the Nambu. It seemed all right, too. He loaded each gun. Then, leaving the guns on a rock lightly covered by one of the bags, he measured thirty paces along the floor of the gully. Taking six small rocks, he placed one beside the other on one of the large boulders. He went back to the guns and picked up the Browning. Pausing, he surveyed the landscape. Satisfied that he was alone, he stood with his feet apart, both arms stretched in front, one hand steadying the other, just as they had taught him at Camp Hale. He fired once, twice, three times. The first three rocks splintered. The sound ricocheted off the sides of the gully. His ears rang. The sound was louder than he had imagined. His heart was beating loudly. He hoped that if anyone heard, they would think it was a premature outburst of New Year fire crackers. The Han had not yet banned fire crackers.

Without waiting, Ari replaced the Browning and repeated the

procedure with the Nambu. Legs apart, arms outstretched, three shots in quick succession. The remaining stones splintered, the sharp cracks echoed around the gully, his ears rang. There was a smell of cordite.

He cleaned and oiled the guns and returned them carefully to the yak-skin bags and replaced the bags, taking care to leave the stones exactly as he had found them.

He did not leave until twilight. No one came. No one saw him depart. His secret was safe.

Every year Ari went to that place. Each year he fired six shots, three from each gun, and he was gratified to know that his aim was as true as ever. He wondered how long it would be before his training could be put to use.

One year, after his fourth or fifth annual pilgrimage, he was walking back to Lhasa when he was overtaken by a convoy of trucks carrying Han youths wearing red armbands and chanting slogans from a small red book. The Great Proletarian Cultural Revolution had reached Tibet.

Everyone knew it was coming. For months Ari and his colleagues had listened anxiously as the loudspeakers in the compound broadcast news of the new madness sweeping China. President Liu Shao-ch'i, once the Great Marxist and Proletarian Revolutionary, had overnight been transformed into a Renegade, Traitor, and Scab. The Soviet Union, they now learned, was no longer the home of the one true faith, but of a new and virulent disease called Revisionism and this was to be reviled at least as fervently as American imperialism. For a while Revisionism seemed to have displaced imperialism at the top of the Han demonology.

A nationwide search began for revisionists. At first it seemed to be a dispute between the newly arrived Red Guards and the Han who lived in Lhasa. They commenced an endless round of meetings from which Tibetans were excluded. Furious arguments were overheard, sometimes degenerating into violence. There were parades. Youths with red flags and armbands marched back and forth waving red books containing the collected wisdom of the Great Helmsman, as Chairman Mao was now known. The Great

Helmsman's portrait was everywhere. In every chapel of every temple. On the roof of the Jokhang. On a huge canvas that stretched across the front of the Potala. It could be seen all over Lhasa. Chairman Mao was on every altar in every household. He was the new God.

Some Tibetans were short-sighted enough to whisper that maybe the Han empire was about to disintegrate. Perhaps the Han would tear each other to pieces and then go home. Such wishful thinking did not last long. There was no escape. Before long the madness would engulf everyone.

It was Sunday. A day of rest even in the Han calendar. From out in the compound Ari could hear raised voices. Han and Tibetan. Someone was being denounced. He ran downstairs. On the way he passed Jamyang, his neighbour, a ruddy-faced youth who drove a truck for the Han.

'What's happening?'

'They are searching for revisionists.'

Ari laughed. 'They won't find any here.'

'There are revisionists everywhere,' said Jamyang. He was not smiling.

Ari went outside. A crowd of Han youths were laying siege to the home of an elderly couple who looked after the compound. They grew sunflowers in their garden. The sunflowers were in full bloom. A youth had snapped one off and was using it to beat the old man about the head. Other youths emerged from the house. Eyes gleaming. One carried a prayer wheel. The old woman was pleading. It was her most precious possession. The youth laughed cruelly and dashed it against the wall. The old woman was beside herself, kneeling on the ground trying to scoop up the precious relics that had fallen from inside the prayer wheel. A butter lamp was thrown from an upper window. The Han youths cheered. Someone emerged with a picture of the Dalai Lama. The old man made a grab for it. He was pushed aside. The picture was held aloft for all to see. Someone lit a match. The mob cheered as the flame took hold. The old couple were out of their minds with grief at the sacrilege.

By now the mob had turned to the other houses in the

compound. They were hammering on every door. Those that did not open immediately were smashed down. The list of items deemed revisionist grew longer as the afternoon wore on. Prayer beads, earrings, scarves, butter lamps, holy pictures, heirlooms that had been in families for generations lay scattered across the courtyard. Almost anything Tibetan seemed to be revisionist. Even *chubas*. In the new China, it seemed, everyone would be dressed in the drab blue or grey overalls of the Han.

The more the owners pleaded, the greater the destruction wrought upon their homes. One young Red Guard emerged carrying a set of lama's robes, evidence of the owner's earlier incarnation. Even worse, the man had tried to conceal the robes under his mattress. This earned him a sound beating, following which he was paraded round the compound with a dunce's cap on his head.

Ari was ready when the hammering came on his door. He had removed his watch and concealed it in a drainpipe on the roof (it was well known that Red Guards did not always confine their attentions to manifestations of the old order). Ari's *chuba* and boots, the ones Sonam had had made for him in Kalimpong, were suspended by string from the back window.

The Red Guards searched his room. Their leader was a girl. Her hair had been sheared. It came to a ragged end halfway down her neck. She had been pretty once.

'We are destroying the old society,' she said.

She could not have been much older than sixteen. What did she know of the old society?

'Who told you to do this?'

'Our beloved leader, Chairman Mao.'

There was no sense in arguing with Chairman Mao. Other Red Guards had crowded in behind her. Some wielded sticks. They were crazy, these Han.

They searched thoroughly. Ari's bed was overturned. His quilt ripped open. His few possessions scattered on the floor and picked over. They confiscated a book of folk tales and a Nationalist Army water bottle. He had bought them in Chengtu.

'Is that all?' They seemed disappointed with their haul.

'I am a poor man.'

As they were leaving the girl noticed the cord around his neck.
'What's that?'
'It's nothing.'
'Show me.' They stared at him. Ari had frozen to stone.
'*Show us.*' One of the youths made a lunge for the cord. The piece of Phuntsog's thighbone emerged from beneath Ari's shirt. The boy jerked the cord. It snapped. He held it up for all to see, eyes gleaming in triumph. The bone dangled.

'What is it, greenbrain?'
He might have told them that was his most precious possession. He might have told them that it was all that remained of his best friend and teacher, but they would not have understood. These were the children of an age that had no time for sentiment.

'You can't take that,' said Ari lamely.
But they could and they did. 'One day you will be grateful to beloved Chairman Mao for freeing you from superstition and ignorance.' They laughed at him as they departed.

That night Ari wept for Phuntsog and for Tibet. 'Oh Phuntsog, are you out there? Can you see what they are doing to our country? These crazy Han will destroy everything. They will crush us like ants. How can we save our beautiful country from these madmen?'

Old Phuntsog was up there somewhere. His answer came back clear as crystal: 'You must kill their beloved Chairman.'

So, when Ari heard that he was to go to Peking, his heart leapt. Fourteen years he had waited and now, at last, his chance had come. A chance to repay the Han on behalf of all Tibetans. It was a big responsibility, a great honour. He had been chosen and he must not fail. He would not.

As for old Phuntsog, he was up there somewhere, arranging everything.

24

CROCKER HAD NEVER seen Director East Asia in such a state. These Harvard types usually made a big deal out of staying cool. But not this one. He paced the floor in Crocker's tiny living room like he was expecting to go to the Chair at dawn. The ashtray on the mantelpiece was piled high with half-smoked Stuyvesant. A pall of smoke lingered.

'If that guy don't sit down soon, he'll wear a path in your carpet,' whispered Neumann. He was ignored.

'Have you told Henry?' asked Crocker.

The very mention of the National Security Adviser was enough to cause Director East Asia to throw a wobbly. 'Have I *what*?'

'I thought, maybe –'

'Listen, Harvey, have you any idea what he'd do to us if he finds out about this? And as for Nixon . . .' Director East Asia shuddered. The possibilities were too awful to contemplate.

There was an awkward silence. Outside it was a hundred degrees. The air-conditioner hummed. Then Neumann had a brainwave. 'Why don't we just slip word to the Chinese? Kinda private like. They could pick the boy up quietly. Save us a lot of trouble.' The suggestion, like its predecessor, was not well received. 'And supposing they don't wanna do it quietly?' Director East Asia had stopped in his tracks again. 'Not everyone in China's thrilled to bits by the prospect of a visit from Tricky Dicky. Supposing, just supposing, word gets round that the CIA is trying to take out Chairman Mao at the very moment when every other agency of the Administration is bending over backwards to be nice to the old bastard. That wouldn't look too good, would it? Matter of fact, the Chinese might just use it as an excuse for cancelling the President's entry visa.'

Neumann said he hadn't thought of that.

*

In due course a plan was decided. The boy would have to be taken out. Crocker said maybe it wouldn't be necessary to waste him. Perhaps they could just talk the boy out gently. Set him up with a tea shop or something in Kathmandu or Denver. A Tibetan tea shop would go down a treat in Denver. 'We owe it to the boy to give him a chance. After all, he is on our side.'

'Not any more, he's not,' whispered Neumann.

Director East Asia was having none of it. 'Nice idea, Harvey, but we ain't got time for kid gloves. We are now in July. The congress opens in November. It will take us at least a month to recruit our killers and train them and another two to infiltrate them through the Himalayas. We're cutting it fine as it is.'

Crocker shrugged and said it was a pity. He felt kinda responsible for that boy. After all, Fire Monkey had been his baby.

Crocker didn't give up. Later he suggested that Neumann and himself take a trip to Kalimpong to see if they could track down any of the boy's relatives. Maybe they could get word to him that the operation had been aborted.

Director East Asia lost his temper at that point. 'Now listen, Harvey, let's get one thing straight. If it wasn't for you, we wouldn't be in this mess. I don't want to listen to any more of your damn fool ideas. As far as I and everyone else at Langley is concerned, you have retired. RETIRED, do you understand? From now on, we're going to do things my way.'

'Ain't you forgetting one teeny-weeny detail?' Crocker's tone was insolent.

'What's that?'

'Just this: that all Fritz . . .' he indicated Neumann, whose weathered features were severed by a thin smile '. . . and I need to do to blast you clean out of the water, is to tap out a little memo, mark it strictly personal, stick it in a plain brown envelope, and sent it to Henry . . .'

Director East Asia called them all the names under the sun . . . And then said he'd do it their way, after all.

Brother-in-law Sonam was still to be found in Kalimpong. He had diversified. Nowadays he was into precious stones, antiques, and carpets, as well as just about everything else. He had carpet factories strung out along the Himalayas from Darjeeling to Dharmsala. Lately, he had acquired a controlling interest in a tea plantation in Assam. He had even negotiated an arrangement with an antique dealer in St James's, London, through which he auctioned the treasures of his civilisation. Drolkar had borne four children, including two healthy boys who were being educated at a boarding school in Geneva. In due course they would inherit all that Sonam possessed. Reports reaching Langley spoke of unconfirmed allegations that he had been taking a cut of the Agency's contribution to the liberation of his country. He was a Tibetan for whom the coming of the Han had been something less than a disaster.

Sonam had the respect of his fellow Tibetans, but not their love. That would be too much to expect. Bodyguards – huge oafs from his father's estates in Kham – watched over him night and day. In the courtyard, snarling mastiffs strained on their chains at the approach of strangers.

Crocker and Neumann could hear the snarls even as the taxi deposited them at Sonam's gate.

A servant showed them to a room draped with faded *thankas* and thick with carpets. Two gold Buddhas reclined upon a little altar. A window opened onto a garden of chrysanthemums. Beyond, Kanchenjunga loomed, and the sunlight on the snows was dazzling.

'Now I call that some view,' said Crocker.

'Courtesy of the American taxpayer,' said Neumann.

There was a movement behind. They turned to see a portly oriental, hair trimmed to a crew cut. He was dressed like a Wall Street banker on his day off. Slacks, a vivid shirt that hung loose at the waist, golf shoes, a Cartier watch. Crocker had noticed golf clubs, incongruous among the *thankas* and the gold Buddhas.

'Welcome, gentlemen, to my humble home.' Humble, my ass, thought Crocker.

Sonam advanced, hand outstretched. The files at Langley showed pictures of a man who was much thinner. They shook hands. Sonam indicated a sofa strewn with cushions. 'How can I help you, gentlemen? I thought that America had lost interest in us Tibetans.' His smile betrayed a hint of bitterness.

Crocker came straight to the point. 'We have come about Ari.'

'Ari? He died years ago. You know that.'

Crocker cleared his throat. 'Er, no sir, not exactly.'

'Not exactly what?' Neumann thought he might have a chance to try out his Tibetan, but Sonam had learned good English during his years in Kalimpong.

'Ari is not exactly dead.'

Sonam looked as though he had been hit square across the head with one of his golf clubs. When he recovered he said, 'But we were told . . . You told us.'

'At the time it was necessary. There were reasons, good reasons.'

'Where is he?'

'In Lhasa.'

'Lhasa? How do you know?'

'Sources,' said Crocker mysteriously.

'Why are you telling me this?'

'Because we want him back, urgently.'

Sonam said he would see what could be done. These days almost no one passed between Kalimpong and Lhasa, but there were people in Bhutan who might be able to help. It would take time and cost money.

'Time we don't have. Money's no problem,' said Harvey. He regretted the words as soon as they were out of his mouth.

Sonam's eyes gleamed: 'A lot of money.'

Crocker and Neumann stayed in Kalimpong long enough to arrange a down payment for Sonam and to provide him with a contact in Calcutta who would onpass messages. They then retired to Neumann's condominium in Florida to await events.

Six weeks passed. Director East Asia called every day demanding results. A couple of times they had their man in Calcutta take a run up to Kalimpong to see how Sonam was making out. He returned with nothing except bland assurances that the matter was in hand.

Then, one afternoon in the fall, Director East Asia rang to say there had been a development. He would not go into details on the phone, but suggested a meeting that evening in Neumann's Washington apartment. 'That guy sounds as if he's cracking up,' said Neumann as he replaced the receiver. Crocker said he wouldn't be surprised. These Harvard types were all the same. Cool on the surface, but weak as piss inside.

They caught the first available flight to Washington. Director East Asia awaited them in the lobby. His eyes were dark caverns.

The Director didn't waste time on pleasantries. 'Take a look at this.' He thrust a print-out under Crocker's nose. It was Lhasa Radio monitored in Hong Kong, dated September 22 – three days ago. It said: '*Amid joyous scenes of popular enthusiasm the Tibetan delegation to the National People's Congress left Lhasa today for Peking. They will travel overland via Chamdo, Chengtu, Chungking, and Wuhan. They are expected to arrive in Peking five days before the Congress opens. On arrival, they will report personally to Chairman Mao. They will tell him of the great strides made by the people of the Tibet Autonomous Region.*'

Crocker read the report and passed it to Neumann. 'Boy,' he said, 'have you got trouble.'

25

THE CROWD THAT gathered for the departure of the delegation was sullen. School children and factory workers dressed
in their best clothes, under orders from the Han.

The children wore Chairman Mao badges and the red scarves of
Young Pioneers. Marshalled by their teachers, they marched in
perfect order and chanted mechanically. These children knew
nothing of their rich heritage. They were being turned into young
Han. The very sight of them filled Ari with sadness.

Only the Potala was unchanged. It loomed huge and magnificent. Thirteen floors, one thousand rooms, illuminated in the
early morning sunlight. On the roof the golden tombs of the Dalai
Lamas glinted. The Potala was the one place those crazy Red
Guards had not destroyed. Inside, it was cold and empty, a
mausoleum for a dead civilisation.

Ari knew he was supposed to look happy. He did his best, but it
was not easy. He was looking at Lhasa for the last time. In this life,
at least.

The children were singing a song about Chairman Mao. These
days all songs were about Chairman Mao. A Han photographer
passed among them taking pictures. 'Smile,' he whispered. He
wanted only pictures of happy Tibetans.

The delegation was lined up in front of a small bus, a new bus,
made in Japan and brought to Lhasa especially for the occasion. Its
automatic doors and two different speeds of windscreen wiper
were the subject of much admiration. The driver was a Han of
exceptional arrogance who demanded the respect due to the driver
of a foreign-made bus. To be a driver in Tibet was to be a very
important man.

There were speeches. Much talk of the beloved Motherland and
of Chairman Mao. A Han in a grey tunic with pens protruding
from his top pocket was speaking into a microphone. There were

loudspeakers on trees. The Han was a vice chairman of committee for the Tibet Autonomous Region. He came from Shanghai. Everyone knew that. Of the fifty-six members of the committee, Ari could count only a handful of Tibetans. It was incredible. Twenty years had passed since the Han first entered Tibet and they could not find more than half-a-dozen Tibetans to serve even as figure-heads.

They boarded the bus amid flowers and handshakes. Cameras whirred and clicked. The children cheered. The workers, faces blank, stood at attention with placards proclaiming their love of the Motherland and of Chairman Mao. Loudspeakers emitted 'The East is Red'.

Ari was seated at the rear of the bus in his new boots and *chuba*. A month before departure everyone in the delegation had been given extra ration coupons for cloth and food. The Great Helmsman who, so far as anyone knew, had never set foot in Tibet, wanted to see only well-dressed and healthy Tibetans.

As they drove away Ari looked back at the Potala until it disappeared. He glanced around at the others. They were jabbering excitedly. They had a right to be excited. They were going to places where few Tibetans had ever been. And, unlike Ari, they expected to return.

He felt the gun hard against his body. It was concealed inside his new *chuba*. Did the bulge show? He had done his best to pad the lining with yak hair.

Ari had selected the Nambu. The Browning he had left in its hiding place beneath the rocks. It would remain there for ever, like a relic buried in the floor of a holy place. He had waited until the last moment to collect the gun, making his way out to its hiding place one Sunday in the early morning. He had oiled and tested the gun and it worked perfectly.

By the time he had got back to Lhasa it was dark. Ari hoped no one had noticed his absence.

He had sat up half the night sewing the gun into the lining of his *chuba*. The bullets he stored there, too. He had brought only a dozen. Any more would be useless. He would be lucky to get two shots at the Chairman and one for his own head. The bullets were the kind that exploded on penetration. One hit would be enough. He thought of his own skull exploding and prayed that the Buddha would give him courage.

The poison he had concealed inside a jar of headache pills purchased at the medicine counter of the Lhasa Number One Department Store. He had emptied enough of the pills to make a space for the phial. He prayed that the poison would work. Unlike the gun, it could not be tested.

The bus bumped out of Lhasa. Past the Norbulingka, once the summer residence of His Holiness. Ari remembered the procession to the Norbulingka on his first summer in Lhasa. That was Ari's only glimpse of the Dalai Lama. A shy young man, about the same age as himself, borne aloft in a sedan chair, peeping from behind curtains at the ragged crowds held back by monk-policemen with staves. Ari had been surprised to see that the Dalai Lama wore glasses.

They passed the light-making factory at Nachin. The handful of foreigners who visited Lhasa were told that Nachin had been built by the Tibetan people inspired by love of Chairman Mao. Liberated serfs. That was how the Han referred to Tibetans. It fooled foreigners, but it did not fool Tibetans.

Once a foreigner had visited the school where Ari worked. Before he arrived there was a meeting (there were many meetings in those days). 'A foreigner is coming,' said the Han in charge of receiving foreigners. Who the foreigner was or where he came from no one said. Only that everyone should wear their best clothes and be on their best behaviour. Tibetans should speak only when spoken to. If asked about the independence they were to reply that it would not be a good idea because life had been bad in the old society. They should talk a lot about the wickedness of the old society: foreigners liked that.

And if anyone was of a mind to complain about the rigours of life under the Han, he should bear in mind that the foreigner would be accompanied at all times by security cadres in civilian clothes. 'Remember,' the Han official had warned, 'the foreigner will go home, but you will stay.'

*

'Cheer up, Ari. You look so miserable.'

It was Pema, the girl from Shigatse. Her father had been with the Han since the time of the Long March. He was one of the only true Tibetan communists. Even so, the Red Guards had given him a rough time.

Although she was representing Shigatse, Pema had been living in Lhasa for two years. This delegation represented no one. It was a charade.

'You should be happy that we are going to Peking.'

Ari assured her that he was.

'What are you thinking?' If anyone else had asked that question, Ari would have been suspicious. But not of Pema. Throughout the madness of the Cultural Revolution she had somehow retained her innocence.

'I was thinking of my mother,' he lied. 'She was called Pema, too.'

'I know. You told me.' Of course he had. One Sunday afternoon by the lake in the park beneath the Potala. They had been walking out together ever since. He had tried not to encourage her. To do so would be cruel. He had no prospects in this life, but she was not to know. That was his secret.

Several times he had planned to break off seeing her, but he could think of no good reason. He considered telling her he had a wife and children in Litang, but she would not have believed him. He even thought of telling her that he did not love her and never could, but she would have seen the tears in his eyes and known that he was lying. In the end he let it drift. They had first met in early summer. The season of picnics. Each Sunday she would appear at his door with a bag of *tsampa* and apples from her uncle's garden. They would go down to the river or to the gardens of the Norbulingka. The gardens had recently been opened to the public – an act which the Han represented as evidence of their extraordinary magnanimity.

Although they never discussed such matters, Ari suspected that Pema, too, hated the Han. Once, on a Sunday in the gardens of the Norbulingka, they had opened a door in a high wall. It led to one of the old palaces, deserted and decayed. There they came upon a courtyard piled high with relics – statues of the Buddha, prayer wheels, *thankas*, and tapestries. Smashed and defaced with red paint. Piled higher than a man. Thousands upon thousands. Looted from every temple in Lhasa.

They had retreated hastily. As though the place were cursed. Not until they re-entered the park had Ari noticed that Pema was crying. Tears streamed in rivulets down her cheeks and dripped onto her dress. 'What have they done to our country?' was all she would say. 'What have they done to our country?'

It had not occurred to Ari that Pema would be coming with him to Peking. His blood went cold when she told him that she, too, had been chosen for the delegation. 'Three months,' she kept saying. 'Just think, we will be together for three whole months.'

Ari did his best to look happy at the prospect. He knew that she wanted to marry him. He would have liked that. It would have been as good a way as any to spend the last three months of his life. But so unfair to poor Pema, to make her the widow of Chairman Mao's assassin. In the years to come even to have known him would be a disaster. He wanted to warn her. 'Stay away. I am contaminated.' But to do that would be to invite questions for which there were no answers.

'I don't understand,' Pema was saying as the bus climbed out of the Lhasa valley. They passed peasants reaping barley. They waved as the bus passed. High upon a hillside overlooking the road, characters were written in stone: 'MAO CHU HSI WAN SUI' – 'Mao Tse Tung, ten thousand years.'

'For weeks now you have been so gloomy, just when we have so much to make us happy. In ten days we will pass through Litang. You can see your family.'

Ah yes, Litang. Until two days ago Ari had not realised that they would take the road through Litang. Another catastrophe dressed up as good news. Was his mother alive or dead? Were his sisters still in Litang or had they escaped to join Sonam in India? Even if they were in Litang, he could not see them. He was, after all, supposed to be dead.

26

DIRECTOR EAST ASIA said things had gotten out of hand. He was going to have to tell the guys on the seventh floor. He guessed that meant curtains for him, but there came a time when one had to make sacrifices for one's country and this was it. He figured he would take the wife and children to Europe for a while. Nixon's America was no place to bring up children.

'If there's anything Harvey or I can do, just call,' said Neumann as he saw the Director into the elevator.

'Thanks, but you guys have done quite enough already.' The elevator doors slid shut. Whether or not Neumann detected the irony in his voice was unclear. Sensitivity had never been Neumann's strong point.

As soon as they got word, Langley declared a red alert. The Director cancelled all engagements and summoned the Agency top brass to a conference in the safe room adjoining his office. A signed portrait of the founder, the late William 'Wild Bill' Donovan, had pride of place on the wall. There were no windows and the room was sealed by a sliding steel door, which operated on a code punched into a panel underneath the table by the Director's seat.

Before discussion commenced the Director had had the room swept by a team from Security.

'Who the hell does the old man think might be bugging us?' asked Jack Finkelstein from Evaluation.

He was overheard. 'I'll give you two clues, Jack,' growled the Director. 'It ain't the Soviets and it ain't the Chinese.'

They listened open-mouthed as the Director outlined the problem. Director East Asia sat chain-smoking and staring blankly at the wall. Had the ground opened up and swallowed him, he would have given thanks to the Almighty.

The Director made a point of remarking that the Head of East Asia Department had known for nearly three months. 'But,' the Director drawled, 'for reasons best known to himself, he has not seen fit to share the problem with either myself or his colleagues.' The Director's every word implied that East Asia was overdue for a drastic shake-up. There had long been mutterings to the effect that East Asia was pursuing a foreign policy independent of that of the United States government. This was the final straw.

It was not, however, a time for retribution. Right now, they had more urgent business. There were, said the Director, three items on the agenda. They were, in order of importance: 'One, do we inform the President? Two, do we inform the National Security Adviser? Three, how do we get to this lunatic before he takes out the Chairman and us with him?'

On points one and two there was unanimity. Under no circumstances should anyone breathe a word to the White House or the National Security Adviser (it was taken as read that no one should tell the State Department).

Item three was more problematic. 'Do we know how long it will take the kid to reach Peking?' asked Sam Silver from Covert Action.

'Three, four weeks. Depends on the route.' Director East Asia was speaking in a whisper.

A map was sent for and unfurled. They stood over it while Director East Asia outlined the possible routes. 'So far as we know, they are heading East through Kham. It's rough country. Up hill and down dale. You have to make allowances for landslides, floods, and other natural hazards. The road diverges at this point, here . . .' He indicated Bamda near the Salween River. 'From there, they can either head north through Chamdo or take the southern route through Litang where, incidentally, our boy comes from.'

'Our boy,' snorted Finkelstein.

'Either way, the road converges again at Kanting. After that it's downhill all the way to Chengtu and Chungking. From there they could either fly or take a boat through the Yangtse river gorges to Wuhan. From there they can take a train to Peking. Our impression is that they are in no hurry so they'll probably take the scenic route.'

'Can we hit him on the road?' asked Finkelstein.

Now that his opinion was sought, Director East Asia had temporarily regained his old confidence. 'Unlikely, even if we could pinpoint him, we'd have trouble getting a team in and out. That terrain is some of the toughest in the world.'

'Quite apart from which,' added Finkelstein, 'no one here will need reminding of the consequences should a team of our agents, armed to the teeth, be caught five hundred miles inside China three months before the arrival of our beloved President on his mission of goodwill.'

There was a momentary pause while they reflected upon the consequences. Sam Silver broke the silence. 'So we've got to get him after he arrives in Peking?'

'I guess so.'

'How long do we have?' They had resumed their seats. The map lay half-unfurled in the centre of the table. A phone rang. The Director made a grab for it. He did not wait to find out who was on the line. 'I gave instructions that we weren't to be disturbed . . . Oh, well, I guess we could use some. Send them in.'

He tapped out the code. The steel door slid open to reveal his personal assistant, Mrs Simons, wheeling a trolley piled with sandwiches and flasks of coffee. Cups rattled.

'Thank you, Jan. Just leave them there. We'll look after ourselves.' Mrs Simons flashed them a steely smile and departed. She hadn't seen the Director so agitated since the night they had lost that nuclear submarine in the Pacific.

No one dared make a move for the coffee.

'So how long do we have?' demanded the Director as soon as the steel door slid shut behind Mrs Simons.

'The congress opens on November 15. Our boy will arrive in Peking anywhere between five and ten days before. Unfortunately, sir, that's not the full extent of the problem.'

'Oh?'

'Sir, the usual practice is that delegations from the national minorities are granted an audience with the Chairman prior to the opening of the congress. My guess is that when our boy, if I may use the expression,' Director East Asia glanced at Finkelstein, 'will make his move.'

'Jesus, Mary, and Joseph,' said the Director, who was not a religious man.

'Amen,' added Finkelstein, who was not even a Christian.

They helped themselves to coffee and sandwiches. In accordance with the Director's first memorandum on assuming office, the bread was wholemeal.

'So who have we got in Peking?' asked the Director, when they had stirred in their brown sugar. The answer he already knew.

'Sir, we've got no one, right now.'

'So what do you suggest?'

'Of course,' added Silver, 'there's an advance team going in to prepare for the President's visit.'

'And Henry's going in for another preliminary.'

'Maybe we could tack someone onto his party.'

'Oh, sure,' said Finkelstein. 'We could go to him and say, "Please, Henry, we got this problem which is so sensitive that we can't tell you about it right now but, next time you go to Peking, would you mind taking in a couple of assassins to do a little job for us?"'

There was not so much as a flicker of a smile. This was no time for jokes.

'Well,' said Silver, 'if we're that hard up, there's always the Brits.'

27

S IR PHILIP CARRINGTON was preparing for a weekend in the country when he received word that the Americans were coming.

'Coming where?' he boomed.

'Here, sir.'

'When?'

'First thing tomorrow morning, sir. Touch down at 0530. They suggest a working breakfast at, say, 0700.'

In Sir Philip's book there was no such thing as a working breakfast. Breakfast was a time for running an eye down *The Financial Times* share index over a plateful of kippers. On Saturdays breakfast was to be taken in bed.

'Won't it wait until Monday?'

'Apparently not, sir. Most urgent. The Director's coming in person. He would have spoken to you himself, except that you were at luncheon. They want us to call back and confirm within the hour.'

'Bang goes my weekend,' sighed Sir Philip. 'Very well, Hawkins, do the necessary.'

The Americans touched down at Heathrow twenty minutes early. There were just two, the Director and Jack Finkelstein. They travelled under assumed names on a scheduled Canadian airlines flight from Montreal. 'Very irregular,' said Sir Philip when he heard of the arrangement. Secretly, however, he was relieved. Sir Philip's first thought had been that the Yanks had found another spy at the embassy in Washington and that they were coming to rub his face in the excreta. The fact that they were travelling incognito, instead of arriving at Northolt courtesy of the United States Air Force, suggested, however, that they had something to hide from their own people. His suspicions had been confirmed when he spoke to the Director in person. 'We're counting on you, Philip, to maintain absolute secrecy. Above all,' the Director had insisted, 'not a word to the embassy.'

Hawkins had laid on a car. From Heathrow they were driven to Sir Philip's country home in Somerset.

'Now that's what I call a house,' said Finkelstein as they rounded a corner in Sir Philip's long driveway. Before them, rising from the early morning mist, lay a Tudor mansion complete with deer grazing in the foreground. By comparison the Director's Georgetown residence looked like a Mexican shanty. 'Sir Philip's family go back a long way,' said Hawkins as though that explained everything.

After a breakfast of orange juice and kippers at which they discussed matters ranging from Sir Philip's golf handicap to the cost of maintaining country houses, the Director suggested they take a little walk. No offence, he said, looking at Hawkins, but what he had to say was for Sir Philip's ears only. Hawkins said he was happy to stay behind with *The Times* crossword. Alternatively, he might help Lady Carrington with the washing-up since he gathered the housekeeper didn't come in at weekends.

Sir Philip rummaged around in the scullery and came up with a spare pair of Wellington boots for the Director and galoshes for Finkelstein.

'Size elevens, will they do?'

Finkelstein said they'd be just fine. The Director's Wellingtons were a size too big, but Lady Carrington solved the problem with an extra pair of socks.

They set off across the south lawn. It was soggy underfoot, but the mist had lifted. Sir Philip insisted on taking his dog, a labrador called Lama.

The dog's name caused Finkelstein some amusement. 'Ironic,' he smirked, 'in view of what we are about to discuss.'

The Director outlined the problem. It was all Sir Philip could do to keep from gloating. 'Hmmm,' he said eventually, 'you chaps have got yourself in quite a pickle.'

Finkelstein outlined the solution or at least what he hoped was the solution. Sir Philip listened impassively. 'Let me see if I've got this right,' he said eventually. 'You want me to send one of our chaps to Peking to murder some poor sod whom you set up in the first place to take a pot shot at Chairman Mao. Speaking personally, I'm inclined to wish the fellow good luck.' Sir Philip was one of the old school. His family had been bankers in Shanghai in the good old days.

The Director said: 'Philip, your service and mine have been together through some rough times. We had expected you to take a more sympathetic view of our predicament.'

Roughly translated this read: 'In view of Burgess, Maclean, Philby, and all the other googlies you numbskulls have bowled us, we think you owe us a favour and we have come to collect.'

It did not take Sir Philip long to decode. He stooped to pick up a stick, which he tossed for Lama. He pondered while the labrador retrieved the stick and deposited it at his feet. His conclusion was long awaited but concise: 'What you chaps need,' he said, smoothing the corner of his moustache with the tip of his little finger, 'is a killer who speaks Mandarin. I'll see what I can do.'

Nowadays there wasn't much call for Timothy Ogilvy's special skills. At thirty-nine he was past the peak for his profession. He was also contemplating marriage – to the daughter of a Presbyterian minister. Indeed, he was in the arms of his beloved, at his croft on the shore of Loch Etive, when the call came to say that he was wanted urgently at Century House.

A four-hour drive to Glasgow, the plane to Heathrow. By late afternoon, Ogilvy was being ushered into Sir Philip Carrington's functional office on the top floor.

'Ah, Ogilvy, so good of you to come.' Sir Philip peered at him over half-moon glasses. 'This is Mr Finkelstein. He is from America.' He indicated a man with a shock of prematurely grey hair and a frown etched into his forehead. Co-operation having been agreed in principle, the Director had returned post-haste to Langley, leaving Finkelstein to sort out the details.

'How do you do?'

'My pleasure,' said Finkelstein. His handshake was vice-like.

'How shall I put this?' said Sir Philip. 'It's about China. I suppose you know there's been this, ahem, change of line?'

'Yes, sir.'

'Well it appears, ahem, that there are one or two loose ends to be tidied up.'

'Oh, aye.'

'Mr Finkelstein will explain.'

Finkelstein explained. Sir Philip was impassive. 'It goes without saying,' Finkelstein concluded, 'that, if you succeed, you will be handsomely remunerated.'

'Not, I'm glad to say, out of my budget,' muttered Sir Philip.

Finkelstein ignored the interruption. 'The target's name is Ari Paljor. He came from Litang in eastern Tibet. We brought him out in July '58, put him through a course at Camp Hale and dropped him back about four months later. He's lived in Lhasa ever since. Right now these are the only pictures we have. He was aged around eighteen when they were taken.' Finkelstein passed a couple of black-and-white mugshots across to Ogilvy. They showed a long-haired youth with wide cheekbones and flashing teeth, one of which appeared to be chipped. The boy's eyebrows joined over his nose.

'Never trust a man with joined-up eyebrows. That's what my father used to say.'

'This boy's proved too damn trustworthy,' said Finkelstein.

A third picture showed the youth with his arms around two Americans.

'Who are these fellows?'

'Those are the jerks who trained him. Apparently they took that as a souvenir. Strictly against regulations. If it wasn't for them, we wouldn't be in this mess.'

'What's this?' Ogilvy was pointing to the cord around the boy's neck.

'According to his minders, it's a piece of bone. A chip off some old friend of his. Don't ask me. Those Tibetans have some funny customs.'

'Thirteen-year-old photographs. That's all we've got to go on?'

Finkelstein shifted uneasily. 'We're hopeful of getting an up-to-date picture of the delegation leaving Lhasa. It's a question of getting our hands on a copy of the *Lhasa Daily*. Our information is that it takes about a week to show up in Peking. The reproduction is likely to be poor, but it should be possible to identify our guy on that. Your people in Peking,' he nodded in the direction of Sir Philip, 'will have it couriered down to Hong Kong where we can have it blown up, reprinted, and sent back to await your arrival.'

'What cover are you proposing?' Ogilvy did not attempt to conceal his incredulity.

'Well, that's a sore point. We favoured attaching you to the embassy in Peking, but your people,' he nodded again towards Sir Philip, 'aren't having any of that.'

'Too damn right we're not,' snorted Sir Philip.

'So, instead, we're thinking of sending you on a friendship tour,' beamed Finkelstein. 'It just so happens that there's one coinciding more or less exactly with the period when our target will be in Peking.' He thrust a brochure into Ogilvy's hands. It read: 'The Society for Anglo-Chinese Understanding is pleased to announce its first young persons' tour of the People's Republic of China.'

'It says young people. Where do I fit in?'

'We've made inquiries and we understand they are prepared to stretch a point. Seems they're having trouble filling all the places. The cost's a little high for youngsters.'

'It also says they're going in overland, via Moscow and Mongolia.'

'So? That means you get a nice long train ride and a chance to acclimatise in the company of all those one-hundred-and-ten-percenters.'

'And the weapon? You don't seriously imagine I can carry a gun across the Soviet, Mongolian, and Chinese frontiers?'

'We had hoped you might get by without a gun but, if necessary, Sir Philip has agreed –'

'Against my better judgement, I might say.'

'. . . to bag one in to the embassy. You can pick it up on arrival and return it after you've finished.'

Ogilvy said he would want time to think it over. He had been on some crazy operations in his time, but this one took some beating. Besides which, he was contemplating marriage. Finkelstein made a little speech the gist of which was that the future of the world was at stake. The word 'remuneration' featured several times, though no figures were specified. Sir Philip said nothing until Ogilvy was out of the door.

When he had gone, Finkelstein said: 'Sir, I just want you to know how much my people appreciate what you're doing for us.'

Sir Philip was unmoved. 'If you must know, I find this whole affair deeply distasteful.'

Finkelstein nodded gravely, as if to say, 'Don't we all'.

Ogilvy thought the proposition over and said 'Yes'. Privately, he determined it would be his last operation. When it was over he would settle down and have children who (he had promised his prospective father-in-law) would be brought up as good Presbyterians.

Finkelstein was over the moon. 'You won't regret this,' he kept repeating. 'We'll set you up for life.' Clearly, Finkelstein was used to dealing with mercenaries who knew nothing of pride in a job well done, of facing a challenge for the hell of it, of defending values that money could not buy.

Ogilvy was a unique phenomenon in the secret underworld. A killer who relaxed to Handel's 'Water Music', a collector of first editions, and a product of the Edinburgh Academy and Balliol. Had he graduated, the world might have been spared the unusual talents of Timothy Ogilvy. No one doubted his intelligence. His tutors had testified to that. Quite apart from which, he was an asset to the college rugby fifteen. The incident that put paid to his academic career occurred one cold November evening when he had put two local youths through the window of Blackwell's bookshop. Afterwards no one could recall the origins of the dispute. Ogilvy claimed that one of the youths had struck the first blow, but no matter. He had struck at least the last half dozen. About that there was no dispute. One of the youths was in hospital for a week.

The Bursar seemed more upset about Blackwell's window. 'Why Blackwell's?' he kept asking. 'Had it been any other shop in Oxford a scandal might have been avoided. As it is, Ogilvy, I am afraid we have no choice . . .' Ogilvy had been sent down. The

Bursar had hinted that he might be allowed back after a year, but by then Ogilvy had moved on. He had enlisted – as a private – in the Parachute Regiment. There, his special talents had been instantly recognised and he was whisked off to the SAS at Hereford. Events moved swiftly after that. A spell in Aden, where he had quickly picked up the rudiments of Arabic, a year under deepest cover in Ireland, and then to Hong Kong where he taught himself not only Cantonese but Mandarin.

On leaving the Army, he had immediately been snapped up by the secret world. 'It's not every day we come across a chap who can kill in four languages,' the man from the MoD had remarked at his induction course.

Mostly the work had been routine. Bag jobs in Berlin and the Eastern Bloc (God knows why they needed someone who spoke Arabic and Chinese). Apart from some unpleasantness in Beirut a couple of years back, life was looking distinctly dull. Until this job came up.

One telephone call to the Society for Anglo-Chinese Understanding produced an application form. He gave his name as Saunders and was provided with a passport in that name together with an address on a Kentish Town council estate. He was asked to supply one reference. He gave the name of a tame academic at the School of African and Oriental Studies.

In the space marked 'Occupation' he wrote 'Welder (self-employed)' – reasoning that they were bound to want to include a token representative of the working classes on a trip to the People's China. Not for the first time, Ogilvy's Scots accent was an advantage when it came to concealing his origins. No one south of Newcastle could tell the difference between a welder and a product of the Edinburgh Academy.

In due course he was invited to an interview. The SACU offices were in Warren Street, a place of second-hand Rolls-Royce dealers. Hard-faced men, in pin-striped suits that didn't quite do up at the middle. SACU itself was up several flights of a dingy staircase in a building ear-marked for demolition.

The interviewing panel was presided over by a genteel, elderly lady with snow-white hair tied in a bun. No doubt she kept fit climbing the stairs to the SACU office each day. Ogilvy bet himself that her parents had been missionaries in Tientsin and that she'd been hooked on China ever since (it transpired that her parents *were* missionaries and that she'd been raised in Harbin).

'And now, Mr Saunders, perhaps you'd like to tell us why you want to visit China?'

Ogilvy gave a little spiel about his father having been a staunch socialist who had brought him up to believe that the revolution in China was the greatest event in human history. He mentioned that he had worked in Hong Kong in the Sixties (they did not ask what he had been doing there; had they asked, he would have told them he had been helping to construct the Castle Peak power station) and had picked up a smattering of the language there. When it came to his aptitude for languages, he erred on the side of modesty, implying that he spoke just enough to impress them as to the seriousness of his interest.

'What books have you read?'

'Everything I can lay my hands on.' This much at least was true. He mentioned a few of the obvious authors, Edgar Snow, William Hinton, C. P. Fitzgerald. They seemed pleased.

'Are you interested in any particular aspect of China, Mr Saunders?' This from a bearded man of indeterminate age. Ogilvy put him down as an academic.

Ogilvy said he'd always had a soft spot for Tibet.

'I am afraid we won't be going to Tibet, Mr Saunders. Not this time at any rate.' They smiled pleasantly at him.

'No, but I thought we might get a look at one of the minorities' institutes. The one in Peking perhaps.'

They thought that this was very possible. The elderly lady who presided suggested he request such a visit on arrival in Peking. It seemed to be taken for granted that he would be going. She added: 'You'll find the Chinese very willing to oblige.' If only they knew, thought Ogilvy.

There was a spring in his step as he made his way down Warren Street, weaving in and out of the second-hand Rolls-Royces.

28

ONCE THEY WERE clear of Lhasa the road began to dip and dive. They skirted the Yamdrok lake, blue and empty. Distant snow mountains fringed the horizon. A cloud of dust rose behind them, engulfing everything in their wake.

They passed desolate houses with pats of yak dung drying on the walls. No prayer flags fluttered. No dogs barked. People scurried about as though afraid of their own shadows. No one waved, not even the children. It was not like the old days. A curse had come down upon the land.

The political cadre, Mr Chen, studied each of them in turn and made notes in a little book. He had a high forehead and delicate hands, which suggested he had come unscathed through the Cultural Revolution. Behind his back they called him the Amban, after the official who, in days gone by, had been the Emperor's representative in Lhasa. Although he had been at his post for five years, no one had ever heard Mr Chen utter more than six or seven words of Tibetan. He made a desultory effort to converse in the Han language with the young Tibetans seated nearest to him, but they regarded him warily and responded only with polite generalities.

Pema talked non-stop. About her brother who was studying at the minorities school in Chengtu. About the bananas and other exotic fruits said to be available in the lower valleys. About the heat in China. About the snow in Tibet. About the glaciers, which from time to time menaced the highway. About every subject under heaven.

'You aren't listening,' she said eventually.

Ari did not respond.

'I said, you aren't listening.' She kicked him.

'I am thinking.'

'About what?'

Ari had been wondering if Mr Chen had noticed the bulge in the lining of his *chuba* where the pistol and the ammunition were stored. Whenever he looked up, Mr Chen seemed to be staring at Ari. He was seated at the front of the bus, near the door. His seat was sideways on to the others, giving him a view of everyone in the bus. Did he know? Surely not.

'I was thinking that you have beautiful eyes.'

They passed the night in one of the Han forts built at intervals along the road. It was like the compound the Han had built at Litang. A high wire fence. Loudspeakers broadcasting thoughts of Chairman Mao. A single flag fluttering from a tall pole. Pale, shivering Han youths in the padded uniform of the People's Liberation Army, cursing the bad luck that had brought them to this place.

There were guards on the gate. Mr Chen explained that it would be better if they did not leave the compound since there were still some bad elements active in this area. He did not say they were forbidden to go out, only that they were advised not to. Contact with the locals was discouraged. For the time being, they were to be considered honorary Han.

On the second day they crossed a high pass. So high that Mr Chen's face began to turn blue and his breathing became irregular. He put away his notebook and dabbed at his forehead with a white handkerchief. From time to time the driver gave him anxious glances. Pema debated whether to offer him one of her herbal pills, but decided not to on the grounds that, when he recovered, Mr Chen might denounce her as a greenbrain.

A pile of stones marked the top of the pass. It was surmounted by prayer flags of recent origin. Mr Chen was too ill to note this latest evidence of superstition. Several of the Tibetans took advantage of Mr Chen's temporary indisposition to mumble the customary prayer on the safe crossing of a high pass.

They descended. The road was a series of hairpin loops, zig-zagging down the mountain. Far below they could see a convoy of PLA trucks climbing towards them. It was an hour before they passed. The soldiers waved. In twelve hours they passed no other traffic.

When they had reached the bottom of the valley, the road straightened and ran beside a fast-flowing river, strewn with huge boulders. At times the road was so close to the river that the roar of the water drowned their conversation. In places the river had eaten into the road so that it became a narrow ledge, scarcely wide enough to accommodate a single truck. At such places Pema would grab Ari's arm and hold it tightly, murmuring exhortations to the Buddha and earning disapproving looks from Mr Chen.

More than once, the driver had ordered them to get down from the vehicle and walk behind while he negotiated a particularly perilous stretch of road. Later they passed teams of Han soldiers and Tibetan labourers, mainly women, rebuilding the road. Several of the women were wearing Chairman Mao badges. They stared blankly at the passing bus.

The second night, like all that followed, was spent in another of the Han encampments that straddled the road at regular intervals. They mostly consisted of the long barrack houses, enclosed by high wire fences and guarded by shivering Han youths. Most were illuminated by dim electric lights powered by a rattling generator. The food came from green PLA ration tins. Lukewarm rice and fatty lumps of pork washed down with the thin Han tea. The food was the subject of much complaint. On the second night, Ari was delegated to inquire if they might at least have butter tea. Mr Chen promised to see what could be done, but no butter tea materialised. At the stop-over on the third night, Ari, Pema, and several others ventured out, ignoring the advice of Mr Chen and, after a short walk, came to a small settlement. The people were cautious. At first they remained in their homes, refusing even to respond to a knock on the door. Eventually an old woman plucked up the courage to speak. She was bent double with pain in her back. After some negotiation, butter tea was produced in return for Han cigarettes and some of Pema's herbal pills. The old woman invited them to sit by the fire in her house. They choked on the smoke. It was so thick that they could hardly see one another. It reminded Ari of Litang.

The woman was surprised to hear that they came from Lhasa. In the old days, she said, there had been many pilgrims and traders travelling to and from Lhasa. Several families in the village had made a living providing food and lodging for travellers, but nowadays no one came. No one except Han and they always stayed with the soldiers. Some people made a living working on the Han road. For this they were paid a small ration of barley. Poor-quality stuff, riddled with chaff and stones. She guessed the Han obtained barley by taxing the farmers in the lower valleys. The farmers did not like paying taxes and so they put stones in the barley so that the Han would break their teeth. 'They are not to know that the barley is for us, not the Han.' She laughed bitterly.

Was there a school, asked Pema, indicating the ragged children who crowded the doorway for a glimpse of the visitors.

The woman gave another harsh laugh. 'School? There is no school. Not since the Han chased away the lamas.' They sipped their tea. Since the woman did not have enough bowls to go round, they shared. The fire was the only light and their shadows danced on the walls. 'Once,' said the woman, 'in the centre of the village, we had a big *stupa*. Inside were the relics of a holy lama who had lived a hundred years ago. People came from far away to say prayers and ask for good fortune. Then, four summers ago, an iron horse full of Han youths arrived. They assembled the village people in front of the *stupa* and made long speeches. We could not understand what they were saying so they went away. We thought they had gone for good, but the next day they came back with a Tibetan boy who spoke the Han language. He translated. They wanted us to spit on the *stupa*. One by one they lined us up, shouting at us all the time. Everyone was crying. Even the boy who was translating. To show us an example, they each took turns in spitting on the *stupa*. One of them opened his trousers and pissed against it. "See," they said, "no harm comes to us. There is no curse. Your gods are powerless."

'Still, none of us would defile the *stupa* and the Han youths became angry. They took some magic sticks and tied them to the *stupa*, then they made a long string leading away from it. Then one young Han set light to the string.'

She paused to stir the cauldron of butter tea. 'There was a man called Jamyang whose family looked after the *stupa*. He had a daughter. She is still here. Maybe you have seen her outside. He pleaded with them not to destroy the *stupa*. He even went down on his knees, but the Han youth only laughed at him. The first time the fire was lit, he ran forward and stamped it out. The Han youth were furious. They tied him to a tree and beat him. Then they lit the fire again, but first they warned us that, if anyone tried to stamp it out, they would tie him to the *stupa* and blow him to pieces too.

'There was a big explosion. Bits of rock showered everywhere. One came through the roof of my house.' She pointed upwards into the gloom. 'Then everything was quiet and when we looked, the *stupa* was gone. Completely destroyed. Not a stone was left upon a stone.

'The people were crying and wailing, but the Han youths just laughed. We should be grateful to them, they said, for ridding us of superstition. After they had gone, everyone in the village got down on their hands and knees, searching through the rubble for the relics of the holy hermit whose bones had been inside the *stupa*. We found some pieces and that night, after it was dark, we buried them in a secret place on the mountain, in case the Han came back.'

The old woman refilled their tea bowls. 'And the curse?' asked Pema, ever curious.

'The curse? Oh, yes. It fell upon the family who looked after the *stupa*. Jamyang was so upset he could not speak to anyone. After a few days he disappeared. We found his body a week later, smashed against rocks at the place where the river flows fastest.

'Soon after he disappeared, his wife became ill. We summoned a holy man who had been a lama. He was hiding from the Han in a cave on the mountain. We had kept him supplied with food. He said many prayers for the woman. Prepared many medicines. But it was no good. "It is the *stupa*," he said. "She is cursed. This family has taken the curse for the whole village." Very soon she, too, was dead. Soon afterwards, her daughter became crazy. The daughter lives by herself in the house next to the place where the *stupa* used to be. You can see for yourself. Maybe we should destroy the house so that the curse will go away, but what will happen to the daughter?' She shook her head as if to say there was no accounting for the anger of the spirits. Her hair was matted.

Unwashed over several generations. Tibetans were the dirtiest people on earth, thought Ari. At least the Han were right about that.

The glowing embers and the smoke gave the woman's face a ghostly aspect. 'Of course,' she said, 'that was not all.' For the first time she emitted a smile of genuine warmth. Gaps showed between blackened teeth. 'The Han youth departed from the valley three days later. We saw their truck going up the road towards the high pass. They were waving red flags and singing songs. No doubt they had gone in search of other holy relics to destroy.

'Some days later word came that their truck had fallen off the road into a deep canyon. They were all killed. Every one. The soldiers made some of us go with them to bring back the bodies.' She chuckled. It was good to know that the spirits were able to exact retribution even from the Han.

After the cursed village the road sloped steeply. Down, down, down, into bottomless gorges where demons lurked. Soon they came to trees. At first no more than stunted bushes, but before long they were travelling through damp forests where water dripped from hanging creepers.

Mr Chen, who had by now made a complete recovery from his earlier sickness, devoted several hours each day to the study of Mao Tse-tung Thought. He looked with disapproval upon the chattering Tibetans, as if to say that they, too, should be studying Mao Tse-tung. On occasion, he was frank enough to say so.

Early one morning, at one of the PLA encampments along the way, Pema had caught sight of Mr Chen exercising in his long underwear in time to commands from the loudspeakers from which all Han seemed to take instructions.

News of her discovery kept Pema and her friends amused for several hours. Repeatedly, as the bus bumped along, she was called upon to describe the scene to the others. She did so in whispered tones, with anxious glances in the direction of Mr Chen, who stared disapprovingly at the young Tibetans doubled up with laughter, unaware that the joke was on him. For the next few mornings much sport was had trying to spot Mr Chen exercising in his long underwear. In due course, however, he must have realised what the fuss was about for when next espied exercising, he was fully clothed. After that, he spent some hours scowling at Pema and scribbling furiously in his notebook.

As they descended, so the climate changed. The sun was hotter than ever. Their clothes began to stick. The men took off their jackets and sat with their sleeves rolled up. All except Ari. He had grown used to the weight of the gun by now and Mr Chen's long stare, but he dared not wear anything but his sheepskin *chuba*. Perspiration rolled down his face. It reminded him of the day they had been delivered to the East Pakistan border. He dismissed the thought as quickly as it had arisen. That was in another life. Too dangerous even to think about.

'Why do you wear you thickest *chuba* in this weather?' asked Pema.

Ari said he was fine.

'You are hot. I can see you are hot.'

'I am fine. Please leave me.' He wanted to scream.

'What's the matter, Ari? Why are you angry with me?'

He tried to smile. If only he could share his secret.

Eventually, Ari relented. Not to have done so would have aroused suspicion. He packed away his *chuba* at the bottom of his bag, watching carefully as the driver loaded it on to the roof. He felt Mr Chen's eyes upon him and tried to look unconcerned.

They were in rain forest now, so thick that no one could see more than a few feet into it. Pema had never seen anything like it and remarked on every flower and every insect they passed. Now and then they caught sight of a monkey swinging in the trees or a rare bird. They whiled away the hours, scanning the jungle for wild-life. Even Mr Chen set aside his book of Mao Tse-tung Thought and joined in the sport.

The jungle gave way to terraces of young rice, emerald green. Mr Chen was visibly cheered by the sight. It reminded him, he said, of the village where he was born. He became so carried away that he was even persuaded to produce a photograph of his wife and two children. It was passed round for everyone to see. Mr Chen's wife was a thin-faced, serious woman, with a pudding-basin hair cut. She stood stiffly to attention as all Han seemed to do in the presence of a camera. Even the children, a boy and a girl, wore serious expressions. Mr Chen's wife was several years younger than he. She was a school teacher in a small town near Peking. He had not seen his family for three years. When they reached Peking he would apply for leave to visit them, but he could not say if his request would be granted. That, he said stoically, was up to the party.

Pema said she felt sorry for Mr Chen. The Han system was so cruel.

The houses now were made of timber. The people, although Tibetans, wore fewer clothes. Many of the men had bare shoulders and the children were practically naked. Ari was not surprised by the changing scenery. He, after all, had passed this way before. With Aten, many years ago. In those days, of course, they had travelled on foot.

Was Aten still alive? Ari had neither seen nor heard of him since that day at the Nachin reservoir. If Aten were alive today, he would be in some labour camp on the high plateau. Was it possible to survive so long in the camps? Ari thought not. So few people had come back. Over the years Ari had met one or two. On each occasion he had inquired discreetly, but no one had heard of Aten.

Ari was haunted by his last sight of his friend. Squatting among the prisoners as Ari's truck pulled away, a single tear trickling down his face. Was Aten in another life? He hoped so. Maybe they would soon be together again.

On the eighth day the road began to climb again. Rice paddies gave way to barley fields. The rain forest to pine trees. Bananas disappeared from the diet at the Han camps along the way. Ari wore his *chuba* again. He was happier to feel the gun against his chest. He sat away from Pema so that she would not brush against it.

As the road climbed and the air thinned, the colour began to drain from Mr Chen's face. His book of Mao Tse-tung Thought which, if the Han were to be believed, was the answer to all afflictions, remained unopened in the pocket of his tunic.

They came to a river, which – according to Mr Chen in a rare moment of lucidity – was the Yangtse.

'*Yang-si*,' Pema practised the word. It was a distant memory from school days in Shigatse. The Han teacher had talked about this river as though it were a wonder of the world. To look at, it seemed nothing special. No wider than the Kyichu. They noted with satisfaction that the bridge was guarded.

'In case of bandits,' said Mr Chen, reading their thoughts. 'In this region there are many bandits.'

The sight of the Yangtse had caused Mr Chen to make a temporary recovery. 'We will see the Yangtse again,' he said. 'When we reach China . . . That is to say,' he corrected himself hastily, 'when we reach the lower part of China.' The Tibetans cupped their hands to their faces and smiled. Even Mr Chen could make mistakes.

'Where are we?' asked Pema. The road had levelled. It ran along the floor of a broad valley, fringed by distant hills. Young willow trees, planted by the Han, lined the road. Pigs and sheep nosed among the stubble of the lately harvested barley. By comparison with all they had so far passed, this was a prosperous place. The houses were of stone and white-washed mud. The young men walked with swagger. Even the older folk were not so bowed down.

'This place is called Batang,' said Ari. 'It is the last town before my home.' And as he spoke, he could hear his heart pounding.

29

COMPARED TO BATANG Litang was a town of ghosts. The narrow streets were all but deserted. Windows were firmly shuttered. Here and there a ragged creature scuttled across the path of the bus and disappeared through an unseen doorway or into a dark alley.

The market place was empty, save for a handful of nomads huddled around a stone upon which were displayed a few emaciated ribs of yak meat. The men averted their eyes from those of strangers, as though afraid a spell would be cast upon them.

The tea houses once thronged with the travellers and wild nomads of Ari's youth were gone. So too were the Han merchants selling spices and bricks of Double Thunderbolt tea from China. The little tailor shops, run by Indians from Darjeeling and Kalimpong, were boarded up and plastered with Han big-character posters stuck one upon the other. A new layer added with each new round of denunciation.

What struck Ari at once was the absence of lamas. He should have known, of course. In Lhasa there were no more lamas except a few ancient men who lingered on as caretakers in Drepung and Sera. In ten days of travelling they had not glimpsed a single figure in the purple robes of a lama. Not even an ancient caretaker. Nor had they seen a single intact lamasery. At Batang, Markham, Rawu, and a host of other little towns and villages along the way, they had noted with silent anguish the empty shells of once great lamaseries. Looted of their treasures. Holy shrines defiled. The lamas fled. Timbers taken for firewood. Even stones had been taken away for building.

Pema said the dereliction was the same along the road from Lhasa to Shigatse. Han Red Guards had organised the local youth to destroy everything. In Shigatse itself, only the Tashilhunpo lamasery survived. Unauthorised visits were forbidden. The vast

Dzong, which had overlooked the city for centuries, had been dismantled stone by stone. Only foundations remained. Poor Pema, she had only the dimmest recollection of life before the coming of the Han. In one more generation, two at most, Tibetan civilisation would be extinct, except for Sera, Drepung, and the Potala, which were preserved for the Han to show to foreigners.

Ari should have known that Litang would be no different. There was no reason why the Litang lamasery should have fared any better than the others. On the contrary. Over the years word had drifted back to him that the Han had not waited until the Cultural Revolution to exact revenge on Litang for the rebellion that had caused them such inconvenience. Perhaps it was because Ari could not envisage Litang without its lamasery that he was still able to be surprised by the spectacle that greeted him.

As always, the lamasery was visible from a long way off. A town within a town. Houses and temples advancing up the hill towards the cave where, according to old Phuntsog, Ari had lived in a previous incarnation. The same hill up which Ari and Aten had made their escape on the last night of the rebellion.

The road approached across a flat grassland dotted with yellow and blue poppies. Yak and sheep grazed. Not so many as Ari remembered from the old days. By now the nomads should have brought their animals down from the high pastures.

Ari scanned the horizon, looking for the glint of sunlight on the golden roof of the prayer hall, but could see none. As they drew closer, he looked for the turquoise tiles on the Abbot's quarters, but there were none. The Litang lamasery had gone the way of all the others.

They drove through the town without stopping, the Han driver hooting continuously despite the empty streets. Litang, he remarked loudly, was a no good place, full of thieves and robbers.

They passed the south gate of the lamasery, through which a constant stream of small servant-monks had once passed back and forth, laden with buckets of water from the river. It was deserted. There was no sign of the beggars who once sat in lines outside the gate, seeking offerings from the pilgrims. No sign, either, of any of the bent old women who, each dawn and dusk, hobbled along the holy walk around the lamasery, twirling prayer wheels and accumulating merit. They were all gone. Instead, Ari glimpsed only the ruined shells of buildings and weeds rising between the flagstones in the Abbot's courtyard. The place where, long ago, he had first set eyes on the Red Han who had come to inform the Abbot that Litang had been liberated.

'You are home?' Pema said quietly.

'Yes.'

'You are not happy to be home?'

'No.'

'You will see your family again?'

'I don't know.'

After which Pema said nothing. Even she had sensed that this was no time for talk.

They drove straight to the Han encampment. It was bigger than before. The area enclosed by the compound had been expanded. Stone turrets manned by soldiers interrupted the high wire fence at intervals. The rows of stone barracks had an air of permanence, which – in Ari's day – they had lacked. There were huge fuel tanks and a park full of battered trucks presided over by Han technicians in grease-stained overalls. Vegetable gardens stretched down to the bank of the river. There was even a tea house and a tailor's shop.

The centrepiece of the encampment was a three-storey, whitewashed building bedecked with red flags and big-character posters. A portrait of Chairman Mao adorned the entrance. Underneath was the ominous slogan: 'HARDSHIP ONLY EXISTS TO TEST THE WILL OF THE PEOPLE.'

The world had been turned upside down. The lamasery was gone and in its place the Han had built a citadel complete with temples to their own gods.

As they passed between the town and the encampment, Ari strained to catch a glimpse of his home, near the river. The flower pots in which his mother grew chrysanthemums were gone. So were the prayer flags.

The door was ajar. Someone was living there.

*

Ari waited until dusk. To have gone earlier would have meant being recognised. There was sure to be someone in the town who remembered him and Ari did not wish to be remembered. The Han soldiers in the sentry post at the gate ignored him. Their interest was with who came in, not who went out. He walked along the road towards town. The wind was cold and he pulled his *chuba* tightly around his body. He had forgotten how cold the nights could be in Litang.

There was no traffic. The Han did not travel after dark and most Tibetans did not venture out at night for fear of evil spirits. He walked a short distance towards the town and then took a path leading to the river. He followed the river until he came to the place where, before the lamas had claimed him, he used to play hide-and-seek with his sisters among the rocks. The Paljor house was a black shape some distance to his right. By approaching from the river he could avoid the prying eyes of neighbours.

He crossed what had once been his mother's barley field, good for only one poor crop a year. Grass and weeds were all that grew there now.

He crossed the yard behind the house where Pema Paljor had laid out her barley to dry in the sun. Chickens pecked at dry earth. In the distance a dog barked. From within came the sound of voices. A woman's voice, but it stirred no memories. An oil lamp burned dimly.

He had no plan. At first he had intended only to observe the house from a distance to see if he recognised the occupants. He wanted only to satisfy himself as to what had become of his mother and sisters. To do more would place them all in danger. When his mission was complete, everyone who had known him would be questioned. If it came out that he had visited his family only two weeks before, they would immediately be suspect.

But as he drew near the house he knew he could not resist knocking. What had become of his family? He had to know. Suppose they still lived here? Then he would have to go inside. What reason could he give for not doing so? That he was on his way to assassinate Chairman Mao? Anyway, by then it would be too late. They would know he was alive. The shock of seeing him again would probably kill his old mother. He would swear them to secrecy. They must not breathe a word to anyone. Not now, not ever. They would find out why soon enough.

Another voice. This time a man's. The husband, perhaps, one of his sisters. Ari's hand was shaking as he tapped on the door. Once, twice, lightly so as not to alert the neighbours. His heart was thumping.

'Who's there?'

The man's voice. It came from the roof. Where Ari's mother passed the long summer evenings looking towards the lamasery that had stolen her son.

'Who's there?'

Ari did not answer. He tapped again. A head appeared over the parapet and then retracted. It was too dark to make out a face. From inside there came the sound of cursing and then of someone scrambling down a ladder.

The door was in two parts. The top half opened inwards. A man was standing with a lamp. A rough man. His face was pock-marked. Surely Dechen or Nyima had done better than this for a husband?

'Are you deaf? Didn't you hear me calling?'

'I'm sorry.' Ari took a step back to escape the glow of the lamp. From inside came a smell of roasting *tsampa*. 'I'm looking for a woman. An old woman who lived here once.'

'Dead,' said the man. That was it. A single word and Pema Paljor was disposed of. Not how or when. Just dead.

The man had all but closed the door when Ari found his voice again. 'And her daughters? She had two daughters.'

'Gone,' he snarled. The door was all but closed.

'Gone where?'

'To India.' The door slammed. There was the sound of a crossbar being secured. From within there came the sound of a woman laughing. It was an unpleasant laugh. Ari's sisters did not laugh like that.

There were many other questions he might have asked. Such as what this uncouth man was doing in the house that Ari's family had occupied for generations? Or when and how his mother died? And had she ever mentioned a son who had deserted her? Any neighbour could have provided answers. He had only to knock on any other door and he would have been welcomed like the long-lost son he was.

But it was too late. Ari knew all he needed to know. His mother was dead. Dechen and Nyima were in India. Gone to other lives. As he walked back across the barley stubble to the river, Ari felt no emotion save relief. Whatever became of him, his family would be safe from the retribution of the Han.

30

TIMOTHY OGILVY, ASSASSIN (alias Dick Saunders, self-employed welder), was waiting on Moscow's Yaraslavl station for the train that was to take him to China. His accent had been carefully adapted to obliterate all traces of his expensive education. He was the only member of the SACU party who claimed to be a worker. The others were mainly students or young academics with addresses in London NW3 or NW11. Several studied Mandarin (or North China dialect, as they liked to call it) at Cambridge, but their Chinese was not a patch on Ogilvy's. A fact which he did his best to conceal.

Ogilvy had, however, come clean about speaking the language. He didn't want the news slipping out halfway through the trip. That would arouse suspicion. In any case, a working knowledge of Mandarin would come in handy in Peking and he didn't want to manoeuvre himself into a position where he was unable to use it. Besides which, never tell a lie unless you had to. That was the first thing they drummed into you in the Secret Intelligence Service. He'd learnt his Mandarin at night school in Hong Kong, he told them. That was true, too. One or two small lies had been necessary, of course. Like telling them he had been working in Hong Kong as a welder when in fact he had been interrogating refugees from the mainland.

The others seemed pleased to have a member of the working classes on the trip. The workers featured a lot in their conversation, but Ogilvy got the impression that most of them had more experience of Chinese than of rubbing shoulders with genuine members of the British proletariat. His cover was unlikely to be blown.

'You're a real find. We're so glad to have you,' the genteel old lady at SACU had said during the coffee break at the introductory session the previous weekend. 'We tried awfully hard to make our tour more attractive to the working class. We did have a few inquiries. There was a docker from Bermondsey, but he dropped out when he heard the price. We even discussed offering him a reduction, but some of us were against that on the grounds that it was patronising. It is such a problem. Next time we're going to have to rethink our position.'

Ogilvy had nodded sympathetically. If SACU wanted a token member of the working classes for their first young people's tour of China, he was only too happy to oblige. Even to the extent of knocking a couple of years off his age.

It was a Chinese train. On the side of each carriage was a painted sign listing in Russian, Chinese, and Mongolian the three principal stops – Moscow, Ulan Bator, Peking. Above each sign was a plaque depicting the Gate of Heavenly Peace and four red stars. A Chinese steward in a spotless Mao suit and matching blue cap stood at attention by each door.

A thunderstorm hovered over Moscow as they boarded. Inside, unseen loudspeakers played 'The East is Red'. The compartments had lace curtains and table lamps. Four comfortable bunk beds converted into seats during the day. Ogilvy found himself sharing with a youth called Toby and a girl called Melissa. The fourth bunk was empty. Melissa explained that she had to share with men because there was an odd number of women. She hoped they didn't mind. Ogilvy said that was fine with him. Toby seemed positively overjoyed and it soon became apparent that he and Melissa had something going between them.

The walls in the corridors were decorated with glossy colour pictures of beaming peasants in paddy fields, each capped with a quotation from Chairman Mao in a different European language. The caption under the picture outside Ogilvy's compartment was in German. Mao was described as '*Der Grosse Führer*'.

Lightning lit the sky as they pulled out of Yaraslavl. The platform was crowded with Russians and Mongolians waving off relatives and friends bound for unpronounceable destinations. Melissa said she had never been so excited in her life. Toby concurred. Ogilvy did some mental arithmetic. The National People's Congress opened in Peking in twelve days. They would be on the train for six days and seven nights. That gave him six days and five nights to track down and eliminate Ari Paljor.

'We will soon arrive in Chungking,' said Mr Chen. The train moved as slowly as a stately water buffalo. Outside a blood-red sun was rising above thatched cottages in groves of bamboo and eucalyptus.

'Soon,' said Mr Chen, 'we will see the Yangtse again. In Tibet it was only a stream by comparison. Now it is a mighty river.' He allowed himself a thin smile. Everything in China was bigger and better. Back on the burning plains of China, Mr Chen was his old self again. Scribbling furiously in his notebook. Devoting hours to the study of Mao Tse-tung Thought and advising his Tibetan charges to do likewise.

He also lectured them on good manners. They were representatives of Tibet, said Mr Chen. If they wished to make a good impression on the Han people, they would have to behave. Until now he had allowed certain indiscretions to pass without comment. From now on, however, anyone engaging in unsocialist behaviour could expect to be severely criticised.

Pema had never seen a train before, let alone travelled in one. Ari had explained that the engine, which belched thick black smoke and was decorated with a portrait of the Great Helmsman, worked by coal and steam. The Han, he assured her, were not the only people who possessed the secret. There were trains in India, too. And in certain other countries.

'Which countries?' demanded Pema.

'Many,' said Ari vaguely. Adding hastily that he had read about such things in magazines. It was not wise to appear too familiar with the way of life in other countries.

'Chungking,' Mr Chen continued, 'is one of the three furnaces of China. Hotter even than Chengtu.' He paused to let them absorb the information and then added, 'Fortunately for you, the worst is over for this year.' The heat was a subject upon which Mr Chen had discoursed on a number occasions since they had reached the burning plains of China. It was his revenge for the rigours of Tibet.

'We will stay two days and one night at Chungking. There will be sight-seeing. A ball-bearing factory and a carpet factory. The house where Mr Chou En-lai lived at the time of the Anti-Fascist United Front. And, of course, the Museum of Mao Tse-tung Thought.'

Pema was at the window, pointing out children and buffalo wallowing in village ponds. She was as wide-eyed as Ari when he had first gone down to the plains of Bengal.

'There are no yaks in China?'

'No.'

'And so many people?'

'Yes.'

'And no gods?'

'No. Han people have abolished gods.'

'Unless, of course, you count Chairman Mao?'

'Shhh, Pema. Such talk is dangerous. Han people do not have a sense of humour like we Tibetans.'

But Pema only smiled. She was a child in a wicked world. It was hard to imagine anyone less prepared for the disaster that Ari was about to inflict. But what could he do? His fate had been determined long ago.

'You don't look to me like a welder,' said Melissa. They were twenty-four hours out of Moscow. The Urals had passed in the night. The birch forests were endless.

Ogilvy shrugged.

'Come to that, you don't sound much like a welder.'

'Met a lot of welders, have you?'

Melissa giggled. She giggled whenever she was stuck for something to say. Which was not all that often.

On day two, Toby had produced a book of Chairman Mao's thoughts and proceeded to read selected extracts to Melissa. They sat for an hour discussing the finer points. It was all Ogilvy could do not to throw up.

'Do you believe in dictatorship of the proletariat?' asked Toby.

'Never given it much thought,' said Ogilvy. He had other things on his mind.

'I thought your father was supposed to have been a communist?'

'My father was engaged at the sharp end of the class struggle. He didn't have time for that kind of crap.' As to which side of the class struggle his father had been on, Ogilvy forbore to mention. 'And while we're on the subject, what does your father do?'

Toby's cheeks flushed. 'I can't see what that's got to do with anything.'

'Oh, go on, Toby, tell him,' said Melissa.

'If you must know, he's a professor at the London School of Economics.'

'Aye,' said Ogilvy. 'That figures.'

In the evening Ari went walking in Chungking. He was not alone, for it is never possible to be alone in the teeming cities of China, but he was without Pema and the ever-vigilant Mr Chen.

Chungking was damp and crowded. It was the place where the Yangtse and Jialing rivers met, surrounding the city on three sides. Mist engulfed the little houses clinging, one upon the other, to the steep river banks.

There were so many Han. More in this one city than in the whole of Tibet. Thronging the streets so densely that most cyclists dismounted rather than try to weave a path through the multitude. Vehicles moved at little more than walking pace. Drivers blasted their horns, sweating and cursing. Men and women, harnessed to carts, dragged awesome burdens up impossible inclines. The Han often sneered at the backwardness of Tibetans, but in Tibet such work was done by yaks.

It was late when Ari returned. Pema had been in bed an hour. She lay awake until she heard his footsteps in the corridor.

The Siberian forest was endless. It rolled by for hour upon hour, night and day. Now and then a tiny settlement or a solitary log cabin broke the monotony. Here and there the train stopped for five minutes at remote outposts where no one got on or off. Once they spotted two old men with white beards extending almost to their waists, sitting at a station. When Toby had tried to photograph them, an official had appeared and tried to confiscate his camera. Fortunately, the train moved off before the dispute could be resolved. The two old men were almost the only sign of life in that vast wilderness.

Every twenty-four hours or so, a huge city loomed, Sverdlovsk, Omsk, Novosibirsk . . . Mirages in an eternity of forest.

The stewards in charge of Ogilvy's carriage were called Li and Wang. They were of indeterminate age. High cheekbones exaggerated their smiles. They shared a tiny room, emerging at intervals to patrol their domain and top up the flasks of boiling water that graced every compartment. Toby spent half an hour trying out his pidgin Chinese on Mr Wang, but was able to discover only that he came from Nanking, had two children, and made the round trip between Peking and Moscow twelve times a year. On all other matters Mr Wang was genial, but vague. Ogilvy stayed out of the conversation, having no wish to draw attention to the fluency of his Mandarin.

He did his best to stay out of everyone's way, although it wasn't easy. Some bright spark decided they should elect a leader. The Chinese would expect a leader, they had been told. The post was hotly contested and the best part of a day was taken up with debating the relative merits of the candidates.

They were intelligent kids, but they confirmed Ogilvy's worst fears about the children of the middle classes. Privately, he divided them into two categories. Those who had satisfied themselves in advance that every aspect of life in the People's Republic would be perfect – these he labelled Rave Babes. The others were only ninety per cent convinced that the sun shone out of Chairman Mao's backside. These he christened Capitalist Roaders.

Someone nominated Ogilvy for leader on account of his sound class background and the fact that he was alleged to speak Chinese. (Perversely, the fact that no one had heard Ogilvy utter more than a few words of Chinese seemed only to enhance his reputation.) Melissa said she'd vote for him, even if he did show signs of being ideologically unsound. To general disappointment Ogilvy declined, leaving a run-off between a Rave Babe and a Capitalist Roader. The ballot was secret. Ogilvy voted for the Rave Babe just for the hell of it, but the Capitalist Roader won by a single vote. By the time the election was over, they were approaching Irkutsk.

31

At Chungking a boat awaited. It lay at the foot of two hundred steps leading down to the muddy waters of the Yangtse. The name was inscribed on the side in large red letters. It was called *The East is Red Number 40*, in keeping with the Han habit of numbering everything.

'So big, so big,' Pema kept repeating. She had never seen a boat bigger than the rafts and yak-hide coracles on the Kyichu.

There were four decks, each crowded with travelling Han. Loudspeakers played patriotic music, interspersed with exhortations to passengers to avoid spitting and on the proper use of the toilet facilities.

They were housed in two large cabins, one for the men, one for the women. Mr Chen had a cabin to himself. As they later learnt, most Han passengers were confined to crowded bunk-rooms below the bottom deck. It was unheard of for a Tibetan to live better than a Han. They were privileged.

They sailed in darkness. A light mist hovered. Lights twinkled. Horns, bells, and other sounds of Chungking street life drifted down. Hammers pounded upon metal like the chimes of a prayer gong in a lamasery. By and by the sounds faded. The city was behind them and the only lights were the stars in heaven and the occasional oil lamp in a farmer's cottage. A breeze relieved the damp heat.

Ari stood by himself watching Chungking recede into the mist. Forbidden memories stirred. The steamboat waiting by the river. The crowds, the chaos. He was with Aten, Lotse, and Muja. Dressed in turbans and Punjabi pyjamas. Their hands were chained. Arrogant Sikhs stood guard. There was an American. What was his name? Hank, that was it. Captain Hank. Like Mr Chen, Captain Hank had had a private cabin.

Such a great secret to carry for all those years. Soon there would be no more secrets. Ari was nearing the end of a long road. He smiled to himself. His mind was made up. A burden had been lifted. If he ever had doubts, they were resolved.

'What makes you smile?'

Ari started. It was Pema. He had not seen her. She missed nothing.

'Am I not allowed a smile?'

'Of course, but there must be a reason. Why won't you tell me? I am your best friend.'

Oh no, dear Pema. You are not my best friend. The holder of that honour is Aten who was sent away to the camps on the desert of ice. If he is alive, then you are my second-best friend. If he is dead, then you can claim the title. But only in this life.

'Why won't you answer? You are deep, Ari Paljor. Deeper than the Yangtse River.'

Poor Pema. It was unfair. He would have reached down and kissed her cheek, but for the sudden appearance of Mr Chen.

After Irkutsk the train skirted the southern shore of Lake Baikal. Still and deep. According to Toby, it was the deepest freshwater lake in the world. Ogilvy said he'd heard that, too.

He was pretending to read. Edgar Snow's *Red Star Over China* was open on his knee. The page remained unturned. Ogilvy was thinking about that boy. He should have reached the Yangtse by now. Three days, four at the most and he would be in Peking. By that time Ogilvy would be there too. Waiting.

He would have to move fast. The boy might not have to wait until the congress opened for his first chance to take out Chairman Mao. According to those who knew about such matters, an audience with the Chairman could come at any time, day or night, depending on whether the Great Helmsman was enjoying one of his lucid periods. (Latest intelligence suggested that the Chairman had recently suffered a stroke and that his speech was impaired.) As Finkelstein had said, 'If I were you, Tim — I can call you Tim, can't I?'

'I think we should keep this formal, *Mister* Finkelstein.'

'Okay by me, *Mister* Ogilvy.' But it clearly wasn't. The American had looked hurt. Anyone would think they were discussing golf handicaps, not assassination. 'As I was saying, you ought to get to the boy in the first twenty-four hours, just to be on the safe side. After that you can relax and enjoy the tour. I'm told the quis-een's pretty good, even if the politics is a mite tedious.'

'And if I haven't caught up with him by the time we leave Peking for the provinces?' Ogilvy had inquired.

'Then you have to stay put. Up to you what excuse you make. Sickness, accident, anything. Just remember, you aren't goin' to China for the sight-seeing.'

As to the method. Every operative had his own preference. Ogilvy preferred his hands. A single blow to the windpipe, a sudden pressure behind the ears. These were far more effective ways of killing than a gun. No mess. No weapon to be disposed of.

In this case, however, a gun was inevitable since Ogilvy could not guarantee to get close enough to the target to use his hands. A Tokarov fitted with a silencer had been bagged to the embassy and awaited his arrival. A Tokarov would not have been his first choice, but the man in Special Effects had insisted on a weapon widely available in China. You didn't need to be an Einstein to see the sense in that. They had considered other possibilities. Special Effects had offered to fit him out with a Chinese umbrella adapted, along lines said to be favoured by the Bulgarians, to eject poison pellets. 'Who knows,' said the man with a wan smile, 'the Chinks might even pin the killing on the Bulgarians. Now that would be an added bonus.' Ogilvy had thanked him politely, but rejected the offer. He wasn't going to entrust his fate to the clowns in Special Effects.

Around noon on the first day the *East is Red Number 40* stopped at Fuling, a miserable town with houses shrouded in mist and coal dust. Mr Chen offered a little local colour. 'Fuling,' he said reverently, 'is where the First and Sixth Red Armies joined up at the start of the Long March.' People and packages were unloaded along a narrow gangway. After thirty minutes they moved on again. Past junks with tattered sails, loaded with coal and oil drums. Once they saw a junk being towed upstream by five ragged men who stumbled along the shoreline attached to long ropes.

Pema expressed surprise that there were Han who lived worse than Tibetans.

Ari seemed more relaxed than at any time since they had left Lhasa. Indeed, more than at any time in the five years she had known him. He laughed at Pema's jokes and made a few of his own. He did his best to answer her questions. He made no effort to move away when she placed her hand on his as they stood at the side of the ship watching the world slide by. Only on one matter was Ari not forthcoming.

'Last night in Chungking, where did you go? Mr Chen was asking.'

Ari's face clouded. 'What did you tell him?'

'That I did not know.'

'I went for a walk.'

'Where?'

'Just a walk. That is all.'

'Why?'

'To see the city. To sit with the old men in the tea houses and look at the river.'

'Mr Chen is very suspicious.'

'Mr Chen can jump in the Yangtse for all I care.'

It was dark when the train reached the Mongolian frontier. The customs post was built in the style of a temple. It was cold and empty. Dead-eyed officials scanned the passports. They had learned their trade from the Soviets. All cameras were opened. Exposed film was confiscated. One of the Capitalist Roaders attempted a mild protest, but he was ignored. Ogilvy was ordered to empty the contents of his wallet. They counted out the money and noted the total. They lingered over his photographs of Priscilla. One taken in the garden of her parents' cottage in Perthshire. Another on the beach at Cannes in attire which, by Mongolian standards, must have seemed positively indecent.

It was gone midnight when they were allowed back onto the train. Ogilvy fell asleep immediately but was aroused in the early hours by the unmistakable sounds of Toby and Melissa, humping.

*

The *East is Red Number 40* stayed in mid-stream, swept along by the current. Lesser boats were tossed in its wake. Once a man, struggling to retain control of his fragile craft, paused to shake his fist at the passing monster. Pema said the incident reminded her of the times she had seen Tibetans choking by the roadside in a cloud of dust kicked up by a passing Han truck.

Ari wasn't listening. He was half the world away with Bill and John. Remembering the night they had broken the news that he wouldn't be going back to Tibet with the others. Recalling the long journey to America. The time John had offered him chewing gum and Bill had protested that he was teaching Ari American habits. How they had taught him to play poker and how, one night, he had cleaned them out of cigarettes. The look of relief on John's face when Ari had agreed to play the role they had allocated to him.

Had they forgotten him? Thirteen years was a long time. Many things could change in that time. But this, had this changed? Surely not. What was it the Colonel had said on that first night? *'Americans and Tibetans are brothers . . . America does not enter lightly into alliances. We always stand by our friends.'* Ari remembered the warmth with which John had shaken his hand on that final journey in the iron bird. Minutes later he had stepped out into the darkness over Tibet and they had vanished for ever.

Did they know he was on his way to meet Chairman Mao – at last? At the time it had seemed to Ari that Bill and John were important men who controlled events and made decisions. Lately it had occurred to him that maybe they were like him. Small men beholden to mysterious forces over which they had no influence.

Either way, it didn't matter any more.

32

CROCKER SAID THAT maybe the time had come for him and Fritz Neumann to lie low for a while. Neumann said that was a fine idea. Nowadays Washington gave him the creeps.

They decided to head over to California and look up Gerry Bannister on his grape farm. Gerry was one of the old school. It would be good to be amongst friends again.

Before they set off, Crocker dropped in at Langley for a pow-wow with Director East Asia. The man was as jumpy as a kangaroo on heat. His eyes were haggard. Since the meeting in Crocker's apartment he'd lost a full thirty pounds. Harvey Crocker was the last person he wanted to see.

'Five minutes, Harvey. That's all I can spare.'

Crocker made a little ceremony of removing his deerstalker and placing it carefully on the Director's desk. These days he never went anywhere without his deerstalker. 'I want to know what's happening,' he said.

'Harvey, I can't tell you nothing. It's out of my hands.'

'Who's dealing with it, then?'

'That's not for me to say.'

'Melvin, how long have you and I known each other?'

Director East Asia heaved a sigh. 'Harvey, I gotta be honest, I wish I'd never set eyes on you.'

'That's not a very nice thing to say, Melvin. Most particularly to someone who treated you like a son from the day you first set foot in this place.'

'Harvey, I don't think you understand how serious this is.'

There was an interval while Crocker picked up his deerstalker and arranged it on his head, tilting it until he was satisfied with the angle as though in front of an imaginary mirror. He looked at Director East Asia as if to say, 'Well, if that's how you want to play it'. Then he headed for the door. 'If you really want to know,

Melvin, I hope the boy makes it. That'd teach ol' smarty pants to go playing footsie with the Chicoms.'

And with that he was gone.

'Wanhsien,' said Mr Chen, 'the last town before the gorges.' The *East is Red Number 40* was anchored for the night. The gorges can only be navigated in daylight.

Daylight brought Ogilvy and friends to Ulan Bator, the loneliest capital city on earth, not counting Lhasa. The architecture was a bizarre mix of high-rise apartments and yurts. A horde of Mongolian grandmothers, uncles, aunts, and cousins had assembled to greet long-lost relatives. They were splendid people, clad in rich silks with burnished, parchment complexions and manes of jet-black hair. In times gone by their ancestors had conquered half the known world. Now their sphere of influence was limited to a few billion hectares of arid grassland.

Off-duty Russian soldiers, bored sallow youths, loitered on the station. Disembarking passengers were swept away in a welter of bear hugs and Mongolian kisses.

After Ulan Bator came the Gobi desert. An ochre waste of burnt grassland. Now and then they passed a settlement of yurts. Children waved. Wild camels grazed. In the late afternoon the train drew alongside a bright-red fire engine of 1930s vintage. It bumped along the dirt track that trailed the railway line, struggling to keep pace. A handful of men clung to ladders, one furiously ringing a brass bell with his free hand. There was no other traffic. No sign of human habitation, let alone a fire. For five minutes the fire engine kept pace. Then it was gone. Fading back into the desert like an image from a painting by Salvador Dali.

After the fire engine, Ogilvy fell to thinking about the man he had come to kill. Before placing his unusual skills at the disposal of the state, Ogilvy had to satisfy himself that the contract complied with his, admittedly somewhat limited, code of ethics. Did the target pose a threat to the way of life that Ogilvy was committed to defending? Was there any means, short of the ultimate, by which the threat could be eliminated? And even if Ogilvy were satisfied on these points, he had other ground rules. For a start, he never killed women.

His other blind spot was the British Isles. Strictly off limits, as far as he was concerned. Excepting Ireland, of course. He had passed his year in Ireland, helping the IRA to organise bank robberies in the Republic. A grateful nation had awarded him an MBE for his services in this regard.

Unlike Ogilvy's other precepts, his refusal to work on home ground was based upon considerations that were purely practical. Sooner or later he planned to marry, retire to Loch Etive, and set up a little consultancy. When that day came, he didn't want his past coming back to haunt him.

So, within his terms of reference, Ogilvy was a man of cast-iron principle. More than once he had turned down an assignment where the target was not one he regarded as fair game. Most of his work had been in remote outposts, helping to preserve what little remained of the British Empire. Ogilvy was a great Empire man. It angered him to see how casually so much had been given away. There were times when, he had reflected bitterly, the Empire might have been better served by the elimination of a Tory politician or two, rather than some ill-educated Third World Marxist.

As he watched the sun going down over the Gobi, Ogilvy began to reflect that he might perhaps have been a little hasty in accepting this commission. By no stretch of the imagination could the target be regarded as a threat to British interests. Unless, of course, one took the view that British interests were identical to those of the United States. Ogilvy was ambivalent on this point. On the one hand, he admired the Americans for having the guts to fight while everyone else in Europe was sitting around wringing their hands. On the other hand, he detested the Americans for their lack of culture and their penchant for spectacular blunders. This being a case in point.

'Can I interest you in one?'

It was Melissa, offering an apple from her grandmother's orchard.

Ogilvy accepted gratefully. Although the train was Chinese, the dining car had been in the hands of the Russians as far as the Mongolian frontier. The menu consisted of meatballs and cabbage soup. Now the dining car was under the control of Mongolians who stoutly refused to accept payment in anything but local currency with the result that it travelled empty across Mongolia. So much for socialist planning, thought Ogilvy. A sentiment he took care to conceal from Toby and Melissa.

Sometime after midnight, the train entered China. The Mongolian dining car and engine were detached. A steam engine, bedecked with flags and a red and gold portrait of Chairman Mao, hauled the carriages at walking pace across a fifteen-kilometre stretch of no-man's-land. The unseen loudspeakers played 'The East is Red'. Toby was clutching his book of Mao Tse-tung Thought.

Melissa declared for the umpteenth time that this was the most exciting moment of her life. Ogilvy said nothing. He had a lot on his mind.

33

THE *EAST IS RED NUMBER 40* entered the Qu Tang Gorge soon after dawn. 'This,' said Mr Chen, 'is the first of three.' His glasses were misted by spray. 'Before Liberation the rapids in this place claimed an average of three lives each day. Now they have been tamed by dynamite. And also . . .' he added, '. . . by the correct application of Mao Tse-tung Thought.'

The sides of the chasm were sheer and dark. Thick, grey mist hovered in the aperture where the sky should have been. There was no hint of sunlight. The Yangtse was narrower, muddier, deeper. The water flowed so fast that the crew seemed almost to have abandoned the ship to the mercy of the current. Suddenly the ship didn't seem so big any more.

Pema said she was feeling sick. Ari held her close, ignoring the disapproving glances of Mr Chen.

LONG LIVE THE GREAT CHINESE COMMUNIST PARTY.
LONG LIVE OUR GREAT LEADER CHAIRMAN MAO.
The slogans were in English and Chinese, in letters a foot high, illuminated by red and yellow light-bulbs. As the train drew up to the platform at Erlian, a score of officials in blue overalls and peaked caps waited to receive the visitors from England. Each member of the welcoming committee clutched the thoughts of the Great Leader in his or her right hand, which they waved in unison while chanting slogans, like the chorus in a revolutionary opera.

A man with two fountain pens in his breast pocket made a little speech of welcome. The Capitalist Roader whose election had occupied most of the time between Novosibirsk and Irkutsk responded on behalf of the visitors. Formalities were few. Passports, vaccination certificates, that was all. No one bothered to inspect their luggage. They were taken to a small reception hall where girls with long plaits and ready smiles offered tea and cigarettes. There was much talk of undying friendship between the English and Chinese peoples. There were references to the status of Taiwan. American imperialists and all their running dogs were repeatedly denounced by the man with the fountain pens. Everyone nodded vigorously. Melissa brought out her grandmother's apples and offered them round. She was met with unanimous, but polite refusal.

The *East is Red Number 40* entered the Wu gorges in the teeth of a howling gale. Pema said she wanted to lie down. Ari took her to her cabin and returned to the deck. The eyes of Mr Chen were upon him.

The walls of the gorges were not sheer, but sloped steeply, receding into distant mists in shades of purple and green. They passed a junk being hauled upstream by trackers, ragged men bent double. Mr Chen remarked that, when the socialist transformation was completed, such work would be abolished.

In mid-morning they emerged from the Wu gorges and docked at Padung. Several hundred steps led up from the river to a huge mosaic portrait of Chairman Mao. Ari went to check on Pema and found her sleeping.

Ogilvy slept soundly and awoke to find the Gobi desert giving way to villages of yellow mud.

'Shansi Province,' said Toby, who was studying his *Daily Telegraph* map of the world. Melissa had chided him. 'I do think you might have found something a little more appropriate. Now if it had been a *Guardian* map . . .'

Toby said he didn't think the *Guardian* produced maps.

As they went south it grew hotter. The poor soil was lacerated by deep clefts from dried streams that, in winter, flowed from distant mountains. Production brigades of peasants laboured in fields beneath red flags. Once, when they stopped, a crowd of children assembled and stared goggle-eyed at the foreigners, ignoring attempts by a railway official to shoo them away. Melissa spent the morning trying to capture the landscape with her camera.

At around noon Toby went to consult the stewards, Messrs Li

and Wang, and returned saying that they would be in Peking by late afternoon.

The narrow path through the Xi Ling gorge was indicated by yellow marker buoys. The *East is Red Number 40* navigated with care, dodging niftily around rapids and whirlpools. At times they passed so close to the wall of the gorge that they seemed about to be dashed against it, only swerving away at the last moment.

'Before Liberation,' said Mr Chen, 'passengers had to disembark with their luggage at Padung and leave the crew to guide the ship through the gorge. Since Liberation, this is no longer necessary.'

'Thanks to the correct application of Mao Tse-tung Thought,' said one of the Tibetans.

Mr Chen was not amused.

Sometime during the morning, Ari disappeared. Mr Chen made inquiries, but the best anyone could offer was that he had gone below to look after Pema. Mr Chen checked. Pema was sound asleep, there was no sign of Ari. He looked into Ari's cabin. A sheepskin *chuba* lay, dishevelled, on one of the bunks. A bag lay half unpacked. There was no sign of Ari.

Ordinarily Mr Chen would have paid no attention to the temporary disappearance of one of his charges. There was, after all, a limit to the mischief even a Tibetan could cause on a steam-ship in the middle of the Yangtse gorges but, where Ari Paljor was concerned, Mr Chen had his suspicions.

34

T HERE WAS A time when Ogilvy would have given his eye teeth for a trip to Peking. He had spent three years commuting between Hong Kong and Macau, studying the tea-leaves. He had taught himself Cantonese and Mandarin. He had patrolled the wire fence that divided the two worlds. He had observed through binoculars. Each evening in his Mid-Levels apartment, he had tuned to Radio Peking, listening to what passed for news in that most mysterious land. He had stood on the platform at Shatin watching the fortunate few come and go, envying, interrogating, and sometimes wining and dining an official of some foreign mission in Hong Kong for a few days' R & R.

Now he was there. Actually standing outside the main railway station in Peking listening to the loudspeakers chanting Mao Tse-tung Thought in between news of arrivals and departures. Listening to another speech of welcome. More talk of undying friendship between the British and Chinese peoples. Another denunciation of American imperialists and their running dogs. Listening to Toby, Melissa, and the other Rave Babes saying that everything was wonderful.

And yet Ogilvy felt no emotion. Neither elation, irritation, nor fear. For now he was operating on auto-pilot. He had a job to do and it would be done. His senses absorbed only the information relevant to the task at hand. Ogilvy was thinking that, within the next two or three days, the target would arrive at this very railway station. There would not be more than two or three trains a day from Wuhan. This would be the place to pick up the trail.

Ari reappeared within twenty minutes. He had, he told the others, been making tea for Pema. She was feeling better and might even be well enough to eat the evening meal with them. It was an unnecessary lie and Ari regretted the words as soon as they were out of his mouth. Mr Chen took careful note.

Mrs Wu, the guide, was a care-worn woman in late middle age. She spoke perfect English, learned many years ago, at Oxford. She wore a skirt that came down to mid-calf and that, it soon became apparent, made her different from almost every other woman in China. There was also Mr Chu to whom Mrs Wu pointedly referred as Comrade Chu. He was a genial balding man who smiled a lot, but said little. Largely because, it soon became clear, he did not speak a word of English. His presence was, therefore, something of a mystery although there was no doubt that he was a person of significance. He had three pens in his shirt pocket and devoted much time to notetaking.

Occasionally Comrade Chu could be seen in whispered conference with Mrs Wu, but beyond that he took no part in the proceedings. Attempts by Chinese-speakers in the party to engage him in conversation proved fruitless. From the outset, Comrade Chu took a particular interest in Ogilvy.

By nightfall they had reached I-Chang, the city at the head of the gorges. The Yangtse had suddenly become flat, calm, and wide. Pema made a miraculous recovery and ate a hearty meal of rice, pork, and vegetables. Her first in two days. Almost at once she noticed a change had come over Ari. He was more relaxed than she had ever seen him. He laughed at her jokes, answered her questions, and even kissed her without being prompted. Mr Chen also noted the difference and recorded the evidence in his notebook.

Ogilvy said he needed to call on the British embassy. It was his fiancée's birthday and he wanted to surprise her with a telegram. Mrs Wu looked doubtful and consulted Comrade Chu who, surprisingly, gave his consent. Mrs Wu offered to arrange a taxi. Ogilvy thanked her, but said he would rather walk, if she would only show him the way.

Mrs Wu sketched out the route to the legation quarter on a piece of hotel notepaper. Past the cathedral, now a light-bulb factory, right down Chang-An Avenue for about thirty minutes, and then left.

Ogilvy set out in twilight. Foreigners stuck out like sore thumbs in Peking and before long he had a posse of children in his wake. So far as he could tell, no one else was following, but then how would he know?

Chang-An was clogged with cyclists. All without lights. A continuous flow. Once or twice there was a cry of 'foreigner', but by and large he went unrecognised in the darkness. Ogilvy quickened his pace and the children gradually fell behind.

It took nearly an hour to find the embassy. A sentry outside flashed a torch in his face, asked his name and where he was staying. No doubt Mr Chu would receive a report in due course.

There was a car parked on the drive. A black Rover with local number-plates. A bicycle leaned against a wall. In accordance with local custom, it also had number-plates. Ogilvy climbed the steps and rang the bell. A light came on in the hall. Doors opened and closed. Footsteps. A key turned. The door opened just wide enough to reveal a polished toecap and a mop of sandy hair.

'My name's Saunders. I'm looking for Miss Kershaw.'

'Not here, I'm afraid. I suggest you come back tomorrow. We're open between ten and twelve. I suggest you telephone first, just to be on the safe side.' The toecap receded a centimetre or two. It would have been withdrawn altogether had not Ogilvy's foot descended.

'What the hell do you think you're doing? Remove your foot at once.'

'Listen, dickhead, I haven't got time to play silly buggers. I want to see Miss Kershaw, *now*.' In a trice Ogilvy was inside. Beneath the sandy hair were the clean features and rosy cheeks of an English public schoolboy on his first overseas posting.

'There really is no call for that.'

'Sorry, chum, but I do need to see Miss Kershaw.'

'Wait here.'

The lobby was empty save for a standard issue picture of the Queen and a coffee table with out-of-date copies of *Punch* and the *Illustrated London News*. Somewhere in the distance a muffled voice was speaking into a telephone.

Five minutes elapsed. A clock struck a quarter-past the hour. Then a crunch of tyres on gravel. The sound of a car door being slammed. Footsteps. A key being inserted in the lock. Ogilvy stood up. She advanced upon him from the shadows, hand outstretched. 'You must be Saunders,' she said. 'I'm Miss Kershaw.'

A severe woman. Elegant in a way. Auburn hair swept back into a pony tail held in place by a satin bow. A gold bracelet, inscribed. A parting gift, perhaps, from a rejected lover. Tall, trim, efficient, with a whiff of Ivoire. Very un-Peking.

Ogilvy followed her up a staircase lined with prints depicting scenes from the Boxer Rising. Many doors had to be unlocked and locked before they came to her office.

'I wanted to send a telegram to my –'

'No need for that nonsense, Mr Saunders.' She cut him short. 'We were swept last week. Clean as a whistle. The Chinese don't seem to go in for that sort of thing any more. Not since they kicked out the Soviets. They've got other ways of keeping tabs on us.'

There was a wall safe with a combination lock. Miss Kershaw opened it and withdrew a package about the size of a cake box. It was sealed inside waxed sacking. She handed it to Ogilvy. The parcel was heavy for its size.

'This arrived in the bag last week. My instructions are to hand it over and ask no questions. God knows what use you are planning to make of it. Frankly, I'd rather not know.'

'Scissors?'

She rummaged around in the top drawer of her desk and came up with a pair of scissors.

'Oh yes, and there's this. We had it sent down to Hong Kong for a blow-up. Well, we could hardly put it in at the local Boots, could we?' It was the photo from the *Lhasa Daily*. 'Far from perfect I'm afraid. But the best we can do in the circumstances.' There were two prints: a blow-up of the boy and a print of the entire delegation lined up ready for the long journey to Peking. 'The chap in whom you appear to be interested is second on the right in the back row.' Miss Kershaw indicated the place with a manicured fingernail. 'I must say he looks harmless enough to me.'

The boy had changed a lot in thirteen years. His hair was short now, almost cropped. Close inspection revealed the joined-up eyebrows. He was taller than the others, but for that the chances of recognising him would have been slim. Ogilvy hoped to hell the delegation would be wearing their Tibetan gear around town.

He cut open the sack. It contained a Fortnum and Mason cake box, someone at the Department's idea of a joke. Inside, tastefully displayed against a background of yellow foam-rubber, was a Type 64 Tokarov automatic, snug in a leather holster. A magazine of rimless 17 mm bullets lay alongside.

Miss Kershaw peered at the gun and pulled a face. 'Is that the best they could do?'

Ogilvy explained that he needed something that wouldn't get anyone into trouble. The gun was not much bigger than the palm of his hand. It was oiled and ready for use. He loaded the magazine into the butt, checked the safety catch, and holstered the pistol. Then he stood and unzipped his trousers. 'Excuse me.'

'Be my guest.' Miss Kershaw did not avert her eyes.

Ogilvy strapped the holster to the outside of his left leg above the knee, adjusted the straps until he was satisfied and pulled up his trousers.

'If you don't mind my asking,' said Miss Kershaw, 'do you have to drop your trousers every time you want to use that thing?'

Not to worry, said Ogilvy, he would cut a hole in the pocket. Anyway, that was his department, not hers. He would, however, be grateful for an opinion as to whether the outline of the weapon was visible to the casual observer. He took a practice walk across Miss Kershaw's carpet and, after some minor adjustments, she pronounced herself satisfied.

'That just leaves the map,' said Ogilvy.

'I hadn't forgotten, Mr Saunders.' As if Miss Kershaw ever forgot anything. She produced a much-used street map of Peking, complete with coffee stains. 'I wouldn't flash this about, if I were you. Not many of these around these days. They stopped selling them to foreigners six years ago.' She spread the map out on the desk. It was in English. 'We are here.' She pointed to the place. 'And, where did you say you are staying?'

'The Hsin Chao.'

'Could be worse,' said Miss Kershaw. 'The Hsin Chao is here. Does a very good lobster, I'm told.'

'The railway station?'

'Here, ten minutes' walk from your hotel.'

'And the National Minorities Institute?'

'A bit of a hike, I'm afraid. In the north-west. Here.' She indicated the place on the map.

'And how would I get there?'

'The hotel would probably get you a taxi. I imagine they might be a wee bit curious as to why you wanted to go there. But then, aren't we all? Alternatively you could get a bus, but don't ask me where from. When it comes to buses, it's all I can do to get from Kensington High Street to Hyde Park Corner.'

'A nine, a fifty-two, and a seventy-three,' said Ogilvy. Miss Kershaw looked amazed.

They went out the way they had come, unlocking and locking doors. As they went down the stairs Miss Kershaw said: 'Mr Saunders – if that's what your name is – I don't know what you're up to, but I ought to warn you that HMG's heart isn't entirely in this.'

'What makes you think that?' Ogilvy tried to sound surprised.

'HQ went to great pains to set limits on the assistance I was to offer you. My instructions are that, if anything goes wrong . . .'

Ogilvy said he was perfectly capable of looking after himself, thank you very much. They had reached the front door. There was no sign of the freshman who had opened it.

Miss Kershaw offered her hand. 'No offence, Mr Saunders, but I never wish to set eyes on you again.'

35

O NCE THEY WERE through the gorges a great calm settled over the river and the surrounding countryside. The land was perfectly flat and the river meandered between high dykes on top of which a man and his water buffalo were silhouetted against the sky. 'Before Liberation,' Mr Chen began . . .

Liberation. A bitter word. Perhaps the Han only used it to mock Tibetans. Litang before Liberation had been so full of life. The great fairs each summer. The dancing, the horse races, the archery contests. The sounds of the lamasery coming to life each dawn. Metal pots clanging on cold stone. A cock crowing. The conch horn summoning lamas to prayer. That was in the days before the accursed Han had descended upon the land. Now there was only silence and wind whistling through ruins.

'Before Liberation,' Mr Chen was saying, 'this place was the scene of one of the greatest natural disasters in world history. More than three million people died when the Yangtse changed course. But now this problem has been resolved thanks to the correct application of . . .'

Maybe Liberation was good for Han. If so, let them keep it. The Americans had used that word, too. '*We will help you to liberate your country,*' the Colonel had said. In his first talk at the training camp in . . . Ari knew not where. '*Our friendship will last, not for one or two years, but for many,*' the Colonel had said. Where were the Americans now?

According to Phuntsog, if Tibetans were ever to defeat the Han, they must find another country to help them. One that also had iron birds and talking machines. Ari had followed Phuntsog's advice. And here he was, alone.

In those days Ari had been ignorant. So much had changed since then. And in the space of one short life. Was it possible to live three lives in one? Phuntsog would have known.

'When we get home,' Pema was saying, 'I can tell everyone that I have travelled on an iron horse that pulled ten carriages and carried five hundred people at one time.'

When Ari and Aten had escaped from the besieged lamasery they had thought they were going to walk to America. What simple people they had been.

Pema was saying: 'No one will believe me when I tell them we have travelled on boats higher than ten men and which can move without oars.'

Ari was thinking that he should never have agreed to the crazy schemes dreamed up by the Americans. If only he hadn't listened. If only he had insisted on going back to Kalimpong. If only, if only . . .

'Poor Tibet,' said Pema. 'We are so ignorant behind our mountains. We know so little. Isn't that so, Ari?'

'I'm sorry. I was far away.'

'Oh Ari, you are always far away.'

Ogilvy rose at first light and set out for the railway station to meet the train from Wuhan. He had no plan except to identify the target and, if possible, trail him. If necessary, Ogilvy would visit the station each morning and evening until the Tibetan arrived. He had to come soon. The congress opened in six days.

Supposing the Tibetan was already in Peking? Supposing he wasn't staying at the Minorities Institute? Supposing he wasn't coming by train, after all? The more Ogilvy considered the possibilities, the more he wished he had stayed at home with Priscilla.

It was a fine, clear day. Cyclists passed in a continuous flow, muffled against the autumn cold. The air was misty with their breath. Old men paused from their callisthenics to stare at the passing foreigner.

The station was bustling. Children and old women with tiny feet waited by mountains of luggage. Peasants carried trussed-up chickens and television sets on bamboo poles. Minor functionaries rushed hither and thither blowing whistles.

Three girls were sitting behind a long marble-topped counter, bare except for a sign saying 'Information'. They wore identical

234

peaked caps and blue jackets with red armbands. Shoulder-length plaits, tied with red ribbons, protruded from under each cap.

'I am looking for the train from Wuhan.'

'We are sorry, but we do not speak foreign languages,' they replied in unison.

'I am speaking Chinese.'

They looked at Ogilvy dumbfounded.

As Miss Kershaw had predicted, the train arrived dead on time. Ogilvy stood by the barrier and watched the passengers disembark. Amazing how many people could be squeezed onto one train. He waited until it was empty. There was no sign of anyone vaguely Tibetan.

By the time Ogilvy was through at the station it was often eight-thirty. He jogged back to the hotel. Mrs Wu and Comrade Chu were waiting in the lobby. 'You have missed your breakfast, Mr Ogilvy,' said Mrs Wu. Comrade Chu nodded icily.

The *East is Red Number* 40 passed the day skirting the vast Tungting Lake. In places the river was so shallow that islands of mud protruded.

Ari borrowed a needle and thread from Pema. Needed, he said, to repair the lining of his *chuba*. Pema offered to sew it for him, but Ari said he could manage alone.

Finally, under cover of darkness, they reached the triple city of Wuhan and dry land. 'In thirty-six hours,' announced Mr Chen, 'we shall be in Peking.'

Crowds followed Ogilvy and his party everywhere. In the Forbidden City the presence of fifteen foreigners attracted so many people that they had to take refuge in the Hall of Complete Harmony until order could be restored. Melissa said it was like being a pop star.

Mrs Wu was embarrassed. 'We are not used to seeing foreigners,' she said. 'It has been so long.'

Mrs Wu, it transpired, had recently returned from re-education in the countryside. She was vague about the details, but implied that her husband had not survived his re-education. That would account for her sadness.

Where re-education was concerned, Toby and Melissa seemed to have bought the whole package. Toby said he thought it would be rather fun to spend a year or two in the countryside. Melissa said she would have been a Red Guard, had she been in China at the time.

'When we go home perhaps we could start a Cultural Revolution of our own,' said Toby, who was already sporting a Mao badge.

'Starting in Hampstead?' suggested Ogilvy.

'Super idea,' said Melissa. She did not appear to realise that he was taking the piss.

In the early evening Ogilvy set out for the Minorities Institute. The bus routes were marked on his map and they were easy to follow. He was less conspicuous now, having bought himself a blue cotton jacket and peaked cap at the Friendship Store. Melissa, Toby, and most of the others were similarly kitted out.

The appearance of a foreigner on a public bus caused a sensation and people were falling over themselves to offer their seats. In answer to the many inquiries as to where he came from, Ogilvy always gave the same answer: 'Bulgaria.'

The walls of the Minorities Institute were thick with big-character posters, layer upon layer. By the main gate a large, brightly coloured hoarding depicted the Great Helmsman surrounded by peoples of all races who gazed up at him in awe.

Old women sold bowls of steaming noodle soup and sweet-meats. Oil lamps glowed. Youths and girls sat round, clutching satchels, talking, laughing, and noisily sucking soup from tin spoons.

Ogilvy ordered himself a soup and sat down by the largest group of students. Only from close up was it apparent that they were not Han. They eyed him cautiously at first and continued jabbering in a language he did not understand. Ogilvy smiled and asked if he could borrow the soya sauce. They stared wide-eyed as he liberally dosed his noodles. The Han stall-holder paid no attention. As far as she was concerned they were all foreigners.

Ogilvy was halfway through his noodles before one of the students plucked up the courage to address him in Mandarin. 'Excuse me, sir, you are a foreigner?'

'Yes.' The noodles trailed over his chin.

'Where is your country?'

They had never heard of Bulgaria, so Ogilvy explained that it was a small country in Europe, next to the Soviet Union.

They laughed and said that relations between the Han and the Soviets were not good, but not to worry because they were not Han. They were, they revealed proudly, Uighur from Turkestan, a place of great deserts and mountains and the finest yoghurt on earth. In hushed tones, they told him that the Han were not popular in Turkestan because they had destroyed all the mosques and forced the nomads to settle and grow wheat.

'How many nationalities are there in this place?' He nodded towards the gate.

They counted on their fingers: Kazaks, Mongolians, Yao, Yi, Hmong, Lolo . . . Just about every species of human being except Bulgarians.

'Tibetans?'

'Oh, yes, many Tibetans.' One of them added quietly that, even more than the Uighur, Tibetans hated the Han. Then, sensing that he had gone too far, the boy changed the subject.

They offered Ogilvy a conducted tour of the campus.

'Isn't that against regulations?'

'Yes, but no one need know.' They seemed to relish the idea of outwitting the Han.

They smuggled Ogilvy into their dormitory and insisted he sample their yoghurt. Afterwards they showed him the concert hall, the gymnasium, and the place where, during the Cultural Revolution, Han youths had pushed an elderly professor from a fourth-floor window.

Finally, they showed him where the Tibetans lived.

'Can we go in?'

'Not wise. Many spies,' they whispered. 'This place very

crowded. Special delegations coming. For the congress, next week. You know about this congress?'

'They stay here?'

'Mostly, yes.'

'Including the Tibetan delegation?'

'They arrive tomorrow.'

36

PEKING AT LAST. Now that he was almost home, Mr Chen was suddenly overtaken by an air of informality. He started referring to the Tibetans as his 'dear friends'. Dear friends, indeed. Ari was indignant: 'He has spent the last two weeks spying on us.'

Mr Chen even talked of seeing his wife and children again. Of course, it would be up to the party, but he would apply for leave. His daughter would be thirteen now. Almost a young woman. He had heard she had taken up the violin at school. The Tibetans stared blankly, until Mr Chen explained that the violin was a musical instrument with strings and a bow. It rested on the shoulder. Like so. He gave a demonstration and everyone laughed, mainly out of relief at seeing Mr Chen in such good humour.

He gave a little speech. They stood in a corridor while he addressed them. Unseen loudspeakers played 'The East is Red'. Outside they passed stone villages and fallow fields. 'Dear friends,' Mr Chen began. 'After a long journey we are about to arrive in our glorious capital, Peking. Please remember that you are here as representatives of your people and that it is up to you make a good impression. We will be staying at the Peking Institute for Minority Nationalities where students from all parts of China come to study Mao Tse-tung Thought and to learn about the socialist transformation of the Motherland. You will be very tired after your long journey so, on the first day, we will rest. After that there will be sight-seeing and next week we will attend the National People's Congress, which will be opened by our Great Leader, Chairman Mao. Do you have questions?'

Pema said she had read that there were great palaces in Peking, bigger even than the Potala. Did Chairman Mao live in a palace – like His Holiness the Dalai Lama?

Mr Chen smiled uneasily. Chairman Mao, he said, lived modestly, in keeping with the principles of socialism, of which he was the foremost living exponent. For good measure Mr Chen added that only imperialists and reactionaries lived in palaces.

'Will we meet Chairman Mao?' asked one of the others.

Chairman Mao, said Mr Chen, was a very busy man. He was also very old. It was not possible to say for certain that he would receive them, but in Mr Chen's humble opinion it was likely. 'It is well known,' he alleged, 'that the Tibetan people hold a special place in the affections of Chairman Mao.'

At the mention of Chairman Mao, a nerve in Ari's face began to twitch.

Peking was not like Chungking or Wuhan. The air was cold and clear. Pema said it reminded her of Lhasa. Ari wore his sheepskin *chuba* and boots, Pema her warmest dress and best apron. She had spent the last half hour of the journey combing her long hair. Undone, it fell nearly to her waist. Ari had helped her plait it. Tears had welled in his eyes. He hoped she would not notice.

There was a reception committee. It was headed by a Tibetan. An aristocrat in an elegant *chuba* with a fine array of fountain pens protruding from the pocket of his shirt. 'Ngabo ,' whispered Ari. It was indeed Ngabo. The former governor of Kham who had crossed over to the Han. The stooge produced by the Han whenever they wanted to prove to the outside world that all was well in Tibet. A man so reviled in his homeland that he had not dared set foot there for five years.

Ngabo shook hands warmly with Mr Chen and then, less warmly, with each Tibetan. He made a short speech and then applauded. Everyone joined in. That was the Han way.

Outside a bus awaited. Ngabo and Mr Chen led the way, up a staircase and across a marble concourse. They each carried their own baggage. Pema gazed about the station in awe. It was bigger than the Jokhang.

Pema noticed him first. She stopped dead in her track. 'Ari,' she almost shouted. 'A foreigner.'

Once, when Pema was fifteen, the Han had brought a foreigner to Shigatse and shown him the Tashilhunpo lamasery. The visitor had caused great excitement. Half the town had turned out to stare at him. Pema and her sister had followed from a distance until the

Han police had chased them away. That was the only foreigner Pema had ever seen. Until today.

This foreigner was wearing a blue cap and cotton jacket, exactly like those worn by the Han. You had to look twice to be sure, but there could be no doubt. The round eyes, the narrow cheekbones, the white skin. He was no more than five paces away.

It was a shock for Ari, too. In thirteen years the only foreigners he had seen were pictured in Han magazines.

'Ari, he is staring at you.'

'Don't be ridiculous, Pema.'

But it was true. The man was looking straight at Ari. Even when his stare was returned he did not avert his eyes. At least not for some time.

The others were almost out of sight. Ari and Pema had to run to catch up. As they boarded the bus, Pema turned to look again.

'Ari, he is still there.'

He was, too. Standing now at some distance, eyes firmly trained on Ari. It was a cold, hard stare. A tiny thought stirred. Had they come to make sure he carried out his mission? Did they know he was here? How could they?

The man was still watching as the bus pulled away. The nerve in Ari's cheek twitched uncontrollably.

Ogilvy could scarcely believe his luck. He had spent the afternoon trailing around the Peking Number Five Textile Factory, listening to Melissa prattling on about class struggle. A revolutionary opera had been threatened for the evening, but he had escaped, saying he wanted to soak up some atmosphere in the old city. His repeated absences were remarked upon. Melissa was loudly expressing the view that it was the height of bad manners to absent oneself from any part of the programme laid down by their hosts. Ogilvy's behaviour was setting a bad example. Other Capitalist Roaders in the group were beginning to disappear for strolls on their own. It was bad for morale. 'You are a very independent man, Mr Saunders,' Mrs Wu had remarked as he returned from one of his pre-breakfast trips to the station. Whether or not this was intended as a criticism was unclear. Ogilvy had a hunch that there was more to Mrs Wu than met the eye. He awarded her one of his smarmiest smiles and promised himself that, after his business was complete, he would be a model tourist.

The evening of the third day saw Ogilvy's fifth visit to the station. He couldn't keep it up much longer without arousing suspicions. He arrived to find half-a-dozen significant-looking men pacing up and down the platform. They seemed to be some sort of reception committee. If Ogilvy was not mistaken, several of them were wearing Tibetan national dress.

The train was dead on time. The Tibetans emerged from the fourth or fifth carriage dressed exactly as they had been in the *Lhasa Daily* photograph. They were instantly recognisable. Ogilvy surveyed the scene from a pedestrian bridge over the track. He did his best to appear casual, leaning forward and resting on his forearms. Had anyone asked, he would have explained that he was train spotting. In his country, he would say, there were no longer any steam trains.

The welcoming committee took its time. One of the officials was making a speech. There was clapping and hand-shaking. Around them the platform had cleared. The party approached across the empty expanse. The tallest Tibetan was the obvious candidate. From a distance it was hard to tell, but he seemed to be about the right age. He was with a girl. They lagged behind.

When they had all passed, except for the man and the girl, Ogilvy moved in. Without going closer he could not be certain. He approached from an angle, just outside their direct line of vision. They were preoccupied and paid him no attention.

Suddenly the station seemed empty. A space had opened up around them. The couple were no more than twenty feet away, fifteen, ten . . . If Ogilvy had been sure, he might have done it there and then. One blow from behind and then run like hell. But then, damn. The girl had spotted him. They were looking right at him. For a second the Tibetan held his stare. Yes, that was him. No doubt about it. The cropped hair, the chipped tooth. Exactly as in the photograph.

Too late now. They were hurrying away. Through the portico and out to where the others were waiting. Ogilvy trailed them from a distance. He stood watching as they boarded the bus. As she mounted the first step the girl turned again. She had seen him. They both had. He could see them looking back at him as the bus pulled away.

37

O GILVY HAD A plan. Strictly unofficial. The boneheads at the
Department would have been horrified had they known. Not
to mention the Yanks. But what did Ogilvy care? This was his last
mission. A life of married bliss awaited. As a family man, he had a
responsibility to return home in one piece.

He would kill the Tibetan only as a last resort. This was, of
course, entirely in keeping with Ogilvy's (though not necessarily
the Department's) personal philosophy. But if he was honest, there
was a more practical reason. He had not counted on the girl. She
had seen him, too. Should the Tibetan be found in a back alley with
a broken neck, she was bound to report the presence of a suspicious foreigner at the railway station. True, he had laid a false
trail with the Uighur students, but the Chinese were not daft. Once
they had eliminated from their inquiries the handful of Bulgarians
in Peking, the net might spread further afield. Comrade Chu was
already taking note of his repeated absences and they just might
put two and two together and come up with Ogilvy.

Something more sophisticated was called for. Ogilvy proposed
instead to set up a meeting with the Tibetan and do his best to talk
him out of assassinating the Chairman.

No doubt the Tibetan spoke Mandarin at least as well as Ogilvy,
probably rather better, so there would be no language problem. It
was a matter of appealing to reason. The line, Ogilvy would
explain, had changed. Many years had passed. Much water had
flowed under many bridges. His masters in America were grateful,
but they wanted out. Of course, Ogilvy would say, he realised this
would come as a surprise. A shock even. That was only natural.
Holed up in the mountains all those years, the Tibetan was not to
know that the United States and China were about to kiss and
make up. Frankly, it had come as a shock to people all round the
world. Ogilvy included. There were even signs of a fall-out in the

Chinese Politburo. Witness the recent disappearance of Marshal Lin Piao (talking of which, perhaps the Tibetan could shed some light on the matter. On second thoughts, perhaps not).

As for Nixon, no doubt news of his impending visit would be announced shortly. At next week's congress perhaps. In due course even Lhasa Radio might have a word or two to say on the matter. Well down the bulletin, of course. After all those figures on the production of yak butter.

Speaking personally, Ogilvy would say, he regretted this development as much as Ari. He hoped the Tibetan didn't mind being called by his first name? Was that the practice in Tibet?

Were it up to him, Ogilvy would stress, he wouldn't have gone near the Reds with a sterilised barge pole. Unfortunately, however, policy was made by bigger fish than Ogilvy. People who had to take account of global factors. Geopolitics, that was the American word. No doubt there was a suitable Chinese expression and sooner or later the concept would find its way into Tibetan. One thing he could say, however: everyone at home (everyone in the know, that is) was lost in admiration for the way that Ari, alone behind the Himalayas, cut off from contact with base, had clung for so long and so single-mindedly to his mission. Such dedication, such patriotism was rare these days in a world so preoccupied with the short term. It was an honour to meet him (here, Ogilvy would offer his hand).

And if that didn't work, Ogilvy would change tack. What was the point of killing Chairman Mao? He was old and ill. He would die soon, anyway. If anything, his assassination would unleash even greater repression in Tibet. To say nothing of the fate that lay in store for the family and friends of Chairman Mao's assassin. If the Tibetan did not care what became of himself, he ought at least to think of those he loved. The girl, for example. Was she his wife? Lover? What would become of her? Had he thought of that?

Finally, Ogilvy would say (although he had no authority for doing so) that, if the Tibetan could make it to the safety of India or Nepal, the Americans would express their gratitude by setting him up for life. That was the least they could do. And why not bring the girl along, too? They could settle down and bring up children in Colorado, or Switzerland, or anywhere they cared to name. There came a time when everyone had to come in from the cold. Ogilvy was about to do the very same with Priscilla. He would tell the Tibetan about Priscilla. It might help to create a bond between them. He would paint a picture of two men who had devoted their lives to the service of their country (Ogilvy was not planning to be precise about his country of origin), whose vision of nirvana – he would use that very word – had been thwarted by the manipulations of devious politicians. There came a time, however, when even they had to face facts, however unpalatable, lay down their arms, and take what little solace life had to offer. This was the moment.

Ogilvy reviewed his case as he tucked in to a bowl of steaming noodles outside the main gate of the Peking Minorities Institute on that cold November evening. There was no sign of the Uighur students from his previous visit. If necessary, he would go in search of them. He planned to use one as a messenger. It was a risk, but risks were his business.

Probably his argument would cut no ice with the Tibetan. Goodness knows, he had had long enough to consider the pros and cons of assassinating Chairman Mao in his thirteen years of isolation. Having come this far, he was unlikely to be talked out of killing the Chairman on the strength of a half-hour exposure to the undoubted charms of Timothy Ogilvy. Ogilvy was under no illusions. It was a long shot, but worth a try.

Of course, it was possible that the Tibetan would pretend to go along with Ogilvy and kill the Chairman anyway. Ogilvy had considered that. Fine judgement was necessary here. Ogilvy prided himself that he was an astute judge of human nature. At Oxford he had even dabbled a little in psychology. As evidence of sincerity, Ogilvy would insist that the Tibetan hand over his weapon. He must have a weapon. If not the guns given him by the Americans, then whatever he had picked up since. Also the poison. Ogilvy would demand that, too. He would dump them, together with his own weapon, in the nearest canal. He could then go back to being a tourist. The Tibetan could return to his friends and maybe one day, a year or two from now, he and his girl would appear at a remote outpost on the Indian or Nepalese frontier, seeking asylum. No doubt the Americans would be looking out for him. The Nixon visit would go ahead as planned. As for Chairman Mao, he would be assured of a less glorious end. And it would all be due to the diplomatic skills of Timothy Ogilvy. Who knows, perhaps in time his services would be recognised with the preferment of a knighthood. The citation, of course, would be suitably vague. 'For services to Queen and Country over and above the call of duty.' Sir Timothy and Lady Ogilvy. What more fitting end to a career at the sharp edge of the secret world?

But what if the Tibetan was not open to reason? Or if Ogilvy was not satisfied that his conversion was sincere? In that case, regardless of risks, Ogilvy would do what had to be done. A sudden blow to the windpipe. A snapping of the spinal cord. A single bullet behind the ear. The end would come suddenly, cleanly, painlessly, and when least expected.

Ari, his sleeves rolled above his elbows, was washing shirts when Pema found him. She was beside herself. 'Ari, Ari, the foreigner. The man at the station. He is here.'

'Impossible,' but, even as he spoke, he realised it was perfectly possible. A soaked shirt slid from his hand and landed with a splat on the washroom floor. He made no effort to retrieve it. The nerve in his face began to twitch.

'By the gate, eating noodles. Same hat, same jacket . . .'

'Every Han in Peking has such a hat.'

'. . . and the same eyes. He looked straight at me, just as he looked at you yesterday, at the station. It is him, Ari, I know it is.'

'Okay, so it is him. Maybe he is a teacher in this place . . .' His voice trailed off. The Han had sent all foreign teachers home years ago. The shirt lay in a pool of soapy water. Why would they seek him now, after so long? Surely they would not be so stupid? Not when he was so close.

38

Harvey Crocker said he hadn't felt so good in thirty years. Not since he woke up one morning in Bangkok and discovered he had acquired a Thai wife.

They were having breakfast on Gerry Bannister's patio. The early morning sunshine cast long shadows as they sampled Bannister's home-grown grapefruit. From where he was sitting, Crocker had a clear view of the valley all the way down to the ocean. At night, if there was no wind, you could hear the waves pounding on the beach.

Bannister said he didn't understand why everyone on the east coast didn't simply up stakes and migrate to California. 'Getting out of Langley was the best thing I ever did.'

'I'll drink to that,' said Neumann, raising his glass of papaya juice. Crocker pretended not to hear. The truth was that he missed Langley. The gap in his life was too big to be filled by golf or trout fishing. Maybe he should take up growing grapes.

They'd told Bannister about the meetings with Director East Asia. About Operation Fire Monkey. About how the man appeared to be losing his grip. Bannister said that didn't surprise him in the least. 'If I were you, Harvey, I'd forget all about Fire Monkey. Forget those creeps at Langley. Forget that boy. Why, he's probably growing grapes in Kathmandu by now – or whatever they do grow out that way.'

'If it had been any other country,' said Crocker, 'Taiwan, Vietnam, Laos, even the Soviet Union, then we could have sent the station chief a memo telling him to call it off. He would pass word to the operatives in the field. And that would be that. But Tibet's different. For one thing we don't have a station in Tibet. Or anywhere else in China for that matter. And for another, Tibet ain't the sort of place you send memos to.'

Bannister pushed back the table and got to his feet. He hadn't got time to sit around, he said. He was taking a run into town to pick up some fencing for the chicken coop. Neumann said he'd come for the ride.

'What about you, Harvey?'

'If you guys don't mind, I'll stay. I gotta a hunch that something big's coming off today and I want to be near a TV set when it happens.'

Mr Chen appeared while they were still eating.

'Dear friends, I have a very important announcement.' His voice was quivering. 'There will be a meeting. Tonight. With whom, I cannot say. At what time, I cannot say. Please go to your rooms and prepare.'

'Chairman Mao,' whispered Pema.

The twitch in the side of Ari's face was worse than ever. It wasn't Chairman Mao, but the foreigner who worried him. Each evening since they had arrived in Peking the foreigner had been waiting by the noodle stands. Yesterday Pema had reporting seeing him actually inside the Institute, loitering near the entrance to the hostel. He was waiting for Ari. Of that there was no doubt. The final proof had come not an hour before. An Uighur student had searched out Ari. (Thank heaven, Pema had not been around.) 'I have a message,' the student had said. 'From a foreigner who is waiting by the noodle stands.'

'I don't know any foreigners.' Ari tried to sound surprised. He was cold with fear.

'The foreigner wants to talk to you. He says he brings news of your family. From India.' The Uighur delivered his message and was gone. He knew that no good could come of involvement with foreigners.

So it was true. The Americans had not forgotten. Even after so many years, they were still watching. Incredible. Did they understand what they were doing? Surely they knew that contact with foreigners was forbidden. Absolutely forbidden. It was madness. Ari made up his mind. He would not go.

Ogilvy waited an hour. The Uighur did not return. There was no sign of the Tibetan. He could not risk staying much longer.

Already his nightly vigils were becoming the subject of gossip among the students. The Uighurs who had befriended Ogilvy on the first night were now wary of being seen with him. It was only a matter of time before someone reported his presence.

And time was running out. In two days the SACU tour would leave Peking for the provinces and Ogilvy would have to go with them. As a last resort, he could fake illness in the hope of extending his stay in Peking, but that was a high-risk strategy. Comrade Chu's attitude towards Ogilvy was becoming colder by the day.

No, he would give the Tibetan another hour. If he hadn't shown up by then, he was as good as dead.

After some time, Mr Chen reappeared. He was in an even greater state of agitation than before. He ran down the corridor knocking on doors and calling on everyone to assemble downstairs. 'Immediately, immediately,' he kept repeating.

Pema was wearing her best dress and brightest apron. She had spent the preceding hour combing her hair. It hung loose down her back, reaching almost to her waist. Her cheeks were radiant. She looked more beautiful than ever.

Ari, too, had dressed in his best for Chairman Mao. He wore his best *chuba*, washed and pressed, tied loosely at the waist. He had ironed his shirt and brushed every speck of dust from his boots. But he was shivering from head to foot. He hoped that Pema would not notice.

A bus was waiting. The one that had carried them to the Great Wall, the Summer Palace, the Temple of Heaven, and a host of other places. For the first time in three days the Han driver did not have a cigarette in the corner of his mouth. He was wearing a grey tunic without a single button missing. He smiled at each of them as they climbed aboard. It was the most important moment of his life, too.

Ari and Pema sat at the back where Mr Chen could not see that they were holding hands. He gripped her hand tightly so she would not feel him shaking. As the bus pulled away, Pema jumped, as though she had sat on a thorn.

'Ari, look. The foreigner.'

*

Ogilvy had given up waiting. The time had come for action. He looked forward to disposing of the gun. His leg was sore where the holster rubbed.

He walked through the main gate unchallenged. Amazing what a little self-confidence could do. He had almost reached the hostel when he saw the bus approaching.

It took him by surprise. He ran his eyes along the passengers, not expecting to see anyone he recognised. Only when the bus had passed did it dawn on Ogilvy that these were Tibetans. His Tibetans.

He knew at once he was too late.

39

Like the mandarins of old, the rulers of China live behind high walls. When they emerge, which they rarely do, they travel in cars with rear windows curtained like sedan chairs.

They live in the Chung Nan Hai, a walled park adjacent to the Forbidden City from where ancient dynasties ruled the Celestial Empire.

The wall surrounding the Chung Nan Hai is high and wide, painted vermilion in keeping with the decor of the Forbidden City. It has a circumference of many miles, intersected at intervals by gates guarded day and night by armed soldiers.

A citizen of Peking can only hope for a glimpse of the place where his rulers live by climbing the hill in the Bei Hai park, which overlooks the Chung Nan Hai from the east. He will see a lake, trees, and office buildings not unlike those to be found elsewhere in the city but, however hard he strains, he will not see into the inner sanctum.

To this place must come all those who wish to pay homage to the Great Helmsman.

Tien An Men square was empty, apart from a few shadowy cyclists. The Great Hall of the People was in darkness. The presiding portraits of Mao, Marx, Engels, and Stalin were dimly illuminated.

As the Tibetans' bus neared the Chung Nan Hai, Mr Chen got to his feet. His mouth opened, but at first no words emerged. 'Dear Friends,' he said eventually, 'in a few minutes we will visit . . . our beloved Chairman Mao. We will not stay long because . . .' he fumbled '. . . he is a very old man . . . great honour . . . remember this day for the rest of our lives . . .' For once Mr Chen had run out of words. He sat down.

Ari had disengaged his hand from Pema's and was clutching the left side of his chest, as though in pain. His heart was beating like a hammer.

The bus turned right through an arch in the vermilion wall. The headlights picked out a soldier in an olive coat with a fur collar. He motioned the driver to stop and climbed aboard. After a brief conference with Mr Chen he indicated that they should proceed. They did so, slowly. The soldier giving directions with sweeping gestures of his right arm. To begin with they were on a street like any other in a Han city. Modest houses built around courtyards, strolling pedestrians, a cyclist or two, lamps on poles. Nowadays even the streets of Lhasa had such lamps.

After some minutes the houses gave way to a lake on one side of the road and a wooded area on the other. Chairman Mao's house was like others, except that it stood alone. 'So small,' whispered Pema. 'I thought –'

'Please get down now. Hurry.' Mr Chen had found his voice again. The bus had driven to the front door. Someone lurked within. Was it . . . ? They could not see.

'What's wrong, Ari?' In her excitement Pema had not noticed that the blood had drained from Ari's face.

'Leave me, I am all right.' He pulled his *chuba* tight.

'You are ill, I can see. I will tell Mr Ch –'

'No,' he almost shouted. She looked hurt. He wanted to tell her that he loved her, but there was no time.

Outside a car was parked, rear windows shaded by a curtain, as is the way of the Han. Two men got out. They were in Tibetan dress. One was the traitor, Ngabo.

'This way. This way.' Ngabo was leading them up the steps to the door, which was sheltered by a tiled portico. It opened into a sitting room. In a corner there was a ping-pong table. Upon it a ball and bat scattered haphazardly as though a game had been interrupted.

Beyond the hallway there was another room. They could see him now. An old man in a deep armchair. He was dressed exactly as his pictures showed, except that his grey tunic was crumpled.

There was no ceremony. No guards. No one searched them. It was like entering the home of an aged uncle.

The old man rose to greet them. The effort was considerable. A young woman held his arm. Ngabo was fawning obsequiously.

He was a big man – for a Han. In his day he must have towered. Now he was slightly stooped. He took their hands one by one, murmuring inaudibly. Ngabo remained at his side affecting to introduce them. Ari was last in line, one hand inside his *chuba*.

It was the first time in a long while that any of them had been in a room without a picture of Mao Tse-tung.

The old man indicated that they should sit. More chairs were sent for. A girl with plaits served jasmine tea in porcelain mugs with lids. In a corner there was a bed and two quilts neatly folded. Was this his bedroom, too? Every wall was lined with books. There were books in piles on the floor and on the table – papers and notes protruding from between the pages.

So this was the man in whose name Tibet had been ransacked, whose name was chanted by the glassy-eyed young fanatics who had looted the Jokhang and dismantled Ganden stone by stone. Who had gone from village to village, house to house seizing, burning, destroying, denouncing, driving old ladies to suicide. Who had colonised Litang and turned it into a town of ghosts. Who had stolen Ari's youth and dispersed his family.

Ari's tea remained untouched on the low bamboo table, which was all that separated him from the Chairman. He had a perfect line of fire.

The old man rambled on. Perhaps he was unaware what had been done in his name. Perhaps he had never left this place. An air-pocket of tranquillity in the midst of the turmoil wrought by his Thought. Perhaps his name had been taken in vain. Perhaps it was all a terrible mistake. Perhaps, perhaps, perhaps.

His face sagged on one side. He spoke with difficulty, emitting words in short bursts. Each outburst followed by a sharp intake of breath. The young woman by his side translated passages that were inaudible.

He talked about feudalism and progress. Unlike other Han he did not speak in slogans. He made jokes about superstition. Han,

he said, were as superstitious as Tibetans. He talked about mistakes. Oh yes, mistakes had been made, he said. About that he was
clear. On behalf of all Han, he apologised. Yes, he used that very
word. Mistakes would be put right, he promised. But please be
patient, it would take time. In China, he added wearily, everything
took time. Mistakes. How could he know? What guarantees could
he give that they would be put right. Ari wanted to speak. He
opened his mouth, but no words came.

A photographer hovered. Ari's legs were shaking. He hoped no
one was aware of it. His hand was still inside his *chuba*.

The old man was regretting that he had never visited Tibet. Never.
Imagine that. To have absolute power for nearly thirty years over a
kingdom so big that it could not all be visited in a single lifetime. Of
course, said the old man, it was too late now.
   He was a sad old man. As if he knew that the Revolution had
gone wrong. That a new feudalism had emerged from the ruins of
the old and that now he was too frail to do anything about it.
Unlike Tibetans, he had no other life to go to. This was his only life.
It had been big, but it was over. He spoke of his life's work with
disdain. 'I have changed a few places in the vicinity of Peking,' he
said. 'That is all.'

Suddenly they were on their feet. The photographer was arranging
them in a semi-circle. Ari was directly behind the Chairman. Close
enough to touch the old man's head.

A blinding flash. It was over and Ari was glad. Another flash. It
might have been the muzzle of his pistol, had he not left it at the
bottom of the Xi Ling Gorge.

40

LOOKING BACK, ARI could pinpoint precisely the event that changed his mind. It was in Chungking. The night he went walking alone. He had sat for half an hour in a tea house overlooking the place where the Yangtse and Jialing rivers meet, watching old men playing chess. A passenger ferry plied back and forth across the river, only its lights visible in the dark. Somewhere a ship's siren sounded.

Ari was thinking of John and Bill. He had got to know them well, or so he thought. As well as one can ever know foreigners. So far as he could tell, they liked him. They were forever bringing him little presents. A piece of chewing gum, a bottle of Pepsi, that Mickey Spillane book translated by Bill into Tibetan. Yet, like the Han, they were not straightforward. They had waited until the last moment to inform him that he would not be going home with the others. For weeks they had not taken him into their confidence about his mission. And at no point had they revealed their real names. Did they think he was stupid? That he would not notice that they never referred to each other by the names they had given to him. Even to this day he had no idea who they were.

They had claimed that America was a friend of Tibet. Yet America had never given Tibet more than a few old radios and guns to fight the Han. They had planes, but they did not show Tibetans how to drive them. Instead, they sent the Tibetans home four or five at a time, to be killed by the Han.

These were not new thoughts. They had occurred to Ari many times in the lonely years since he had dropped from the sky back into his homeland. Yet none of this changed his mind. It was what he saw that night in Chungking on the walk back to the government guest house which did that. He had passed an exhibition of photographs in glass cases outside the People's Palace of Culture. Such exhibitions were common, even in Lhasa. Usually they were photos of model workers or peasants singing the praises of Chairman Mao and the party. But these were different. They showed foreigners.

There was a crowd. That was nothing unusual. Everything in China attracted a crowd. There was excitement, argument. At first he could not get near. Words he did not recognise floated back. 'Kiss-ing-er . . .' 'Nicker-son . . .' They appeared to be men's names. Foreigners. And then a word he recognised at once.

'Meigoren.'

'Americans . . .'

When at last he reached the front, Ari could not believe his eyes. The Americans were coming. To China. To see Chairman Mao. This Kissinger. He was in Peking. Drinking a toast in the Great Hall of the People with Chou En-lai. There they were, *maotai* glasses raised, drinking to undying friendship between the American and Chinese peoples. And there was another picture. Chou En-lai shaking hands with this Kissinger, as if they were old friends. The same Americans whose deeds were commemorated in the US–Chiang Kai-chek Criminal Acts Exhibition Hall, not a stone's throw from this very place. Only yesterday, Mr Chen had taken them on a guided tour replete with ringing denunciations of American imperialists and their running dogs.

And this Nickerson. He was the President. The same man who had sent Ari to kill Chairman Mao. Now he was coming to China as Chairman Mao's honoured guest.

The next evening, on the boat, he had questioned Mr Chen. At first Mr Chen was devious. Where had Ari heard this? One should not believe every rumour put about by bad elements. So Ari had explained about the photographs in the glass case and eventually Mr Chen owned up. Yes, it was true. He chose his words with care. There had been a change of line. At the moment the situation was unclear, but in due course the party would explain everything. Of that Mr Chen was confident.

Ari knew then that he had been betrayed. Bill and John had used him and, when he was no longer useful, they had tossed him aside like a piece of rotten meat. Maybe it wasn't their fault. Maybe they had also been used. Perhaps their gods had let them down, too.

No matter, he knew what he had to do. Ari had waited until Mr Chen was preoccupied and Pema laid low by sickness. Waited for the moment when *The East is Red Number 40* was in the deepest, darkest gorge. Then he had gone below, ripped open the lining of his best *chuba*, removed the gun, and wrapped it, together with the poison, in an old shirt. Using the sleeves, he tied the bundle tight. Then, keeping an eye out for Mr Chen, he had climbed to the back of the boat and hurled the bundle with all his strength into the swirling waters of the Yangtse. It had landed with a splash and disappeared at once. And with it sank the awful secret that he had carried alone for thirteen years.

Postscript

T HE *PEOPLE'S DAILY* of 2 November 1971 – the Tibetan
 Year of the Iron Boar – carried a front-page photograph under
the headline, 'CHAIRMAN MAO GREETS TIBET DELEGATES'.
The picture showed the old man slumped in an armchair surrounded by Tibetans in national costume. The caption identified
the man seated on the Chairman's left as Ngabo, a vice chairman
of the Standing Committee of the National People's Congress.
Ari's friend, Pema, is seated cross-legged on the floor. Ari is
standing directly behind the Chairman, ideally placed (were he so
minded) to put a bullet behind the Great Helmsman's ear. He is
smiling broadly.

Ogilvy saw the photo in Mrs Wu's copy of the *People's Daily* as
the SACU party boarded a train for Sian. On seeing it he was so
relieved that it was all he could do to stop himself from throwing
his arms around Mrs Wu. For the next three weeks Ogilvy was a
model tourist. His absences ceased, he listened attentively to Mrs
Wu's commentaries, and even managed to strike up a dialogue
with Comrade Chu.

Upon returning to England he handed in his notice to the
Department and married Priscilla. When last heard of he was
running a second-hand bookshop in the back streets of Edinburgh
and spending long weekends at his croft on Loch Etive. There is, as
yet, no sign of his knighthood.

Harvey Crocker's fortunes took a turn for the better. Soon after he
returned from his holiday in California, his Thai wife reappeared
and asked him to take her back. Crocker magnanimously agreed
and the happy couple went to live with Fritz Neumann in his
Miami condo. Nine months or so later Crocker's wife gave birth
to a bouncing baby boy. For reasons unexplained to most of
Crocker's friends, he has insisted on calling the boy Ari. Unkind

people have remarked that the child – now a teenager – does not bear any resemblance to his father, but Crocker isn't complaining. Since becoming a father he has shed thirty pounds and turned teetotal. Those who've seen him recently say he's a new man.

Fritz Neumann enrolled at night school for a course in Tibetan Buddhism and makes regular pilgrimages to the Himalayas in search of the kind of enlightenment unavailable in Miami.

In August 1973, Ari Paljor and Pema crossed into Sikkim and asked for asylum. They later made their way to the Tibetan town of Dharmsala in north-west India where they now run the Yak and Yeti guest house, said to be popular with young Western travellers. They have two children. A girl called Pema (after Ari's mother) and a boy, Aten. So far as anyone knows there has been no contact between Ari and the Agency since his arrival in India.

As for Chairman Mao, history records that he died peacefully in his bed on 9 September 1976.